SIMON & SCHUSTER CHILDREN'S PUBLISHING
ADVANCE READER'S COPY

TITLE: All That I Can Fix

AUTHOR: Crystal Chan

IMPRINT: Simon Pulse

ON-SALE DATE: 06/12/2018

ISBN: 978-1-5344-0888-3

FORMAT: Hardcover

PRICE: $18.99 US / $25.99 CAN

AGES: 12 up

PAGES: 320

Please send two copies of any review or mention of this book to:
Simon & Schuster Children's Publicity Department
1230 Avenue of the Americas, 4th Floor
New York, NY 10020
212/698-2808

Aladdin • Atheneum Books for Young Readers
Beach Lane Books • Beyond Words • Libros para niños
Little Simon • Margaret K. McElderry Books
Paula Wiseman Books • Salaam Reads
Simon & Schuster Books for Young Readers
Simon Pulse • Simon Spotlight

CRYSTAL CHAN

ALL THAT I CAN FIX

SIMON PULSE

New York London Toronto Sydney New Delhi

SIMON PULSE

An imprint of Simon & Schuster Children's Publishing Division
1230 Avenue of the Americas, New York, New York 10020
First Simon Pulse hardcover edition June 2018
Text copyright © 2018 by Crystal Chan
Jacket design and hand-lettering by Sarah Creech
copyright © 2018 by Simon & Schuster, Inc.
Jacket photo-illustration of animal crackers copyright © 2018 by PixelWorks Studios
Jacket photographs copyright © 2018 by Thinkstock (sidewalk and grass)
and Symphonie/Getty Images (bicycle and grass)
SIMON PULSE and colophon are registered trademarks of Simon & Schuster, Inc.
For information about special discounts for bulk purchases, please contact Simon
& Schuster Special Sales at 1-866-506-1949 or business@simonandschuster.com.
The Simon & Schuster Speakers Bureau can bring authors to your live event. For
more information or to book an event, contact the Simon & Schuster Speakers
Bureau at 1-866-248-3049 or visit our website at www.simonspeakers.com.
Interior designed by Sarah Creech
The text of this book was set in font Janson Text LT.
Manufactured in the United States of America
2 4 6 8 10 9 7 5 3 1
Library of Congress Cataloging-in-Publication Data TK
ISBN 978-1-5344-0888-3 (hc)
ISBN 978-1-5344-0890-6 (eBook)

To my country

1

IT WAS A THURSDAY WHEN THE SQUIRRELS FELL
from the trees. I knew I shouldn't have stayed at George's after
school, but she wore a really tight shirt that day, and besides, she
was freaking out over four questions she knew she got wrong on
her AP chemistry test and wanted to cry on my shoulder—how
could I say no? Still, by the time the windstorm started, I was
almost regretting it; shingles were ripping off the roofs and flying down the street. I braced myself against the wind as those
squirrels fell, one after another, claws gripping at the sky, squirrels falling like acorns.

Earlier on that same Thursday, Mr. Jenkins, the crazy guy
on the edge of town, the guy who owned an exotic zoo filled
with tigers, panthers, hyenas, and elephants and the like but who
never fed them very well (they all had ribs poking out like the
black keys on a piano)—he decided to go and shoot himself dead,
but not before opening up all the cages and letting his animals
loose. Of course, in that windstorm, the animals—being caged

up for years and years—freaked out and ran. So there we were, Makersville, Indiana, the sudden focus of TV reporters and animal rights groups and gun rights advocates, thrown in the spotlight when we hadn't hardly existed just a couple hours before. Goes to show what a tiger can do.

So everyone was running around with their cameras and cell phones, then running around some more and telling people not to run around and to stay in their homes. Then a couple reporters got on TV and started talking in Really Excited Voices because two giraffes had been mauled and gnawed on by the Bengal tiger. I mean, really, people? Makes sense to me: The tiger had been starving, windstorm or no windstorm, and it's not like it was going to saunter through the fast-food drive-through and order the double-cheeseburger meal deal. And this hubbub was *before* folks learned that the python was nowhere to be found.

Maybe it should have bothered me more that these animals were on the loose and hungry, but in light of what had happened six months before *that*, I wasn't bothered at all. It's funny how relative life is: If you have a boring life where nothing much happens and suddenly there's some big cat out there, I suppose that would be a good reason to get upset. But if your dad tried to kill himself but messed up and just hurt himself really bad, well, some cat somewhere out there isn't all that awful. I mean, the cat could be anywhere. Your dad lives in your *house*.

I was straining into the wind along Oakwood Road—with the nice network of roads for all the new houses in the new part of the neighborhood so only those who live there could ever, *ever* find their way out—when another squirrel dropped right beside me, making a grotesque cawing sound as it fell. I jumped, scared, then glanced around to see if anyone had noticed.

That was when I saw the boy. He was small, about Mina's size, and he was maybe ten feet behind me, heading in the same direction. I was surprised he wasn't blown away, he was so small; if there were chain-link fences, I'd have encouraged him to hang on to them and crawl his way home.

There was no one else out on the street. Who would be out in a windstorm with squirrels falling through the sky and lions on the loose? Not that anyone here actually uses the sidewalks for walking—they're just big, empty spaces that you have to shovel in the winter or your neighbors get pissed at you and start talking behind your back. They're perfect, these sidewalks, flawless, except everyone uses cars.

I continued to walk home, squinty-eyed into the wind, my face at an angle to the sheer, and I could swear that the kid was following me. He had on a hoodie and was using his forearm to protect his face from the wind.

I turned around and staggered a step toward him, the wind blasted my back so hard. "Where are you going?" I shouted to the kid. "You're crazy for being out here."

He said something, but the wind carried his words away.

"What'd you say?" I shouted.

"Give them back," he yelled.

"What?" I shouted.

"Give them back," he repeated.

"What the hell are you talking about?" I said.

"They're not yours," he yelled, leaning into the wind.

I stared at him like he was an idiot, and he turned his head away. With his hoodie he almost hid it, but I got a split-second look at his face. Pale. Mousy. Intense. And the way he looked at me, I knew—I *knew*—this kid needed something freaking bad.

Maybe if I were a better guy I'd have talked to him, found out what was wrong. But at that point a jigsawed shingle fluttered down the road, branches were down everywhere, and Dad was probably pissed he didn't know where I was, which meant Mom wasn't much better. That's really what I was thinking about, not some little kid falsely accusing me of shit. So I turned around and kept walking.

But he kept right up with me; he made his little legs go twice as fast, and he stayed a couple feet behind. I kept catching him out of the corner of my eye, thinking he'd turn off at Allerton Drive or maybe when we came to the cul-de-sac where that new family moved in last week. But no. He stuck by me like a bad shadow.

I spun around, and he nearly bumped into me. "Go away!" I said, and I still needed to shout because the wind nearly dissolved my words. "I didn't take anything, and I don't know what you're talking about!"

At that point he must have seen that I was getting pissed, and he dropped back about twenty feet. But freaking-A, he still followed me.

I thought again about talking to him. Clearly, he was confused. But what could he be talking about? The thing is, figuring that stuff out takes time; while I was more than happy to let George cry in my arms all day if she'd like, I didn't know this kid, and I'd be damned to let him cry on my shoulder about whatever problems he had. Besides, there were squirrels falling from the trees and a couple cats on the loose.

My house was coming up. In a strange way it was a serious relief with this hoodie kid trailing behind me. He still had that really intense look on his face: the look of pure, absolute need. I didn't know what to do, and I think a part of me stalled a little, like a funky engine, because when I got inside the house and turned to close the door, there he was—just like I knew he'd be—standing outside the door, looking at me like of course I was going to invite him in.

"What do you want?" I said, trying not to show that this was creeping the shit out of me.

"I want your jeans," he said.

"You want *what*?" I asked.

"Your jeans," he said.

"Fuck no," I said. "Now go away."

He stood there.

There was nothing more natural than to close that door in his face. So I did. I locked it for good measure. You never know what people will do, even when they're young. Especially when they're young.

2

THURSDAYS HAVE A THING WITH ME. IT WAS A
Thursday when George told me she saw me only as her friend
and always would. George's real name is Geraldine, but she says
her name is George. Don't ask me why it's not Gabbie or Genna
or even Gigi, for Pete's sake. She wants to be a George. And she's
got that kind of personality where whatever she wants, that's
what she gets, and no one ever questions her. But yeah, she held
my hand and looked me in the eyes and said, *Oh, Ronney, you're
such a good friend. We'll always be friends, right?* That was on a
Thursday, mind you.

It was on a Thursday Dad bought his gun and showed it to us
at the dinner table.

It was on a Thursday that I found out I had flunked algebra
and had to retake it next year with a bunch of pimply freshmen.

Got fired from my job at the Car Palace Auto Shop? Thursday.

The day that my little sister, Mina, threw up on the shoes I had bought with that last paycheck from said auto shop? Thursday.

So when I heard at school that exotic animals were loose and Mr. Jenkins dead, all I had to do was go through my mental calendar. It was a Thursday. Of course.

After I closed the door on that kid, I paused in the foyer. The house was quiet, as usual, except for the wind howling at the windows and the occasional *thump* of a squirrel body hitting the roof. I hoped that some of our shingles hadn't ripped out and were tumbling down the street or floating in someone's swimming pool—then I'd have to spend the next couple days calling the roofers and staying home to let them in. Most normal fifteen-year-olds have parents who do these things—like home maintenance—but when you have a dad who's recovering from trying to kill himself and a mom who's popping pills for her various ailments, some things you gotta do yourself or else that leak in the bathroom will still be there.

But still, it's hard to care about *everything*. So yeah, the roof is important. I care about that. But Dad's attempted suicide, Mom's pills, the kid who wanted to come into my house? Sorry. I used up my caring on the roof. And anyway it's a whole hell of a lot easier to pick up the phone, schedule the guys to come over, and know that because of you, nothing leaks. The roof might have been a pain in the ass, but it's fixed—the family's dry. Dad pointing a gun at himself? How can you fix that?

I kicked off my shoes and made sure they landed right in the middle of the kitchen floor. I'm amazed my parents have never tripped over them or, frankly, thrown them out. A part of me really wants them to do something daring, but my shoes just silently migrate to the edge of the shoe wall, like there are magnets in the toes and magnets in the wall; my parents have never said a single word about them. On the Daring-O-Meter, they'd land a big, fat zero.

On the exact other end of the spectrum, there are George's parents. Her mom is a neurosurgeon, and her dad is some kind of chemical engineer who makes some futuristic plastic for some *save the world the future is now* kind of car technology. They go backpacking in the Andes, and her mom did a year of Doctors Without Borders. I mean, *that's* daring. That's living life. My parents? One's an overworked bank manager, and the other used to sell insurance but now sits at home and does nothing.

I was about to go into my room when I heard some rustling coming from my parents' bedroom.

"Ronney?" That was Dad.

"Yeah."

"Where'd you go?" The door opened, and there Dad stood, holding his bad arm, which was new, but his straight, black hair stuck out at crazy angles, which certainly wasn't. He leaned slightly, favoring the injured side. And though his skin is darker than mine, I could see a razor cut on his cheek. That meant that he had shaved today, which was the first time in days: Mom had probably nagged enough.

Dad doesn't care about how he looks. Just like he doesn't care about the lawn or if the toilet's plugged up or that I flunked algebra. The only thing that he does care about is whether or not I'm home. He always wants me to be home. Sometimes he goes around the house, calling my name, looking in every room, alarmed as if I've disappeared into the ether, and he doesn't stop calling my name until I shout back, "Yeah?" Then he says, "Oh, there you are." Then I say, "What do you want?" And then he says, "Nothing."

With his good hand, Dad ran his fingers through his hair. That meant he was mad, just like I knew he'd be, because I went to George's after school and didn't come directly home. If he raked his hand through his hair a couple more times it might actually look halfway decent, but he wasn't pissed enough to run his hand through his hair twice. I'd have to be in some pretty deep shit to see three times through the hair, but that hasn't happened yet. It'd be freaking funny to get him so mad that his hands would turn into an automatic hair-raking system: He'd be the most groomed man in town.

So yeah, once through the hair. "Where'd you go?" he asked again.

"I was at George's," I said.

"With this wind? And animals everywhere?" Dad asked, staring at me.

"She needed me," I said simply. I grabbed an apple off the counter.

He started to say something else, but I left and went to my room. He didn't stop me, nor did he grab my shoulder and demand more respect. Not that I really expected him to.

Adults like to say that these years of growing up are the best years of your life. That line, by the way, is total crap. They forget that, as a kid, you can't do shit about most things, especially the important things. I wish to hell that I could have told Dad not to go and shoot himself and that he would have listened to me. But no. I watch like some passerby at a car accident, completely helpless, staring at all the death and brokenness. So I focus on the things I *can* do something about—like the house—because if not, who knows? I might end up just like Dad.

My cell phone buzzed. I glanced down to see a text from Jello, wanting me to hang at his place later that night. Jello got his name the day he ate over two gallons of the stuff on a dare, kept it down, and then farted cherry juice for the rest of the day. Every so often kids throw him a box of the dried Jell-O stuff, and he always catches it in one hand with a grin. Nothing gets that guy down. I'd have taken a different name, myself. I mean, really—*Jello?* But he's my friend, and he can do whatever he wants, including naming himself after gelatin. I told him I'd beat up any kid who gives him shit about his name, but he's never needed to take me up on the offer.

I can't make it tonight, I texted him. **Maybe tomorrow.** It was a Thursday. Better play it safe. I didn't tell him that, but if he jiggled half his brain, he'd remember what day it was and why I turned him down.

I opened the blinds in my room and searched for that kid, but he was gone. What kid would stalk someone in a windstorm for a pair of jeans? He had to be a stalker kid. I immediately added stalker kids to my list of things to watch out for. Also on this list were UFOs, random-ass sinkholes, iguanas, and the West Nile virus.

I flipped on the TV; the news reporters were all psyched up and talking stressed out about staying in our houses. In the background behind the reporters, useless TV helicopters were grounded, given the velocity of the wind. You could tell that for these reporters this was the story of their lives. But, seriously. There are tons of deer and geese and shit running around, tons of things for these cats to eat. We can all get along, right? Then Mr. Rockfeller—not *Rockefeller*, mind you, but you can't tell him that—got on camera and declared how these animals were a clear and present danger to our community, to the children. That man always gets me. He doesn't even *talk* to his children, for chrissake; he just cruises around town in the shiny BMW he got in Indianapolis and thinks he's the shit. Rockfeller's the leader of the largest gun group in our county. It's super active, and he gets his guys to vote at every election like lockstep soldiers. He's also friends with the mayor—well, let's just say the man does what he wants. But old Rockie's eyes flicked when he was talking about those cats, just once. He really was scared.

Some guys from the Department of Natural Resources were rounding up a black rhino in City Park when I got bored and flipped off the TV. Jello texted me again:

Are you sure you can't come over?

Not coming.

Then I looked out the window again for that hoodie kid and saw nothing but a couple squirrels hobbling on the sidewalk. Cracked me up. The sidewalks are only used by maimed squirrels, stalker kids, and me.

A knock on my door. "Ronney?"

I didn't say anything. Maybe Mom would go away.

She turned the knob, but I'd locked the door.

"Ronney?" she said through the door. "I talked with your dad."

"Good for you."

"He said you went to George's."

I lay on my bed and closed my eyes. "Yeah?"

Pause.

"Ronney?"

"What?" I said, agitated.

"He was upset you didn't tell us where you were going."

I covered my face with my arm. "George was crying really hard, and I forgot to call."

"Oh."

Another pause.

"Dinner's in a couple minutes."

Like I said, my parents have absolutely no daring. I put on my headphones—the beefy kind that cancel out sound in the background—and hit my favorite playlist. It's a mix of stuff, from the screamers to classical. That classical shit can really take you places, unlike most songs where they whine about how much they want to get laid or how they just got laid but it was crap or how great it was but damn, that went fast, and now they want to get laid again. I mean, *we all want to get laid, okay?* That's a fact. But there are other things in life than getting laid, like making George laugh—I swear, when I can do that, it's like the sky rains down gold—or that day Jello and I had an ambush war in his backyard and pelted each other with raw eggs.

Mom made tofu-and-Spam casserole for dinner. As I sat down, I noticed faint lines under her green, almond eyes—Mina gets her eyes from Mom, just like I get my dark tan skin from Dad, and his straight nose, too. But Mom's face muscles were all tense, and she looked exhausted. Maybe that was why I ate the casserole without complaining—for once—but Mom didn't notice. Instead, we sat around the dinner table and let Mina kick her legs, bop her head and accompanying black spiral curls, and prattle on about how she almost won the spelling bee in class today but she missed the word "perspicacious." For a fourth grader. God, I don't even know what that word means, much less be able to spell it. Sometimes the stuff Mina does drives me crazy, and other times she makes me want to start a fan club for her. The problem is I never know when she's going to make me feel one way or the other, and sometimes I do jerky things I regret. When I go off on her, she gets this awful look in her eyes like I've just eaten her small intestine. It's a look that's hard to shake. The next time I turn around, though, her eyes are all bright and sparkly again, like everyone's forgotten my crappiness, except me.

"And so," Mina was saying, "that means that Janella's won four times, but I've only won three."

The only other sound was the scraping of forks against our plates. Mom slowly pulled out a long, wavy brown hair that had fallen into the casserole. My nostrils flared, and I shook my head.

Mina watched Mom, then twirled a lock of hair around her finger. "I think I'm going to study two nights before the next spelling bee instead of just one night before. Maybe that'll help."

"Don't talk with your mouth full," Dad said.

I ground my teeth. His daughter is telling him how she's going to rule the world one day, and he tells her not to talk with her mouth full?

Dad always used to help me with my homework. Even though school sucked, Dad was there for me. Every night, Mina would zip through her homework, and there I was, stuck with my math and a whole lot of other subjects too. Dad and I would sit at the kitchen table, and he would lean over my math book, reading the chapter's lesson, and then he would turn to me and we would go through my math problems, step by step. Somehow he would be able to explain the ideas to me, and somehow math sucked just a little less.

About two years ago now, soon after Dad got depressed, I was struggling with my math homework, again, and I asked Dad if he could help me; I was also hoping that that would get him out of bed.

"I can't help you," Dad said in this new, heavy voice; it was as if something had sucked the life out of it. Dad was under the sheets, and I couldn't see his face.

"Please," I said, standing in the bedroom doorway. "I don't get what the lesson is saying."

"I can't help you," Dad said again. "Go ask your mom."

"She's not even home from work yet," I said. "Please, Dad," I begged, and I went over to his side and touched him on the arm. "I need you. Who else is going to help me?"

"Don't touch me!" Dad screamed.

I stumbled out of the room, seeing but not seeing, feeling but not feeling, my heart beating wildly in my chest. I didn't know then that that was the beginning of my world falling apart. A couple days later I came home from school and went into my parents' bedroom without knocking, and there Dad was again, a covered-over bump in the bed. I went to him and thrust my math homework in his face. On it was a big, fat F.

"This is what I got," I said quietly. If anything would jolt Dad back into helping me with my homework, it would be this.

Dad's eyes fluttered open long enough for him to see my grade. Then he rolled over onto his other side so his back faced me. "Whatever," he said.

"But, Dad," I said, and tears came to my eyes, "you didn't help me."

"I don't care."

My heart broke as I stood there, watching him absolutely not caring about anything, not even me. I didn't know what to do with my assignment, and I didn't crush it into a paper ball—not then, not yet—instead, I put it on my parents' dresser so Mom could see it when she got home. That same evening, Mina asked Dad to help her with her homework, and Dad refused to talk to her. That was when she started howling like a banshee, with huge tears rolling down her face, and that was when I told Mom what Dad had said to me. Mom went into their bedroom and talked with Dad behind their closed door, and that was the first time that I told Mina that I would help her with her homework, that it would be okay.

"But you're not Daddy!" she said, wiping the tears from her face.

"I know. But you need help, and I'll help you," I said quietly. "I'm here for you."

Little did we know how much of a beginning that truly was.

Mina dutifully nodded at Dad and swallowed her tofu-and-Spam casserole. Then she turned to me. "Ron-Ron? Could you help me run through my words for next week?"

"Sure, Min-o," I said.

She beamed.

I gave a little smile. God, you can really love that kid sometimes.

"And, Ron-Ron?"

"Yeah?"

"Can you spend less time in the bathroom in the mornings?"

My fork froze in midair.

"You spend a lot of time in there."

Dad cleared his throat.

I kicked Mina's chair.

"Ow! What?" she said. She gave me a *you just ate my small intestine* look.

I stood up and grabbed the jar of sweet chili sauce from the refrigerator and smothered my tofu casserole with it. You can eat anything if there's enough sweet chili sauce on it. Some of my classmates think that's bizarre—but then they do the same thing with peanut butter or barbeque sauce. The thing is, that wouldn't happen in my family: We don't eat White People Food because, well, we're not white. And I don't tell people what mix of races we are or how my parents could have possibly met or answer other little prying questions because I hate those questions, it's no one's business, and the answers don't matter, anyway. I will say, though, that my family represents more countries at our dinner table than does a general session of the United Nations.

We were halfway through dinner when my phone beeped. It was Jello—again—begging me to come over. He knows that all he has to do is keep asking, and by the third time I'll change my answer. Even on a Thursday. So I got up and announced I was going out.

"Not with all those animals floating around," Mom said.

Dad didn't look up.

"The last time I checked, a camel won't do anything to me," I said.

"I'm not worried about the camel," Mom said.

"And I think you worry too much," I said.

Mom's back stiffened. Dad scraped his fork against his plate.

"Ron-Ron, don't go," Mina said softly. She tipped her face up to mine.

"I'll be fine," I said, more gently. "I'll be back in a couple hours." I paused. "It's not like I'm going to run into an animal, anyway."

"But you might," she said, and her voice wobbled.

I paused. "If I do, I'll put a rope around it and bring it home so you can train it." I gave her a small smile. "Which do you want: a cheetah, a wildebeest, or a python?"

My parents were silent.

"A cheetah!" Mina said, kicking her legs happily in the air. "It's orange."

I tousled Mina's hair just how she likes.

"A cheetah it is, Min-o," I said.

Dad suddenly grabbed his glass of water and slammed it on the table. Water leaped out and soaked the napkins, pooled on the wood, splashed onto Mom's shirt.

For a moment it was like we were all frozen, glued to our places. The only sound was water running in a stream from the table onto the floor. Dad looked at his plate, his hand still gripped around the glass.

At some point I found my voice. "You know, Dad, it would help if you took your meds," I said. "Oh, I forgot: You aren't."

Mina's eyes grew misty.

"I won't be out too long, Min-o," I told her.

Then I slipped on my shoes and left.

3

JELLO LIVED DOWN THE STREET FROM MARREN'S Corner Store, where I used to steal chocolate bars until the old lady who ran the store with her husband found me out and ratted on me to my parents. I mean, get a grip, people. There are wars and insider bank thefts and warming oceans, and they're gonna hang me for a couple ounces of chocolate? More proof that this world is messed up, bad.

Trees were down everywhere, and it was slow going, biking around all the debris and trying to stay balanced in the wind, which was already starting to die off. I went one house past Marren's, threw my bike under a bush, and crept around the side of the small, yellow house until I saw a lit-up window in one of the basement wells. I jumped into the basement well, slid the windowpane sideways, and dropped in.

Jello was right where I knew he'd be, seated at his computer in front of his wide-ass double flat screens, his back to me. His light brown hair was freshly cut, and his shoulders were wider than I remembered. Jello was streaming the local news, which was lame. I mean, you could stream tons of cooler shit than the local Makersville news, which we don't even officially have, by the way, because we're such a small town. The news area is an eighty-mile radius mostly focusing on Bloomington, a city over an hour away, and the media are still desperate for anything newsworthy. Sometimes they even make news up. Once, the newspaper did this freaking long article on a bunch of Makersville kids who had decided to take a couch and put it outside on the sidewalk and sit on the damn thing for four days straight, getting up only to go to the bathroom. And when the reporter asked them why they were doing this, they said—and the reporter wrote it down—*We wanted to get in the paper.* End of story. That's the kind of activity that goes on around here.

Jello was on his phone, texting away. When he saw me, he put his phone away quickly in his pocket and gave me a broad smile. "Took you long enough," he said.

"You nagged long enough," I said. I sat in the my chair next to him and fake punched him on the arm.

Jello grabbed his arm and fake fell over.

"Serves you right," I said. "What's so urgent that you asked me three times?"

Jello's face nearly shone like the sun—seriously, his pale face was flushed—he was so damn excited. I sometimes wonder what it would be like to be Jello; the littlest things get him going. He pointed at his screens. "Look at this," he said melodramatically.

I glanced at the newscast and groaned. "You gotta be kidding me. I hauled my ass over to your house to watch the stupid zoo outbreak?"

"There's a ton lot of animals they haven't found. A wildebeest. Panther. Hyena. Cougar. Ostrich. A lion. There's a lot more, too."

"Right. So let me repeat: I hauled my ass over to your—"

"Ronney, Ronney, Ronney," Jello said, putting his hands behind his head and leaning back in his chair. "I'm going after them."

"That's the most intelligent thing I've heard all day."

"No, I'm serious. Imagine the shots I'd get!"

"What, you want to be in the *National Geographic*?"

He looked at me. "Why not? At the very least, my photos would be uploaded on all the national networks, with my name attached to them. What better way to get noticed?"

"It is said that normal people go to photography school, get an internship, and get a job."

Jello shook his head. "You don't get it. Imagine us going out and tracking down one of those cats. I can even get some night filters for my camera."

"Us."

"What?"

"You said 'us.'"

Jello looked at me, a little hurt. "Well, yeah."

I shook my head. I swear to God, sometimes he acts like a kid, jumping up and down with ideas like these—he was doing shit like this when we were best friends in kindergarten, and he hasn't stopped. Jello's not dumb; he's just, well, a kid. He never had to seal the windows in the winter or go find his kid sister the day she ran away. Jello's parents are actually pretty normal. Maybe having normal parents means you get the privilege of being a kid. Sometimes, if I have my guard down around him, his enthusiasm is contagious, and for a moment I feel like a kid, too. But then reality strikes, and I'm an adult in a teen's body all over again. For Jello, I don't think reality has ever quite hit him.

I scanned Jello's basement room: His walls were plastered with his framed photos, and his photography gear, tripods, and shit were lined up against his walls all nice and neat. The thing was, if anyone could actually get a picture or two of these animals, it would be Jello. His photos were really pretty amazing, I must say so myself. He was not some normal teenager dicking around with some expensive-ass camera that has two thousand features but he only uses the photo button. No. Jello actually knows what to do with those two thousand features. He's a goddamn prodigy, sitting in the basement of some small town in the middle of nowhere, waiting to be found.

I looked at him again. Maybe he's not waiting anymore.

"So you want me to go with you on a jungle safari," I said. It wasn't a question.

"Who else?" Jello plopped a grape into his mouth.

My eyebrows lifted. "Grapes?"

Jello shrugged his wide shoulders. "Toning up, man."

I groaned. "Serious? You could beat the shit out of me any day."

"You set the bar pretty low, Ronney."

I fake punched him in the arm again, and he fake fell over again. It was true, though: Jello, contrary to his name, did not need to "tone up." He could have all the girls he wanted, if he played his cards right.

Jello turned back to his screens. "Come on. Who else would I want to come with me? Think about it."

"I already did think about it," I said.

"And?"

"And if we were going to find said lion, or said wildebeest, or said whatever the fuck is out there, how are we going to stop it from eating us? It's going to be kind of hungry."

Jello got a thoughtful look on his face. "Huh."

I was in shock. He hadn't thought about this?

"And," I said, on a roll, "how are we going to find these animals in the first place? Make lion calls? Wildebeest snorts?" I waved my arm in the air. "Hell, does a wildebeest even snort in the first place?"

Jello looked impressed. "Well, you are the brains," he said.

"Common sense," I corrected. "And common sense says that this is a no go."

"Okay, okay," Jello said, closing the streaming window. "Fine. Whatever. Don't help."

"Don't be a dick," I said. "Come on. This is your reality check."

Jello opened up a new browser window and started typing something.

I sighed inside. He was so *sensitive* sometimes. I let him pout while I grabbed a bag of stale chips from his bookshelf. Those animals were probably long gone, anyway. It's kind of funny, the things that bug me out—aliens, cell phone satellites, sudden changes in weather. But those animals, not so much. I think everyone's allowed at least two huge self-contradictions in their lives. For me, being not freaked out by wild animals of prey would be one of them. But that kid this afternoon. What did he mean, I took his jeans?

Jello was still clicking away and chuckled. "Here, look at this."

I walked over and looked at the image on his screens. "What the—"

Jello's shoulders squared up with pride. "Yup."

"But how did you—"

He grinned. "It's all in the timing, my dear Ronney."

Jello knows I hate it when he says *my dear Ronney*, but right then I didn't care. Before me was a picture of a squirrel falling through the sky, right into the camera; its forearms and legs were spread-eagle, and it had the funniest damn look on its face, a mixture of astonishment and squirrelly joy, like it was at an amusement park.

It was hilarious.

And it had 792,230 hits.

Jello paused a moment, then refreshed the screen.

810,102 hits.

Jello beamed. "I uploaded it two hours ago."

"Two *hours?*"

"Yup." Jello popped another grape into his mouth. "This is *your* reality check, R-Man. Help me out. This is what I can do with a squirrel. If I get a couple pictures of these animals, my career will be made."

I found myself telling him I'd think about it.

4

THE NEXT MORNING I HAD ANOTHER TEXT FROM
Jello.

Come on, help me, it'll be fun.

Maybe.

**Someone just reported a hyena in the Walmart parking
lot. Imagine if I had gotten a picture of that. A crouching
hyena behind an SUV. Maybe on top of it. Inside of it.**

**This sounds like a ton of fun. I'm sweating with excite-
ment.**

Come on. We'll go down in history. Total fun.

Right.

I couldn't think about Jello's safari for too long, though,
because first thing that day, I had to go on the roof. It was what
I thought: The windstorm had ripped off half our shingles. I
cussed and threw open my parents' bedroom door. He was in
bed, just like I knew he'd be.

"You need to call in for me," I said.

Dad groaned, like I was telling him he needed to push a Boeing jet down the runway with his two bare hands.

"If it rains, we're screwed. They're forecasting another storm in the next couple days."

Dad turned on his back and put his good arm across his forehead. "You need to go to school, Ronney."

The inside of my mouth turned bitter. "You going to call the roofers, then? You going to actually get dressed and wait for them to come?"

"You've been missing too much."

My jaw got tight. "You didn't answer either question."

Silence.

I left their room and grabbed my phone to call Jack's Roofing. The number was still in my phone from last year: Dad was too depressed and Mom was too anxious at the time, so it was up to me to call them when a tornado ripped through the county.

"Jack's Roofing."

"Jack, this is Ronney. I called you last year—"

"Oh, yeah, yeah. We know you, kid." He paused. "Your dad's doing better?" Jack's voice was cheery, in a forced kind of way.

"Nope."

"Yeah, yeah." Jack coughed. "So the storm got you, too?"

"Can you come take a look? Lots of shingles down."

"Kid, we're slammed from the storm. Phone's ringing off the hook. But yeah. Ten o'clock. We'll be there."

"No pressure, whenever you can."

"We'll be there—I got you on the list."

I hung up, embarrassed. I knew Jack was feeling bad for me—for us—but I didn't want pity. I wanted a goddamn roofer. Last year, after the tornado, Jack muttered something about how he'd never had a fourteen-year-old putting in a repair order before. He had totally seen what was going on and didn't say a single word about it. He did give me a crazy-ass deal, though, almost half of what the guys in Listig, the other town over, had quoted me. Did one hell of a job, too.

Sometimes it's lousy to wait all day for some repair crew, but it's not as bad as it seems. In fact, I kind of enjoy fixing up the house, making sure stuff works. While Jello streams stupid cats on his computer, I'm glued to the do-it-yourself videos, the fixing and repairing and grouting and laying—how else am I going to take care of things? I memorized a couple of my parents' credit cards a long time ago, and they mostly keep up on their bills, though with Dad sitting around, it gets tight. Before, we used to go to a really awesome water park at least two or three times each summer, and we even took a helicopter ride over the Grand Canyon once when we were on vacation. But after Dad got fired from his job—it was within the first two weeks of his depression, because he stopped showing up—we started using coupons, and Mom started taking some of our favorite food out of the grocery cart and putting it back on the shelf. She talked more and more about money, and all of her talking made me worry, so I logged into their credit card accounts and saw that we were behind on our bills, which according to the credit card history, we never had been before. Of course, it only got worse once Dad landed in the hospital. That was when I started checking their credit card accounts maybe once a week. Mom doesn't know, but I think she suspects.

Anyway, we don't have a crap house or anything—it's small and nice and a little on the old side—but stuff breaks down, and it's a whole lot cheaper to fix things yourself than to get someone to do it for you. And it doesn't break down all at once, but it will eventually, and you gotta know your shit when it does. No one's ever going to take you by the hand.

People in Makersville know all about us—we're the mixed-race family with two helpless parents, the genius kid sister, and the fix-it son. No one's said a word about it, like they don't say a word about how Dr. Manuel hits his wife or how the Raul family has a seventeen-year-old daughter who sleeps in their car. It's amazing how you can turn a blind eye to stuff sometimes. With practice you can get really good at it.

Dad would call in for me, I knew that much: For him, it would be easier than getting dressed. We have a mutual understanding—I do the things he can't do, like fixing the roof, and he does the things that I can't do, like explaining my absences to the principal. He's been calling in for me for about two years—it started when he got depressed. After the suicide attempt six months ago, they kept him in the psych ward of the hospital for a while to monitor him and get him into therapy. Now we're paying for medications that he doesn't take, which doesn't help, and he's seeing a shrink a couple times a week, but that can't be all that effective either, because he still sits around the house all the time and calls in for me whenever I tell him to.

George would be pissed I stayed home to work on the roof. I texted her to let her know not to wait for me, that I was working on a project. That's what I call the stuff I do around the house. Projects. "But, Ronney," she always says, her lips puckering up in frustration, "you gotta go to *class*. They have projects too."

We have this conversation all the time. "Those projects aren't real," I say back.

"Of course they are," she says. This is when she usually shakes her head and the gorgeous mane of her hair. It's so thick I gotta shove my hands in my pockets or I'll reach for it, I swear. "You get real As, then you get real scholarships, then you get into a real college without really going broke, and then you get a real job and a real life."

"Yeah, well, that's for normal people," I say. "For me, if I don't fix that real heating system, my real ass is going to freeze and my real family is going to die. And that happens faster than any little class project due date."

Then a certain look deepens in her eyes, and in that moment I can tell she gets what my life is like. Usually I change the subject before her eyes get all wet, but sometimes I'm not fast enough, and a tear slides down her ivory skin. When *that* happens, I get this sudden, frantic urge to rip open the world for her. That's when I have to walk away, or I'll do something stupid. I don't know what I'd do, but it would be something really freaking stupid. She's never accused me of being a jackass when I suddenly leave like that; sometimes I wish she would, because that would mean she didn't understand, and well, it's kind of weird when girls understand just how hard it is to be friends.

I was going through the refrigerator when Mina bounced in, all decked out in her typical Mina-monochromatic-orange outfit: orange T-shirt, orange pants, orange socks, orange tennis shoes, orange plastic bracelet, and a huge orange scrunchy holding back her spiral curls. Mina says that everyone's favorite colors are green, blue, purple, red—everything but orange, and so she wears orange so it won't feel unloved. Or lonely.

"Ron-Ron," she said, hoisting on the backpack that was too heavy for a fourth grader, "Mom said that school was almost called off today, but then Mr. Rockfeller got on TV and said that everything is under control." She gave a little hop and adjusted the weight on her back. "So now we're going to school. I'm glad, because I want to do well in my quiz." That was when Mina noticed that I didn't have my backpack. "You're staying home today?"

"Yeah, Min-o. The storm really ripped up our roof."

Mina nodded, her face suddenly all solemn. "Mom was worried about that when she left for work this morning."

"Really? What did she say?"

"She said she couldn't handle one more thing."

My jaw tightened.

Mina gave her orange bouncy ball a good bounce on the kitchen floor and caught it with one hand. I had given her that thing from a vending machine a year ago, and she still carried it with her everywhere. "You can fix anything, Ron-Ron."

"Bus is coming," I said. "What kind of quiz is it?"

"Science." She stuck out her tongue. "The teacher treats us like we're idiots."

"That's because the other kids *are* idiots."

"But why do I have to listen to her go over the same stuff over and over?"

"It's the curse of being smart," I replied, turning her around to stuff her sack lunch in her backpack.

Mina went to the door and slipped on her orange shoes. "Dad's still in bed?" she asked. Her voice changed.

I tickled her to get that look off her face. Normally, that's when I would kick her out the door, but when I heard a siren in the distance, I decided to walk her to the bus stop and wait until she got on the bus. Just in case.

By the time Mina's bus pulled away, it was still really early in the morning—I probably could have gone to world history, my first class, and made it home in time, but if the guys came over, I couldn't really be positive Dad would answer the door. So, fuck it. Whatever world history I was missing would still be history when I made it back to class.

I figured I had some time to pick up the debris in the yard

and maybe check out the siding—like if some huge branch had slammed into it or something—when I got a reply text from George:

Another project? ☹ Do you want me to drop by after school with some of Dad's cookies?

This is a question that doesn't need to be asked.

I'll be over as soon as I can. ☺

George's whole family is cool. I mean, hell, her dad actually bakes cookies. Whose dad does that? Her family moved to Makersville four years ago from Chicago to get away from the congestion and crime, George said. I guess being a neurosurgeon in rural Indiana is more relaxed than in a big city, although many times her mom still drives like a freak to respond to emergency calls. The regional hospital is over an hour away in Bloomington, and it's small—nothing like in Indianapolis—but if your brain is going to pop and you need a neurosurgeon, it'll do the trick. Her dad works from home on his various engineering projects and travels a lot. And bakes cookies. The three of them actually play board games together in the evenings just because they want to. Her parents often tell her how happy they are with her, sometimes right in front of me.

I put on my work jeans, grabbed a bunch of garbage bags and my gloves, and stepped outside. Some big branches were down, but nothing that I couldn't haul to the curb, and anyway, while I was outside, it wouldn't be a bad thing to start raking the leaves. The September leaves had just begun to drop, but if I stayed on top of it, the yard wouldn't be so bad. There's something about the air this time of year too—nice and crisp, clean.

That's what I was thinking as I was picking up a branch. Then I heard something behind me. I spun around.

Freaking-A, it was that hoodie kid. Without the hoodie.

I froze.

His eyes were bright. "I'm not leaving until you give them back."

5

THAT LITTLE PUNK WAS JUST A COUPLE FEET away from me, his body all tense, hands clenched.

I took a step back. "What the hell?" I said, almost shouting.

His hair hung over his eyes. "I want the jeans," he said.

"Who said you could come here and follow me?" I asked. I raised the branch in my hand. I swear to God, give me a wandering lion or some other crappy cat, but do not give me a stalker kid in my backyard.

"They're not yours," he said, scowling. His voice was a thin, taut wire.

Now I was pissed. It's not like I don't have enough problems in my life. I was trying to fix the goddamn roof, and this kid teletransports into my backyard and accuses me of shit. "I don't know who you are, and I didn't steal anything," I said through my teeth. "Now I'm warning you: Get off my property or I'll fucking hit you."

His eyes flashed. I had been right not to help him yesterday: Never help a stalker.

The kid lifted his chin as he stared up at me. "I'm not afraid of you," he said.

It was a direct challenge, practically a dare. I raised the branch higher. "Leave."

His eyes squinted into a glare.

I swung the branch at him, smacked him across the side. He staggered and fell a couple feet away on some shingles. I loomed over him and raised the branch again. "I warned you," I said. "Now get off my property."

"But they're not yours," he cried, jerking his chin at my work pants. Then he made this little whimpering sound—the sound Mina makes when she's hurt. My chest tugged when he made that sound; I must have smacked him harder than I thought. I immediately wished I hadn't just clobbered him broadside with a tree. Stalker kid or not, he looked really small right then, huddled on the grass.

"Look," I said, suddenly tired, "I bought these jeans with my own money."

"I'll pay you for them."

I stared at him. "You're freaking weird. They're mine, okay? Now get out of here."

He winced a little, and I stepped back. He hauled himself to his feet and limped away. I kind of wanted to help him walk home, because I felt like shit right then. But more than that, I wanted him out of my yard. I had enough garbage to clear out as it was.

• • • •

"You hit a kid?" George's hazel eyes were wide. She dropped the bag of cookies onto the kitchen table.

"I did warn him," I said.

"You hit a *kid*?" she repeated.

I groaned inside. For some reason I was expecting her to say, *Hell yeah, he had it coming.* "What else was I supposed to do," I said, "shed my jeans right there on the spot and stand in my tighty-whities?"

She paused, then pressed her lips together, trying to hide a smile. "You wear tighty-whities?"

My face heated up. "I meant boxers."

"You wear tighty-whities?" she pressed.

"They give more support," I said. My cheeks were a furnace.

She threw back her head and laughed. Like gold, I tell you. Every time.

I reached for the cookies. She slapped my hand away. "You could have asked him about those jeans, helped him out," she said. "Clearly, he was confused."

"Clearly," I said dryly, and snatched the bag from her. The cookies were warm. I popped two into my mouth. Freaking amazing gobs of chocolate and sugar. "I don't think I broke anything," I said through the cookies.

"Ronney!" She sat down.

I swallowed. "Sorry," I said. "I don't think I—"

"I don't care about eating with your mouth full," George said, rolling her eyes. "I do care about you going around and beating up little kids." She had her brown hair pulled back in a ponytail, exposing her neck. I forced my eyes away.

"I wasn't *going around beating up kids*," I said. "He came onto *my* property—trespassing—accusing me of shit that I didn't know what the hell he was talking about. Twice." I took a bite of another cookie. "And anyway, I only give my clothes away to people I know." I kicked off my shoe and started peeling back my sock. "Like you, for instance. Want a sock?"

George grinned. "I do not want your sock."

"How about my shirt?" I asked, starting to yank my T-shirt over my head.

"Ronney!" She laughed again and stopped my arms.

I straightened my shirt and gave her a look. "When was the last time someone came up to you and demanded you remove your clothing?"

The moment I said *that* my face started heating up for real.

George went to our refrigerator, plunked down a gallon of milk on the table, and glanced at me coyly. A wavy lock of hair snuck out of her ponytail, and she tucked it behind her ear with her finger. Then she drank right from the container. I shook my head admiringly. Mom and Dad have never found out.

"And anyway," I said, pulling my thoughts away from her, "the kid challenged me."

"You could have walked away."

"You don't get it," I said. "He challenged me. I couldn't back down. And can I remind you, it was my property. Where was I going to walk to? Should I have hid in my bedroom and let a ten-year-old take up residence in my backyard?"

George went silent, and her silence was condemning.

"So it wasn't the best thing to do," I said quietly.

"Not 'the best thing to do'? Ronney, that was *awful*."

I threw up my hands. "Fine, I confess. I was an ass."

"Um. Yes. You were." Her eyebrows knit together.

"I even regret it, okay? But I got caught up in the moment."

Her face softened, like it usually does when I give in and admit my stupidity. I'd tattoo all the stupid shit I've done across my chest just to see her face like that every day. She's got these really great eyes, the kind that can look right into you and make you forget where you are. And when you admit that she's right—which, okay, she usually is—you can see her visibly relax, like that tension string inside her goes slack now that she knows that you know that she's right.

But it's more than that. For instance, she gets straight As because, like I said, she's amazing. But last year she was teetering on getting an A- in AP Biology, and she nearly had a mental break-down. She was sobbing that she couldn't lose her perfect GPA. And it was kind of ironic, because I'm in school just enough to keep the principal off my back, and she's moaning about how she'll have a little fly's fart of a scratch on her GPA. When I tried to explain this to her, she cried even harder. George always says that she likes how I can put her grades back in perspective, but that looming A- was somehow an A-bomb to George World.

It has to be pretty precarious, to have only perfection or the abyss as your two real options in life. Whenever I tell her she doesn't have to be perfect, she gives me a look like *How can you expect me to believe that?* But she keeps coming back for more, like she's somehow starving and I'm somehow giving her food. I don't know. Maybe no one else tells her that imperfection is okay.

I could see she was going to say more things about that kid, so I said quickly, "The roofers came today."

Her eyes lit up. "Really? What'd they do?"

"The south side of the house." I gave her a look. "Just repairs."

She grinned. "You mean, you didn't tell them you wanted a vaulted ceiling?"

We both reached for the bag of cookies at the same time. I let her go first. "The guys really like me," I said, "but they wouldn't exactly consider that part of their repair quote."

George was looking up at our ceiling, her eyes sparkling away, imagining some sort of palatial roofing. She's always talking about buildings—she sketches them all the time. Some people know from birth what they want to do with their lives. George wants to be an architect. Once she showed me her list of Twenty Steps to Be an Architect, which she made up when she was nine, which she has taped above her bed, which shows she's on step fourteen.

Then you have people like me, who don't know what to do from one bladder of piss to the next.

She grabbed a handful of cookies and was making some sort of cookie house out of them, pinching the soft cookies at the edges to hold them upright. "You see," she said, "if you tell them to lift the roof over your foyer like this"—she tilted upward the cookies that served as a roof—"and then put in a couple skylights"—she jabbed her pinky through the cookie, twice, I guess to let the sunlight in—"it'll really open up the whole feel of the house."

"My parents, I think, would disapprove," I said.

"And maybe you could add a little loft over the living room," she said, breaking off a chunk of cookie and wedging it into the inside of the roof.

"That's an attic you just made," I pointed out.

"Whatever," she said playfully. I found myself grinning and reaching for a cookie to build with and not eat, despite myself: Somehow George can do that to me.

She licked her fingers and grabbed another cookie. "And you must add a sunroom." Through all of her cookie building, a smudge of chocolate got on her cheek. When I saw the smudge, my grin deepened.

She paused. "Why are you smiling like that?"

I shook my head, trying to stop the stampede of images: Wiping it off. Licking it off. "Maybe one day when my parents are gone for the weekend," I said, "I'll take your advice on the roof. But your folks would have to help me get the lumber."

"No problem," she said. But something in her voice changed.

"What is it?" I asked.

"Nothing," she said. Then she smiled. "Whenever you're going to do it, let me know."

"Sure thing," I said. "And you have chocolate on your cheek."

She wiped the smudge off with the back of her hand. "Gone?"

I nodded. "Gone."

We both knew I wouldn't try to help her take it off myself.

Jello had texted me while George was over.

The hyena was found circling the blood-drive-mobile.

Smart hyena. A blood drive is a flashing neon sign, you know.

It got away. There'll be more opportunities.

Lovely. Just what I was hoping for.

I hadn't mentioned Jello's safari to George because I didn't want her to worry. But the truth was, it was sounding better and better the more I tossed it around in my mind. I mean, okay, so we'll carry some meat along with us, just in case, to distract whatever animals we encounter. In case they're hungry. I mean, if you were hungry and someone threw you a heavy slab of fresh, glistening meat that wasn't going to run away, and then there were these living, crazy humans with flashlights and sticks and shit, which one would *you* go after? These animals didn't survive for millions of years by being stupid. Also, there were still a lot of animals out there—by some reporters' estimates about twenty—so the chances were good that if we went looking, we'd find something.

After George went home, I heard Dad moving around. "Ronney?" he called.

I was still tinkering with the cookie house. I exhaled slowly, closed my eyes, then shouted back, "Yeah?"

"You're here?" Dad called back.

"And my answer implies?"

Silence.

"Is Mina home?" he called.

"Not yet."

Silence.

"Mom's picking her up from school today, so they'll both be late," I said. Our voices carried from one end of our house to the other.

"Do you know what's for dinner?" he asked.

"Nope," I shouted. "Not unless you actually do something and make it."

Dad appeared in the bedroom hallway, still in his pajamas, holding his arm. He watched me add another cookie wall to the cookie house, and I ignored him watching me. I was making a little sunroom off the back; that would be George's favorite room. My hands smelled of butter and sugar. Who thinks of building a house out of cookies instead of just eating them? George. Of course. *I'll surprise her with a monster cookie house when I'm done tomorrow,* I thought.

"What'd the roofers say?" Dad finally asked.

"You didn't hear them?"

Dad shook his head. I wasn't sure if he really hadn't heard them or if he just didn't have the energy to respond.

"Seven hundred," I said.

Dad ran his fingers through his hair.

"Better now than later. Storm's coming," I said. I wadded a cookie into a cookie ball, then popped it into my mouth.

Dad sighed and came into the kitchen, started poking around in the refrigerator. He eventually went into the pantry and grabbed a bag of chips but struggled to open them with one hand. I watched him struggle for a while, debating whether to help him or not. Finally I said, "Got it?"

Dad ignored me, which was nothing new, but it still made me feel like a piece of shit. There was no way I was going to ask him a second time, so I put a bemused expression on my face, and after what seemed like twenty minutes, Dad swore, used his teeth to open the bag, then propped it in the crook of his bad arm. "Visa or Mastercard?" he asked.

"Mastercard," I said. "You get double points on home repair purchases."

"Oh." Dad looked impressed. "Thanks."

I gave a small nod. "We're one-thirtieth of our way toward getting a family trip to Cancún. It's something like a million points. Pack your bags—we're getting close."

I thought Dad would smile at that, but he didn't. "Anyway," I continued, "I want to work on the living room wall. The one with the water damage from last year. The paint's peeled, and there's probably rot behind it."

"You just spent seven hundred dollars, Ronney."

"I'm sure it's nothing with all the new clients you've been signing on," I said.

Dad cleared his throat.

I shot him a look. "That's what you do all day in your bedroom, right? Building up your business?"

Dad stared at me with a blank expression on his face. "It's not that easy, Ronney."

"Nothing is. But some things are easier than others. Like typing." I formed a little cookie chimney with my fingers.

"What's that supposed to mean?"

"Typing with two hands is easier than typing with one." I nodded at his shoulder. "Too bad you didn't think about that before—"

"Stop it."

"They actually quoted me nine hundred dollars, but I worked it down to seven."

Dad muttered something and headed back to his room.

"That mathematical equation means I just saved you two hundred dollars," I called out after him.

He closed his door.

"You're welcome," I said quietly.

It's hard to talk to someone who isn't really there. In this house, we've all wrapped ourselves with such thick metal, it's just one robot talking to another robot. Except for Mina. But she'll learn. I guess that'll be a good day when she does.

I guess.

6

AT THE HOSPITAL THE DOCTORS TOLD US THAT clinical depression is a chemical imbalance in the brain; sometimes it gets better and sometimes it gets worse, but it always was there and always will be. That didn't stop us, however, from wondering why it started when Dad was forty-two, if there was anything that triggered it, and if it was us. Mom said it could have been his old job, which he hated. I said it could've been when he realized he was stuck in a loser life and hadn't saved the world yet. Mina said it could've been when she got that one and only D on her social studies quiz. When she said that, I grabbed one of our kitchen chairs, went outside, and smashed it on the sidewalk until she ran out, sobbing, and begged me to stop.

However it started, the day after that infamous Thursday—six months ago now, while Mom was at the hospital with him—I put in a call and replaced the living room carpet. The smell of blood still clung to the walls like a ghost, and it mixed with that new-carpet smell until the stench was so thick I hopped into my bedroom through my window the whole next week just to avoid it. Mom said I was overreacting. I busted out laughing when she said that, which made her cry and get her pills.

He couldn't even do it right. If his word is worth anything, according to Dad, he couldn't put it to his head like normal people. Instead he held it at arm's length and pointed at where his head should be, but his hand and arm were shaking so hard that when he pulled the trigger, he caught himself in the shoulder.

In the *shoulder*, for chrissake.

Maybe I should have figured it out, because he was nervous as hell the days before. For instance, he broke four glasses washing dishes from dinner one night. That's right: four. How the hell do you break four glasses? I'll never find out, because the only thing I heard was the four rapid sounds of glasses shattering on the floor, and when we got to Dad, there he was in the middle of the kitchen, with soapy hands and a blank look on his face, surrounded by a sea of glass.

Or when he jumped a mile high when Mina slammed the kitchen door coming home from school. Come on; it's *Mina*. Doors slam behind her all the time. Well, like I said, he jumped to the ceiling and then started screaming at her for slamming the door and she started to cry and then Mom came in to see what was wrong and Dad was running his hands through his hair and his arms were shaking and Mina launched herself onto Mom, sobbing. All for a slammed door.

At first it had seemed like maybe there was hope for him after all. For most of my life Dad's done nothing but complain about his insurance job. Two years ago, after he got fired and started sitting around the house, he mumbled something about starting his own business. Online marketing. Something that can *utilize his skill set*. *Where he's in control, for once.* That's how he put it. And in the beginning, his new business was all he talked about, read about, dreamed about. Maybe he realized it was harder than he thought, or that he didn't have the skill set he thought he had, or whatever, because after he couldn't get any clients—well, there were the two clients he did have who decided to "terminate the relationship"— he talked less and less of his dreams and started to sit around all day in front of the computer. That was funny since, new job or old job, he was still sitting around looking at a screen—but with his old job, he'd sit around wearing actual clothing, like jeans. And he'd talk to us: Sometimes we'd watch soccer together or those cop shows. With his new job, he took his laptop into in my parents' room and, well, lived there.

Until he tried to die in the living room. That's ironic—isn't it? Dying in the living room? I called it the dying room while Dad was in the hospital until Mina saw Mom cry and begged me not to call it that again, which I begrudgingly promised, for her.

Mina has never seen me cry; I make a point of that. It was after Dad's depression started that I began to lock my bedroom door because I didn't want anyone to walk in on me when I was crying, not even the chance. There is this small, white, stuffed-animal gorilla that Dad had won for me when I was a kid—it was at Makersville's Fourth of July carnival, on the pop-the-balloon game—and the gorilla always sat on my bed. Holding it made me feel better on the days when I got my report card, which showed me failing my classes, or when Mom would tell Dad that the neighbors were complaining that our grass was too long, and he would walk away from her as if she didn't exist. Those were the times that I would lock my door and hold that little gorilla, and its white fur would grow damp as I held it. I thought this was my secret until one night when Dad had been particularly heartless. I was holding my gorilla when there was a small *tap-tap-tap* at the door. It was Mina. I guess all this time she had heard me crying through the wall that our bedrooms share. I opened the door and let her crawl into my bed with me. That was when she started to cry, and to make her feel better, I took the closest object that I had at hand, an orange bouncy ball on my nightstand, and gave it to her. *It's special*, I said. *Why?* she asked. *Because now it's not alone, now that it's with you*, I said. I guess what I said really stuck with her, because the next day she held it in her left hand from sunup to sundown and did her schoolwork with her right. That had been the first time that she climbed into bed with me, and after that night, I made sure to cry silently.

The Tuesday after the guys fixed the roof, the storm was bad, just like they had predicted. Heavy rains, lightning, more winds whipping around, and whatever debris people hadn't yet picked up was flying around again. *Good thing I got those roofers to come when they did*, I thought. If I'd waited for Mom to do anything about it, we'd be drenched right now. It looked like the storm freaked out some of the animals, too, because the newscasters reported that the ostrich had run out into oncoming traffic, and, well, that was the end of the ostrich.

I tossed my work jeans in the corner of my room, the jeans I was wearing when that stalker kid came to visit last week. I had picked the jeans up at the secondhand store because they had these question marks painted all over them. It seemed pretty apt in the moment. I don't know why. I just liked them, and I even started wearing them on Thursdays, which was a big switch for me.

Anyway, those jeans made that kid hunt me down. A part of me wanted to wait for him to come back so I could throw them in his face and tell him to leave me the fuck alone, but another part wanted to keep those jeans just to make him miserable. In a way I'd be doing that kid a favor: At some point you gotta learn that you can't do shit about most things in life. That's how it is. The earlier you learn that the better.

My phone buzzed.

What you doing?

Nothing much, just admiring a cookie house.

Help me with my safari.

This is the third time.

I know.

A couple moments later he texted me again.

You still there?

Yeah.

Well?

A surge of anger coursed through me. I felt so fucking old right then. Maybe eighty. And here was Jello, enjoying it all.

I'm in. Tell me when and I'll be over.

Later tonight?

I was in the middle of texting him back when Mina bounded through the door, her orange raincoat dripping. "Ron-Ron!" she shouted, throwing her wet-dog body into my arms. "I have a new study buddy!"

I looked to the door, and goddammit, who did I see next to her? Yes. The stalker kid. With a shit-eating smirk on his face. All words choked in my throat as Mina introduced the two of us.

His name was Sam.

It turned out that Mina and Sam Caldwell were in the same class and that he was the only boy who didn't pull Mina's hair. Therefore, Sam was the only boy Mina would speak to. It also turned out that *somehow*, within, oh, the last handful of days, Sam happened to realize that he was failing his math class and, *under great and mysterious ties of coincidence*, specifically asked his teacher if Mina could help him study.

Mina, in gratitude to her non-hair-pulling classmate, said yes. Obviously. And in return for *that*, Sam would help Mina practice her spelling words to perfection. Their fourth-grade teacher thought this was all quite splendid.

Mina gave me a guilty shrug. "I thought you might be busy some nights—maybe you wouldn't have time to help me out with my spelling list. I know every night is a lot." Her eyes pleaded with mine. "But now with both you and Sam, it's better."

Sam smiled.

My jaw suddenly hurt, it was so tight. "And you chose to study here? Why not at Sam's house?"

"My parents don't get home until late," Sam said smugly. "Mina said her dad is always around."

"And there's lots of grown-ups here. Because you're sometimes around too, Ron-Ron," Mina chimed in.

I slammed my hand down on the kitchen table, and the two kids jumped. "Don't you ever call me that in front of him," I said slowly.

Mina froze.

Dad must have heard his name, because he showed up from the bedroom hallway. "They're study partners, Ronney," Dad said. "Leave Sam alone."

I swear to God, I wanted to punch a hole in the wall. Instead, I towered over Sam. "One wrong move, asshole, and I'll finish kicking the crap out of you."

For an instant Sam's eyes widened. Then a determined look came over him, and he met my gaze, challenging.

I knew Mina's face was starting to crumple up, so I didn't look at her. I grabbed my bag and headed for the door. I don't like going out in the rain, and I was early to head to Jello's, but I had to get out of there. I had one more reason to hate my house.

7

THERE'S A LOT OF SHIT IN THE RAIN. THAT'S
what the Internet says. Acid and soot and whatever the hell we
put in the sky, well, it comes raining back down on us. The Statue
of Liberty is green because of a chemical reaction from the acid
in the rain. And if that's what rain'll do to metal, think what it
does to flesh and blood.

But rain or no rain, there was no way I was going to watch that
Sam kid in my kitchen just then. I mean, what the hell? I thwack
him with a tree, and he decides he's going to come to my place
and get all over my kid sister? For what, my lousy jeans? Who
does that?

Suddenly stalker kids listed higher than government-spon-
sored UFOs. Stalker kids now ranked number two, just below
Thursdays. Which was in three days, I might add.

I was biking to Jello's in the full fall of the rain when a white
van with huge lettering, ACTION 2 NEWS TV, pulled up beside me,

windshield wipers swiping away. The passenger window rolled down, and a clean-cut guy stuck his head out the window and stared at me. "Hey, kid! You speak English? *Ingles?*"

I stopped and pointed to my coarse black hair, thin lips, and high cheekbones. "I'm not Mexican, you jackass."

"Oh. I'm Dan. I'm from Action 2 News."

"I figured that out."

"Where's Maricopa Drive? I know I'm close."

"You got an animal?"

Dan could barely contain his excitement. "A couple of reports about a gray wolf. I've been circling around here for twenty minutes, can't find the street."

"Yeah. They design neighborhoods like this for people like you."

He scowled. "Come on, kid."

So I gave him the best directions I could, even though they were kind of shit, since the place is a labyrinth. A part of me wanted to give him shit directions—intentionally, I mean—but then I realized that if I could get tight with the news crew, maybe we could get a heads-up on the locations of these animals so two teenage guys wouldn't have to wander around the county asking people where the nearest saber-tooth was. The news guy looked relieved, and I made sure he knew my name as he pulled away.

Maybe this safari wouldn't be so hard after all.

The only bad thing about using Jello's basement window as an entry is when it rains. His window is two feet from the bottom of the window well, but when it rains and the water is up to my ankles, it gets annoying. If your feet stay wet for too long, then you can get athlete's foot or a parasitic skin disease from Malaysia. Some headline said that. George says that I read the wrong headlines, but whatever.

Jello wasn't in his room when I dropped in, but I could hear footsteps parading above me on the first floor. I slid into his computer chair, and of course he had been watching his falling-squirrel hit count, which was now around a million. I shook my head, but really I couldn't help getting a little excited. If he could do this with a squirrel, what the hell could he do with that wolf? Or a tiger?

My phone buzzed. It was George.

What you doing?

I'm at Jello's, watching his squirrel hit count. You?

Oh, how funny! I'm doing the same thing. Right around a million, right? Minus 182?

Didn't do the math, but if you say so.

I've been watching this thing since he uploaded it—so, so cool.

Yup. And fyi—I put a couple additions on your cookie house, tried to make a little cookie jacuzzi but it didn't do well when I turned the blowers on. I'll give it to you tomorrow.

LOL and so great! BTW, I just decided I'm going to invent a solar-powered window shade that moves with the daylight.

She sent that to me in a text, I kid you not.

You're the best. Remember, best does not mean perfect.

No, you're the best!

Because god knows I'm not perfect.

LOL! But you ARE the best.

No, you are.

No, you are.

No, you are.

I could do that all day.

The basement door opened, and Jello came crashing down the stairs. I swear, he doesn't just go down the stairs like normal people. No. He's a freaking bowling ball.

Jello grinned when he saw me. "Wow, Ronney, you're early." He fake punched me in the shoulder. I fake fell over. "And you pissed all over my computer chair."

"It's the rain," I said, picking myself off the floor.

"And your feet smell like rot. Put your shoes back on."

"They're wet."

Jello fake threw up on my feet.

"There's a wolf in the neighborhood," I said.

Jello snapped to attention. "Really? Where?"

"I talked with this TV guy on the way over, maybe ten minutes ago. He was looking for Maricopa Drive."

Jello snorted. "He won't find it."

"I know. But I gave him decent directions, which means—"

Jello's eyes grew big. "He'll be getting there about now," he finished. He ran around his room, gathering his gear. "R-Man, can you carry some stuff?"

"Sure," I said. "But I want to wear your shoes."

Jello threw me a look.

"Mine are wet," I said. "Socks, too. Clean ones," I added.

"But we're going to get wet once we go outside," he protested.

I shrugged.

Jello groaned. "Fine. Go get them."

I knew exactly where they were. It's not like this was the first time.

One reason why it's impossible to find Maricopa Drive is because it's not really a street. It's actually a hidden driveway for all the new la-di-da houses to branch from so they can feel smug together. Makersville is small, about twenty thousand people, but land is cheap; this part of the neighborhood popped up when folks in Bloomington realized they could build for almost nothing and make the commute. So you have the old side of the neighborhood—where Jello, George, and I live—that has dinky houses, and then the new side, with McMansions. I try to avoid this area whenever I can. George's parents are talking about moving to the McMansion side next year, which blows, so I suppose I'll just have to deal with it.

However, a hungry wolf roaming around the McMansions is another reason to make a visit, if one happens to be on a safari.

Sure enough, by the time Jello and I got over there, our bikes' back tires kicking even more water onto us, the crew from the TV news van was unloading. The distant sound of sirens cut through the rain.

Dan the News Man ran over to us.

"Ronney, right?" He was frantically zipping up his waterproof jacket, which, by the way, I rather envied at the moment.

"Hey." I tried to sound calm.

"You boys need to clear out of here," he said, adjusting the microphone under his jacket. "We overheard a call-in; a guy's been attacked, okay?"

"Really? Who?" Jello's voice squeaked with excitement.

I suddenly remembered we forgot the meat.

The sirens were a lot closer now.

Dan put a hand on my shoulder and turned us back to our bikes. "Go home, kids. The police are going to kick you out, anyway. And seriously. This guy's in bad shape."

"The wolf got him?" I asked.

Dan's lips twitched in the way that said *I'm not supposed to tell you, but my lip-twitching just told you yes* as another of the TV crewmen ran at us. "Dan! Get those kids out of here!"

"I'm trying!" he yelled back.

So we jumped on our bikes and backtracked, passing three squad cars and two ambulances—the most excitement this neighborhood's had since World War II.

A couple blocks away, Jello stopped so suddenly he skidded and almost fell over. "Okay, my dear Ronney," he announced, wiping the rain from his eyes. "Let's turn back."

"What?" I asked. I had heard him correctly; I just wanted him to sound stupid a second time.

"Let's turn back," he repeated. "The wolf's there—that's what the man said."

"You don't know that," I said. "Maybe not anymore. And besides, we forgot the meat."

"We don't need meat," Jello said.

"Like hell we don't."

"The wolf already took a bite out of that guy. So it's probably had a snack."

"A snack," I said pointedly, "does not fill one up."

"You know what I mean." Jello turned his bike around.

Something in his voice pissed me off. "I absolutely know what you mean," I snapped. "It's had a snack. How many snacks a day do *you* fucking have, Jello? You're trying to tell me that we're going there without another little snack for it except our own meaty bodies?" I tightened my hands around my handlebars. "And you know I hate being out in the rain."

Jello looked at me, considering. The sound of sirens wailing was replaced by the sound of dogs barking in the distance. Then he shook his head, like he was stunned that his invincible reasoning had failed to persuade me. "Come on, R-Man. We can't miss this," he said.

"No." I got back on my bike. "That's only the second time, anyway."

As we rode back to my place, we both kept our eye out for the wolf. Just in case.

• • •

That Sam freak was gone by the time Jello and I got home. Looks like he and Mina had reached some sort of study-buddy nirvana, and his brain couldn't take any more. Jello waited around while I hopped in the shower to wash off the rain, and when I got out, I could hear him and Mom talking.

Mom likes Jello. That's a good thing, I guess, since he's over a lot. She's also deemed him "a good influence on me," which illustrates her total lack of judgment. I don't see how someone who would chase down a wolf without a gun or meat could be a good influence on anyone except a maniacal bush hunter. The only parentally admirable thing he does is finish his homework.

For the record, homework is bullshit. Getting As does not guarantee intelligence, and Jello just illustrated that. I don't care that he aces AP Chemistry; if they had a class on common sense, he'd be screwed. He even told me once that I could teach that class, and I'd probably give him an F. I like to remind him of that whenever I can.

Okay, I know what Mom thinks she means. She thinks that since he doesn't do drugs or anything like that, he's therefore a virtuous, upright teenager. And I have to say in that sense she's right. Jello doesn't do drugs because, clearly, he doesn't need to alter his mind any further. However, according to Mom's own definition, my very own pill-popping, mood-altering, some-times-not-so-regimented mother is not, therefore, a good influence on me. I really want to point this out to her one day, but that would only make her take her pills.

Hilarious, isn't it?

Mom's got her good points; don't get me wrong. She puts my shoes away on a daily basis, makes great mango cheesecakes and coconut puddings, and listens to Mina a whole hell of a lot better than Dad. And though she's pretty spineless, sometimes I can't help but feel bad for her. I mean, what Dad did to her. If I were her, I'd feel stupid as hell for choosing to marry someone who would blow out his shoulder while trying to blow off his head. Sometimes I've gotten really mad that she hasn't picked up and left him, and other times I respect the fact that she's still sticking around, which means that she hasn't given up on us all.

Before Dad got depressed, he used to tell us stories of what it was like growing up, and he did it in a funny way so Mom would laugh. Actually, Mom would laugh so hard she would snort, and that would make us start laughing, and us laughing would make her laugh harder and snort more, which would make us laugh harder—that kind of thing. It was a well-known fact in our family that Dad could make Mom snort. I can't remember the last time that happened. Now she's pretty quiet; she only talks when she needs to tell me to put away the dishes or ask Mina to set the table. In the beginning she and Dad would talk in hushed voices behind their closed door, and now sometimes I still hear her voice through the door, but I never hear his voice in return. People in town have told me that Mom is known to snap at her employees at the bank, which I find strange, because she isn't testy with us at home, not even close.

But she does take her pills, and she started that when I was a kid. For anxiety. As needed. I mean, why not do something to calm you down? When I've asked her that, she says it's not that easy. And you know, I get that. I do. It's not always that easy. Still, sometimes she takes her meds more than she should, and then she gets tired and sleeps a lot, and then I have to take care of Mina and the house *and* Mom's pills, and sometimes that's just one thing too much.

The first time I found Mom doubling up on her pills was a couple years ago. She was sleeping, again, and I went in and counted her meds and saw that she only had four pills left, when she had just refilled the bottle the week before. And I couldn't do shit about any of it.

That's when I took that pill bottle, slammed it against the wall, and must have started shouting, because Dad and Mina came to see what was the matter. Dad's mouth was moving, telling me to stop shouting although I could swear I wasn't, and Mina started crying. Mom of course was still sleeping, and all I could hear was this great hissing silence in my ears, and the world went all one, big, angry color until Mina ran at me and hugged me around the waist, and what do you know, a rush of sounds came crashing back down on me, like they had been stuck on the ceiling. Somehow during it all I broke a window in the dining room, although I could swear I hadn't even touched it.

That only happened once. My shouting, I mean. And the window. Mom's done her sleeping thing a number of times since Dad's suicide attempt, but for those I didn't freak out or anything.

I mean, how the hell can I fix any of this? So I do what I do really well these days: focus on my own shit.

Mina has yet to learn this. Once she snuck into my room while I was listening to some Rachmaninoff and was bawling her eyes out. Turns out she thought that Mom was taking her pills because of something the two of us did. She crawled into my lap like some little puppy and just cried and cried, and I think she'd still be crying today if I hadn't told her that Mom's pills are none of our business. Mina didn't quite get that, but she's a kid. It's true, though. What Mom does has nothing to do with us.

Mina also has yet to learn that she can't go around just trusting everyone. Like that Sam. So what that he doesn't pull her hair? Maybe he's not the hair-pulling type. But who's to say that he's not the kind of freak who lures people in and then chops them up when they're not looking? There's lots of different types of stalkers out there; you can't lump them all into one category.

Mom and Jello were watching TV—Dan the News Man's voice was loud and rapid-fire, all crazed—when I went back into my bedroom to get my favorite T-shirt. Rain slashed at the windows. And freaking-A, as I was grabbing my shirt off of the back of my chair, that's when I noticed it, and I almost pissed myself.

My jeans were gone.

8

I BARGED INTO MINA'S ROOM, KICKED ASIDE her teddy bear, and hauled her out of her orange desk. "Where did they go?" I yelled, grabbing her by the shoulders.

Her almond eyes went wide with fear. "What do you mean?"

"You know what I mean."

She shook her head. "I don't know."

"Like hell you don't."

"He told me to." She teared up. "They're his brother Nick's, and you took them. That's what Sam said."

"And you believed that little punk-ass?" My voice pinched. The TV was still blaring in the living room.

"No," she said, choking on the word. "But he said you wouldn't mind."

"That you would freaking steal my jeans? For *him*?"

She gave a little cry. "Stop it!"

I loosened my grip on her shoulders, but not entirely.

"What is going on here?" Mom asked, rushing in. She yanked me away from Mina.

"That little shit went into my room and stole my work jeans," I said. I articulated the words nice and hard.

Mina pressed the palms of her hands to her ears and started to cry.

"You will not call your sister that name," Mom said.

"A little shit? I could call her a lot worse things than that. For instance, I could say—"

Mina started howling.

"Ronney," Mom said.

"I can't help it she can't take it," I replied. "She stole my jeans."

Mom's face hardened. "She's in fourth grade, Ronney."

"Oh, so she can do anything she wants, then? You want to raise a brat?"

Mom turned and yanked Mina's hands from her ears. "Did you steal Ronney's jeans?"

"They belong to Sam's brother," she moaned in a stuffed-up voice.

"I bought them from the secondhand store with my own money," I retorted. "This Nick is a shit for giving them away and wanting them back."

"Ronney," Mom said, turning to me.

"I didn't say that Mina was a—"

"Nick ran away from home," Mina blurted out. "I'm not supposed to tell you."

Mom shook her head. "Now, Mina, you don't want to go around spreading rumors—"

"But it's true," Mina said, swiping at her little pug nose. "Back in the spring."

I gave her a *you are dumb* look. "Then why haven't we have heard of this? No TV? No newspapers?"

Mina gave me a hurt look back. "His parents didn't want a public search. Nick just turned eighteen, and his dad said that if he wanted to come home, he'd come home. And Nick's parents have been giving everything of his to the secondhand store."

"Are you kidding? They're dumping off his stuff?" I asked. That's harsh. Even for me.

Mina dragged the back of her hand across her nose. "Sam's been trying to buy it all back with his allowance," she said.

I whistled and shook my head, impressed.

Now that I thought about it, I had vaguely heard of Nick Caldwell at school; he was two years ahead of me, a senior, and into baseball. We were completely different, except that both our parents sucked ass. I mean, you don't run away from home unless it's really crap. With the size of our town, either Nick didn't tell a soul where he was going or he had some damn good friends with locks on their mouths. If Sam was so stalker-bent on getting those jeans, he and his brother must have been close. Real close. Stalkers can be determined, I realized. Maybe for good reasons.

Dad appeared in the doorway of Mina's room and looked at the three of us. "What's going on?" he asked.

"So nice of you to join us," I said.

"The kids were fighting," Mom said.

Mina sniffled and looked at me.

Dad looked at Mom. "You're taking care of it?"

"Yes, dear," she said, but her voice was heavy.

Dad started to walk away.

"She has to take care of it," I said loudly, "because you're sure as hell not."

Dad stopped but didn't turn and look at us.

I know—I can be a dick. I won't pretend I'm perfect. But it's amazing how you can learn to un-need people if you have to. It gets awkward when Dad is eating chips on the couch. Sometimes I stare at him and wonder what the hell he's doing here. Maybe he feels the same way.

Dad was running his hand through his hair when Jello poked his head into the doorway. "Um, hello?" he said. Jello tried to keep a distance from Dad. "I think I should be going home now. My parents want me home for dinner."

"You're not taking your bike in this storm and with that wolf on the loose," Mom said. "And all the other whatsits." She looked at Dad. "You want to drive Jello home?"

Dad shook his head. "I'm tired."

Mom looked away and exhaled slowly.

"Of course you're tired," I said to him. "It's hard work being tired all day."

"I'll take you," Mom said to Jello.

We shuffled down the hallway, one big pod of us, when Dan the News Man appeared back on the screen. His face stared right into the camera, his raincoat shining from the pouring rain. ". . . the wolf is estimated to be at least one hundred fifty pounds and was shot dead just minutes ago by five deputies with assault rifles, authorized by a shoot-to-kill order from the county sheriff."

That's when Mina started shrieking. I mean, *shrieking*. She doubled over, put her arms over her head like someone was going to hit her, and let loose these ear-piercing screams that no human should ever endure.

This time Mom grabbed Mina by the shoulders. "Mina," she shouted.

"Shoot to kill! Shoot to kill!" Mina sobbed, shaking her head. Her entire body trembled as she gasped for air, only to cough-cry it out again. "I don't want that wolf dead," she moaned.

Dad stood there, stick straight, his lips pressed into a thin line.

"That wolf's gonna be okay, Mina," I said quietly. Mina wrenched herself from Mom and threw herself at me, wrapping her arms around my waist like a vine.

"I don't want to be alone, Ron-Ron," Mina sobbed into my shirt.

"We'll go with Mom and Jello in the car, okay?" I said, rubbing her back.

We all stood around like dumb-asses while Mina drenched my favorite T-shirt. When she was done, the four of us piled into the car and let Dad do whatever he did when we left him. I sat in the back seat with Mina, and Mom drove us over to Jello's in silence. Mina had one hand in mine, and her other hand grasped her little orange bouncy ball. I normally would have been annoyed about her getting my T-shirt all nasty. But not this time.

Mina didn't scream the day Dad shot himself, six months ago on a Thursday. Mom, Mina, and I had gone out to the movies, and when we came back, we found Dad in the living room, the brown carpet all wet and black and thick with stench. Mom rushed over to him, I called 911, and Mina just stood there, staring at Dad on the floor, her eyes big and wide. Mina was still staring when I hung up the phone, and that's when I slapped her in the face like they do in the movies, and she fell onto the floor. I wasn't pissed or anything, but you can't let a kid look at shit like that. I couldn't think of anything else to do in the moment. Mina didn't say anything about any of that, either, so maybe she understood. Like I said, she's smart for a fourth grader. But smart or not, I was glad she didn't see that my hands were shaking. I tried to get them to stop, but they shook for hours after the ambulance took Dad away.

After we dropped Jello off at his place and were headed back home, Mom was driving chauffeur in the front seat with the news radio on. Suddenly Mina said, "Stop the car," loud and firm.

Mom stopped, and before anyone could say anything, a cheetah sauntered in front of us, its long spine undulating up and down with every step it took, like it owned this fucking town. The cheetah paused right in front of our car, turned its head, and stared at us for a long-ass time. Then it flicked its tail and continued on its way.

The news had switched to the wolf shooting, and the announcer was urging listeners to call in any sightings of animals immediately, as they were extremely dangerous. And to my surprise, Mom calmly reached out and turned off the radio. The three of us sat in the car in silence in the middle of the road. It was like that cheetah was still in front of us, although it wasn't. "What do you guys want for dinner?" Mom asked after a while.

"Pizza," Mina said happily.

"Okay," Mom said. She put the car in gear and continued driving home.

That was the coolest thing Mom had ever done.

A few days later, on a Thursday, I was hanging out at George's place, trying to teach her little terrier, Genghis, how to press the on button of the TV's remote control with his paw. I was sitting on the sofa with Genghis under one arm and holding the remote control with my free hand.

"You just go like this," I said to him, and pressed the power button with my finger. Then I took his paw and put it on the power button.

Genghis cocked his head at me.

"I don't know," I said to George. "Maybe Genghis isn't the TV-watching type."

George looked up from the A-frame model of a cabin she was

working on. "I think you're doing it wrong," she said with a sly grin. "You have to get on the floor on all fours and show him how to do it."

I raised an eyebrow. "On all fours?"

George nodded. "If you don't demonstrate it, how is Genghis going to know what to do?"

"You mean I'm supposed to get down on all fours to show your dog how to—"

"Yes." George's eyes twinkled.

Only George would be able to make me do shit like this. "You promise you're not going to tell anyone?"

"Promise." Her hand went to her pocket. "It's just between you, me, and my phone."

"Oh hell no," I said.

"Are you blushing?" she asked.

"Dark-skinned people don't blush," I said.

"Yes, but I could swear that—"

"Fine, fine," I said, getting off the couch and onto the floor on my hands and knees. Genghis sat right down next to me, watching me with curiosity. I put the remote control in between us and put my hand on it, then took my hand off. Genghis cocked his head again and lifted his paw, like he thought I wanted to shake it. George was rolling with laughter.

Suddenly our phones started buzzing at the same time.

It was an all-school text: The man who was attacked by the wolf was none other than Mr. Hendricks, one of our physics teachers. He just died after being in critical condition for a couple days. The principal, who sent the text, announced the loss of one of our best teachers.

I did another mental check: Yes, it was s a Thursday.

George gasped when she read the text. "This is so, so sad," she cried.

I winced.

"He was the best teacher, only to . . ."

"Have his ass chewed out by a really hungry wolf?" I offered.

"Ronney!" George said.

I snorted. I couldn't help it. Mr. Hendricks was known to be one of the toughest teachers in our school. "He got his own ass-chewing. Now that's poetic justice."

George glared at me though her tears.

"It's called dark humor," I muttered, but I could feel my neck getting hot.

"You know what your problem is, Ronney?" she said. She pushed aside the wood pieces of the model she was working on.

I held my breath and braced for the worst. When a girl starts off saying "You know what your problem is?" you know you're screwed. Because she'll be right: You're a dick. And even if she's not right, if you argue with her, you're an even bigger dick for arguing with her—at the very best, you're a jerk-ass dick that just happens to be right in that one instance. And let me tell you, when a hot girl like George walks away with a conclusion like that, it's not really a victory at all.

"The problem with you," George said, getting all in my face, "is you're cold."

"It was a joke," I said, putting my hands up. "I didn't mean it."

She shook her head, her eyes glistening angrily. "You don't joke about things like this," she said. "Mr. Hendricks was the person who connected me with architecture schools. He told me he was going to be my reference when I apply to them."

At that point I wished for nothing more than the ability to take back the last thirty words that shat out of my mouth. But when I didn't say anything, George got even more worked up. "How could you say that about someone who inspired me? Who was violently killed? Who was one of our teachers?" she said.

"I didn't know him," I protested. A tight feeling came over my chest. It was suddenly hard to breathe.

"So that means you can talk like that about Mr. Hendricks? How do you think his wife feels right now?"

"Wait," I said, "what do you mean 'cold'?"

"You think about no one but yourself," she said.

"That's not true," I said defensively.

"Of course it is," she snapped.

"I think about you all the time," I blurted out.

Silence. Her eyes widened as she stared at me.

My stomach dropped. I mean, even if girls say they want the truth, they don't really mean it. They only want you to tell them what they want to hear. Case in point: If a girl only wants to be friends, she never, ever, *ever* wants to hear that you think about her all the time. Especially if it's true.

"I didn't want to hear that," George said quietly.

George's eyes left my face and settled somewhere over her family's flat-screen TV. Genghis waddled over, started walking on the remote control, and looked up at me expectantly, wagging his tail.

"I take care of the house," I said quietly. "You know that."

George sighed. "A house is not a person."

"I take care of the house so the people inside are safe and warm," I said.

"It's not the same," she said.

My mind went blank. I'm sure there were a million things I could have said; this is what came to mind: absolutely nothing.

George fidgeted. "Ronney, I don't know how to say this," she said, curling her hair around her finger. She didn't look at me.

I felt a little nauseous at that point. This could get *worse*?

"My parents don't like me hanging out with you," she said.

Of course it could get worse, considering what day it was. I don't lie about these things.

"Why don't they?" I asked, shocked. The tight feeling spread from my stomach to my chest.

"Since your dad tried . . . to . . . you know," she said. "And you cut classes a lot. My parents don't think . . ."

"I'm stable?" I said icily.

A tear slipped down her cheek. "It's just that—"

"Or maybe I'm not a good influence on you," I finished and stood up. This was starting to piss me off. "Jello, for all of his studious 'good influence,' was the one who dragged me into going after that wolf."

George's eyes grew big. "What?"

"Mom thinks he's smart," I said. "She couldn't be more wrong. Jello's on a safari, hunting down these animals for his photo shoots. We were practically at Mr. Hendricks's house when the wolf got him. We talked with Dan the News Man himself."

Her face dropped in shock. "Ronney, you're crazy."

"*I'm* crazy?" I exploded. "This was all Jello's idea," I said, gripping the back of the living room chair. "In fact, I was the one who turned back because we didn't have any meat. Jello would have fed the damn thing his leg and called it a splendid afternoon."

It was obvious: Jello was crazy, and I was the bastion of reason and logic. I had probably saved my friend's life just then, or at least his left leg. Instead, George's hand flew to her forehead, like she didn't know it was possible I could be so stupid. "My parents would *kill* me if they knew—"

"Knew what?" I asked sharply.

"That . . . well . . ."

My face tensed. "I get that you're into your family," I said, "and maybe one of your parents didn't just take a gun to himself, but where the hell did this come from? When did you get to be such a pleaser?"

Her eyebrows scrunched up. "It's not about pleasing—"

"Like hell it's not. You are—and I am paraphrasing—telling me you don't want to hang out because of what your parents think of me. Not what *you* think of me. Your *parents*."

Another tear slipped down her cheek. "You don't understand, Ronney," she said. She reached for my arm.

I backed away. "I understand more than you know," I said, an edge creeping into my voice. She had absolutely no idea how much she was ripping me up right then: *Her parents think I'm a loser, and she's going along with them.* With *them.* She didn't try to defend me— not even once? Well, if she could hurt me, then I could hurt her.

"And I'm sorry to break your bubble," I said, prepping for the counter blow, "but your parents don't give a shit about you."

"Stop it," she cried.

"It's true," I said. I grabbed my shoes. "They want you to make them happy. And when you stop doing that, you'll see what life is really like. Trust me."

George sank back down in her chair, hands over her face. For the first time, I didn't imagine wiping away her tears.

I left George's house after that, just like she told me to. And even though that cheetah was still on the loose, along with a camel (what the hell is so hard about catching a camel?), the python, and a good number of other animals, I took the long way home. Leave it to George to get all emotional over a joke. It was a joke. It's not like I really wanted Mr. Hendricks to die. But no, she goes from saying I'm cold to telling me her parents think I'm crap. Hell, like it's my fault Dad turned suicidal. How could they blame that on me? How could *she*?

I raced my bike home, jumping curbs as hard as I could. And

what the hell did she mean, I'm cold? I help her make cookie houses, for God's sake. I say one wrong thing, and she turns into a judger.

I knew I wasn't walking away from this smelling like roses, either— I gave her a low blow. I'm not exactly sure that George's parents would dump her if she became the misery of their lives, but hasn't she ever wondered what would happen if she turned off the perfection? If her parents would turn away? Because after watching my family, she sure as hell knows that parents can.

I jumped curbs for a long time because I didn't want to make Mina freak if I came home pissed as hell. Turned out, though, that I bent my back wheel on one of the jumps, so I had to walk my busted bike the last couple blocks. Go figure. As I was carrying my bike to the garage, who else but that little Sam runt showed up again. He stood there awkwardly and watched me like the stalker he was.

But there was something about him in that instant that made him *not* look like a stalker. Maybe it was the way his feet fidgeted like a ten-year-old kid's or the way he scratched his arm. Whatever it was, it hit me: Perhaps I had been overreacting. I guess I was still thinking about how George said I was cold, or how I was worried about how Mina was holding up, or how I was still impressed at Sam buying back all of his brother's shit, or maybe it was just a Thursday and nothing ever, *ever* happens the way it should, but I sighed and said to Sam kind of nicely, even, "Mina's inside." I shoved my bike in the back, by the lawn mower, before turning around. "And look, Sam. Keep the jeans, okay? I'm not going to beat you up."

"I'm not here for Mina," Sam said. He played with the zipper of his hoodie.

I looked at him. "What do you mean?"

He swallowed. "I need your help."

9

SO I WAS WRONG: SAM WASN'T THE STALKING
kind. He was the needy kind, which was almost worse. Because,
you see, since he was needy he was going to want my help, and
then I'd have to tell him: *Hell, no. There's no way I'm going to be
responsible for yet one more thing.* But if I told him to leave me
alone, then I'd feel responsible for whatever disaster happened
because I didn't help. So either way I'd be screwed: Either I took
on his shit and was responsible for it, or I didn't take on his shit
and felt responsible for not taking it on.

Screwed, with a capital *S*. But in the grand scheme of things,
not helping out was clearly still the way to go.

"Not going to help you," I said to Sam, who stood between my
garage and the front door. "I can't help you don't fit into those
jeans. No alterations."

Sam didn't move. "It's not the jeans."

My nice mood was melting off quickly. I threw him a glare.

"And, by the way, you're a little shit for telling Mina to steal them for you."

Sam's chin tilted slightly higher as he looked up at me. I could have sworn that a victorious glint sparked in his eyes, but it sputtered out, replaced with concern. "Mina didn't get in trouble, did she?" Sam asked.

"If you don't consider her face covered in snot and tears, then no," I said. I paused. "Probably a bruise."

Sam flinched.

I made a face. "Yeah. Getting a minion. Clever."

Sam looked at me like he wasn't quite sure what "minion" meant but suspected I gave him a compliment. Made me remember I was conversing with someone in fourth grade. "Look, kid," I told Sam, stepping around him, "I gotta go. But keep the jeans, okay?"

Sam counterstepped so he was still blocking me. "I need your help," he said.

I stared at him. This kid really threw me off. I mean, where the hell did he get his *balls* from? If I had his kind of balls, I would have told George that I wanted to talk to her parents, or told Jello that this safari was a stupid idea and I was out. Who knows, maybe I'd run away from home, Mina or no Mina. For a kid his age, they were small, but freaking made of steel.

In a strange way, though, I understood him; there's not many fifteen-year-olds fixing up a house. Maybe you need different kinds of balls to call roofers, but hell, balls are balls.

For the record, I'm not saying that all other kids on the face of the earth are losers. For instance, Jello pulled me out of a not-quite-frozen-over lake when we were ten. I was thrashing in this water, my legs turning into chunks of lead, and I was grabbing for the ice shelf that kept breaking off in my hands—and Jello somehow got me out. Don't know how he did it, even to this day, but he said it wasn't that hard; I clung to that stick like a leech to warm skin.

But maybe that's what it is. People like me grab what they need because they don't know if another chance is going to come again. People like Jello say *when*. People like me say *if*. There's a world of a difference between those two words.

Clearly, Sam says *if*.

"Go home," I said to Sam. I took a huge step around him—bigger than he could counter—and headed up the little sidewalk to my front door. He followed behind, of course. "Do your math homework," I said, not turning around.

"I don't do math homework," Sam said.

"That's why you're flunking math," I said cheerfully as I pulled out my keys. "Do your homework so you don't have to come by here anymore."

At that point, a lion roared in the distance.

"Some kids in my class got foghorns from their parents so they can scare the animals away," Sam said.

"Wonderful. I can just imagine how much fun recess is going to be," I said.

The lion roared again.

"This is just so weird," Sam said, shaking his head.

I faced him. "You know what's weird?" I said. "You. What the hell you need my help for?"

Sam played with the zipper of his hoodie. "I need to get Nick's poster back. From the secondhand store."

I sized him up. "So it's true? Your brother ran off?"

Sam looked away. "She wasn't supposed to tell you," he said quietly.

"Not her fault," I said.

Sam was quiet. Far away, multiple gunshots went off.

"I'm not going to give you money for the goddamn poster." I paused. "I'm not going to buy it for you either."

"Then go in and take it," Sam said.

I laughed. Steel balls. "Why don't you?" I asked.

"The poster's too big," Sam said. "I've taken other things, but it's framed."

I crossed my arms over my chest. "And what's so important about this poster? Huh? Some hot girl?"

Sam paused. "It's a John Lennon poster. I think Nick wrote down where he was going on the back."

I whistled and pretended I was looking for the house key on my key ring that only had three keys. Why can't people take care of their own problems? Why does everyone come to me? And, can I mention that an hour ago a very amazing and hot girl just told me to get out of her life? I shook my head. "Sam. No. Now go home."

Sam threw me an intense look. For a moment I was afraid he

was going to cry, but then he turned around and headed back to wherever he came from. The kid didn't know he had asked me for help only twice. That was the only good thing that happened, for a Thursday.

The media were delighted over the fact that, despite the police being out in full force for almost a week, there were still that cheetah, a tiger, a panther, a cougar, a hyena, a python, a lion, a wildebeest, and the stupid camel on the loose. Dan the News Man's face was all over TV, telling us, blow by blow, how the polar bear had been taken down in the McDonald's parking lot. Supposedly it had attacked the drive-through window, banging on the glass until the employees started chucking out Filet-O-Fish sandwiches at it.

So I was wrong: Exotic animals do go through drive-throughs.

Anyway, over the next couple days, the wildebeest was found in Mrs. Bruno's backyard, where it had electrocuted itself by chewing on the wires near the garage; the whole neighborhood smelled like a cookout until folks followed their noses and found the carcass. Speaking of carcasses, somebody at the Makersville morgue had propped open the door, waiting for a delivery, and the hyena had snuck in and ransacked the place, including devouring a couple of preserved bodies, for which the mayor told the grieving-again families that the town would hold a special service for the parts that remained. The authorities announced that the hyena was probably dead from consuming the formaldehyde and everything else that was inside the bodies, but nobody could produce the hyena's body as proof. Word on the street had it that the hyena had now turned into a zombie hyena, and kids of all ages went looking online to see if mace could stop a zombie.

The lion had the most unfortunate luck to come across Rockfeller, who was in his BMW at the time, grabbed a gun from under his seat, and blasted that cat six times in the head. The man is an ass, but he's also a straight shot, and six times is a little unnecessary. Regardless, that meant we had to see Rockfeller's ugly face for forty-eight hours on TV, and on the front page of the regional paper, and images of that bloody cat everywhere else you can think of in this wretched town. The worst part was that Rockfeller was suddenly driving his shiny car everywhere, slowly, waiting for people to wave to him like he was his own one-man parade. What a jackwad.

Turns out that other people thought Rockfeller was a jackwad too, because the animal rights group, which had been in town and keeping rather quiet since the zoo breakout, started screaming that his killing of the lion was bloody murder, because, well, it was. Then the gun rights people thought that the people who thought Mr. Rockfeller was a jackwad were jackwads themselves, because he was only exercising his constitutional rights as well as defending himself, which, well, he was. Then the gun control group rallied and shouted that with all these guns and all this fear, somebody was going to get hurt; only the government officials should be shooting anything. A few renegades were yelling that guns or no guns, these creatures were still on the loose and we were not seeing the real issue here, and before you knew it, all these folks started making a little hoo-ha in our downtown city park, which is hilarious since we don't have a downtown, but we do have a downtown city park, and now there was a hoo-ha in it. All this ruckus was quite exciting for the brave and opinionated citizens of Makersville, and no matter what group you belonged to, Rockfeller's downing of that lion was all that anyone could talk about.

Except, of course, for my family. I had unplugged the TV, and no one plugged it back in. Mina went back and forth to school and carried her bouncy ball with her, as usual, but I didn't see her bounce it anymore, which bothered me. One week after Sam followed me to my garage, that Thursday evening, we were eating dinner when Mina said, rather out of the blue, "Sam had bruises on his arm today."

I raised an eyebrow. "Really? You finally beat him up?"

Mom's lips puckered.

Mina rolled her eyes. "Noooooo. I didn't do it. Someone else did."

"Who?" I asked.

"I'm not supposed to say," Mina said, taking another bite.

"You just did," I said.

Mina gave me a confused look. "I did?"

"Sure," I said. I put another spoonful of lamb stew into my mouth.

"Ronney," Dad said finally, "stop confusing her."

"I'm not confusing her," I said, swallowing. "Mina knows exactly who gave Sam bruises. She said it was one of their class-mates."

"No I didn't," Mina retorted. "It was his dad." Then she slapped her hands over her mouth. "You tricked me, Ronney!"

I snickered.

"Ronney," Mom warned.

"What?" I said, all innocent.

"It's true, though," Mina insisted, wide-eyed.

I nodded at Mina. "Absolutely. Dads don't care about harming their kids."

Dad stood up. "I'm done."

Mom looked at Dad. "Honey, you didn't even touch the stew."

I kept looking at Mina. "And dads lose their appetites when you tell them the truth. Their stomachs are just too sensitive."

Mina's wide eyes went from me to Dad's plate of food to Dad. Her bottom lip started to tremble.

"Ronney," Mom said. But her heart wasn't in it.

Dad went to his room.

I remember the exact moment that my sadness and anxiety about Dad turned into anger. It happened about a year into his depres-sion, one long year of Dad staying in bed and of Mom, Mina, and me begging him to do things again—like mow the lawn or just fucking talk to us. Well, Mom got the flu. It laid her up, bad, and suddenly she was in bed all day too, like Dad. And Dad didn't know what to do because she was in his space now, and so the second day of her fever he grabbed the keys, packed up the car, and announced that he was going away on a fishing trip. He didn't say for how long. And he didn't come back the next day, not even when Mom had to go to the hospital because her fever had spiked so high, not even when I called him to tell him that she had been admitted to the intensive care unit. He didn't ask how serious it was; he just said that it was "pretty good" in his fishing town. *But when will you come back? Dad, we need you, please,* I said, and when I said that, I felt a tremor of anger deep in my gut because I realized I was sick of saying that; I'd been saying that for a year straight: That was the very first time there was anger. He never answered the question and hung up shortly after that. Dad ended up coming home three days later when Mom was home and feeling better.

The funny thing is that you would think that would have been the time the anger came. But no. It was in the littlest way: I got home from school one afternoon, about a month after Mom's flu, and set right to work mowing the lawn because the grass was freaking high. And just moments after I had finished, just as I was putting the lawnmower in the garage, Dad came outside into the backyard. He was wearing his pajamas and was walking on the lawn that I had just freshly mowed; the smell of cut grass was still in the air. Dad was drinking a can of soda, and I saw—with my own two eyes—that he tipped the can back and finished it, and then dropped that can of soda right there on the lawn. Like he knew I was going to pick up after him. *What the fucking hell?* I shouted, and he pretended he didn't hear me, so I stomped over to him, but he pushed past me and into the house, into his bedroom, and closed the door.

It was at that moment I realized that the dad I knew and loved was never coming back, never. When I told Mom about the soda can that night, she made some lame excuse for Dad that made me lose all respect for her, too. Around three o'clock that morning, as I was lying awake in bed, it hit me: *He's treating me exactly like a piece of trash. And I will feel like trash only when I trust Dad, when I open up to him.*

Never again, I promised myself. *I will never again let him in.*

And that's when the anger came.

Hearing that Sam was getting bruised up bothered me. I just kept seeing Sam's face and what he would look like if someone were hitting him so hard it'd leave marks. Even though I knew the kid could probably handle it with those steely balls of his, the only thing that really made me feel better was going to the secondhand store that very evening and picking up that lousy John Lennon poster. It was squished behind a My Little Pony poster and some religious crap. It was the only decent poster they had, and I could tell Sam had put it precisely there, because if you only looked at the first twenty poster frames, you'd think they're all junk, which was true, with the exception of that twenty-first one way in the back. Anyway, I picked the thing up for five bucks and got Mom to drive me home with it.

As I was putting it in the back seat, Mom glanced at it and her eyebrows popped up. "I didn't know you liked John Lennon, honey."

"I don't," I said.

She gave a confused smile. "Oh."

"It's a gift, I guess."

Mom smiled again, differently this time. "For George?"

My stomach tightened. It had been a week since she told me I was too high-risk for her perfect little life. "No, not for George," I said, and I left it at that. As we were driving home, we kept an eye out for the cheetah, tiger, panther, python, cougar, maybe the hyena, and the camel, as instructed to by the authorities. I was kind of getting used to having them around. I mean, what's wrong with having a couple exotic animals in the state? Indiana's big. We can all get along. Maybe they just need to spread the animals out a little bit. And if somebody goes down, well, it's all part of the getting back to nature that the climate change people have been harping about. Or maybe the whole "nature" thing is one big scam—because nature, by its definition, is wild, and what we want, at heart, is to control every bit of it.

Of course, Mina saw me haul the poster in from the garage, and of course she asked me if it was for Sam, since she knew he was on the lookout for posters. Of course I said no, and of course she saw through my lie and texted him right away.

I sighed. There is no better surveillance than a kid sister. Secretly, though, I was relieved; it's not like I wanted to contact Sam, anyway. Better that she did it for me.

He was over within the hour. Dad was in his room, and Mom was in the living room, reading her political magazines, when the doorbell rang. Mina materialized out of nowhere, bounded past me, and flung open the door.

"Sam!" she cried, as if this were all a surprise.

Sam smiled at her in a fourth-grade-kid kind of way.

I was a little ways behind Mina. "Hey, Sam," I said as normally as possible.

Sam's eyes shone when he looked at me, like I was the best thing on the face of the earth. I wondered for a moment if maybe that's how he looked at his older brother. Then I wondered where the hell that thought came from and told myself to shut up.

I led him to my room. I didn't know what to say to him—I mean, how do you make small talk with a ten-year-old? I doubted that ten-year-olds even made small talk. Based off of how Mina talks, everything they say carries the weight of the world.

So I didn't say anything until I showed him the Lennon poster, which I had leaning up against my bed. Sam's face gleamed. He was a nice-looking kid when that intense look was taken off his face. That look aged him eighty years, no joke.

We stood there for a moment in silence. Then I said, "Well, take it."

Sam shook his head. "I can't take it home. My parents

wouldn't be happy knowing I'm getting Nick's stuff back."

I fidgeted. "So, I guess you check out the poster here, then."

Sam gave a small smile—almost imperceptible, but I caught it—and slowly turned the poster around. He jiggled the fasteners.

"Do you want help?" I asked.

"No." His voice was somber, quiet.

Was there going to be an address? A phone number? A note from big brother to doting little brother?

Sam carefully slid the poster out of its frame, exposing the back of it, with the delicacy that an art historian must do to some great, lost treasure. He slid it out all the way.

I didn't move.

Sam didn't move.

The back of the poster was blank.

We both stared at it. My stomach tightened.

"He said he'd write his location on the back?" I asked softly.

Sam shook his head. "He said he'd tell me where he was going. He loved this poster. I went through his room, all his papers, checked everything else he could write on. This was the last place I could think of. I could have sworn it would be here."

I looked away from Sam. You can't just watch someone go through shit like that.

My eyes roamed the walls of my room while Sam sniffled. When I thought he had calmed down, I turned to him and said, "Sam, I'm really sorry."

To my surprise, a red-eyed Sam launched himself at me. At

first I threw my arms up in defense, but then I realized he was holding me around the waist. A hug. And then the kid started sobbing. Like a *the end of the world is upon us* sob. And what could I do? Sam's little body was shaking so hard, like he had poured every last bit of hope into this poster, into this last communication he'd ever have from his brother. And somehow, the love that he had for Nick was big enough to hold up the sky.

It's amazing how long you can hold up the sky. Everyone does it. For me it was a year, the way I believed that Dad would snap out of it one day, stop being so withdrawn, maybe kick the ball around with me. The thing is, it's tiring to hold up the sky. It's fucking heavy. And even though you get pretty good at propping it up, you never know when it will all come ripping down.

It sucks when that day comes. Maybe for some people that day will never come, but for those of us who *know*, that day is one goddamn awful day.

I think that's why I awkwardly put my hands on Sam's back and gave a little pat every once in a while. The kid cried on and on. I tried to think of things I could say that could help. *Life sucks, kid. It's one disappointment after another, so get used to it. It might get better from here, but then it might not.* But all of those sounded like something an ass would say, so I just shut up.

After a long time Sam stepped back and wiped his nose with his sleeve. His face was puffy.

"Thank you," he said.

My brow furrowed. "For what?"

"For getting the poster. You didn't have to."

"Oh, that. You're welcome. Even though it didn't help."

Sam's eyes got even sadder, and I kicked myself for talking like an ass anyway.

"But," I said, wanting to say anything to make him feel better, "you can come and hang at our place any time you want."

Sam's face lit up. "I can?"

I swallowed. My mouth went too fast. "Sure, Sam," I said. "Of course you can."

After Sam left, Mom started making dinner, and Dad was actually helping a little and they were talking, which meant he'd had a good day. While they were cooking, I stared for the longest time at the Lennon poster. To my surprise, I ended up hanging it on my wall, just to the left of my dresser. It looked all right, too.

10

ONE OF MY FAVORITE MEMORIES OF DAD WAS when I was eleven years old—a little older than Sam. We were at this lake in Indiana, this big, wide lake that families go to to swim and fish and hike. Mina was just a little runt and Mom was taking care of her, and Dad was taking me fishing. It was my first time fishing, and Dad led me to this quiet little spot with some deep water; he said it had the best fishing on the entire lake. He was in the process of showing me how to hook the worm; it looked really cool and I couldn't wait to stab that worm through its guts, but then Dad said, "Ronney, remember this worm is going to give its life for that fish."

I had no idea what he was getting at, so I said, "Right. Sure," and I grabbed for the worm.

"So," Dad said, taking back the worm from the hook—and from me—and holding it in his hand as he gestured with it so the worm kind of flew around his head, "you need to appreciate life when it gives itself for you, son."

This suddenly sounded too wacky for me, so to stop him from going further I said, "Right. Appreciate life."

Dad nodded his head, his eyes focused on me like lasers. "And when it gives its whole essence, you really appreciate that. Even if it's just a worm."

I squirmed. "Right. That too," I echoed. But I was still thinking of stabbing the worm with the hook.

"Good, Ronney," he said. "I'm glad you understand."

And with that, he stuck the worm in his mouth and ate it.

I started screaming like a lunatic—I shit you not. I ran as fast as I could back to our toweled spot on the sand, where Mom and Mina were playing patty-cake. There I was, howling and screaming and jumping up and down and holding my face with my hands, and Dad was there laughing at me, laughing so hard tears were streaming down his face, and his laugh was big and raucous and free. I'd never heard Dad laugh like that—he was gasping, and through his tears he told Mom what had happened, and she started laughing too, although she had a slightly confused look on her face. I didn't want Dad to touch me, as if his worm germs would somehow infect my body, and my sudden worm fear of Dad made him laugh even harder. "You'll never forget: Appreciate life, right?" he howled.

I wondered if he still remembered that story.

I hated to admit it, but I missed George something fierce. I kept reaching for my phone to text her about something before remembering that she had kicked me out of her life because her parents don't like me. That's so crap. And I'd run into her every once in a while in school—quite intentionally on my part, I might add, as I know exactly the paths she takes to get to her classes.

"Hey, George!" I'd call out to her, and give a little smile.

And every time she'd see me, she'd look away quickly, as if that would make me not see that I'd seen her looking at me.

Goddammit, that girl knows how to make me feel worthless.

To get my mind off of George, I wheeled my bike to City Park to see how the gun factions were getting along. It'd been two weeks since Rockfeller blasted that lion's brain, and some rich dude had gotten an electric fence installed around the park to protect the protesters from wandering, hungry animals; for two long weeks, the animal rights, gun rights, and gun control groups had parked their RVs there (with the city's begrudging permission), lining them up in rows like some sort of triangular Civil War reenactment. The renegades had long gone home, knowing when they looked stupid, I guess.

Anyway, it seemed like the factions weren't even all that into it anymore, except every time a news reporter stuck a microphone in someone's face, the various sides would start waving their signs and chanting their slogans, like their whole purpose had turned into who could be louder, brasher, and just plain right to the world. And this desire to be right overtook the desire to sleep in their beds or even to actually figure a way out of the mess. The mayor kept saying that he was going to "break up the fight," but for some reason nothing ever happened.

It was hilarious, if you ask me. How are kids supposed to figure out how to reconcile on the playground if their parents are taking days off of work to wave their guns and sling insults at each other? Freaking hypocrites.

The craziest thing was, when there wasn't some media dude with a microphone, there actually *was* some intermingling—*do you have some toilet paper* here, *have an extra sandwich* there: I'd even heard rumors that they were raking leaves together as a thank-you to the city. In front of the camera, though, everything melted away into the World War of Rightness, and you didn't know which mask that people were wearing was the fake one. Meanwhile, the only creatures that actually behaved true to themselves were those exotic animals, but there we were taking them down, like we couldn't handle the reality of it all.

When I reached City Park, I knew I had gotten there at the right time; a crowd had already formed around Rockfeller, who was telling the gun rights folks, again, how he had shot that lion, and how that gun had saved his life, and how everyone walking on this country's dirt should have at least one gun each, and how there could never be too many guns in our hands. He said all of this loudly, so the gun control folks were booing and trying to shout over him and drown him out, which just pissed off the gun rights folks, who started shouting themselves and tried to shut up the gun control folks, and the animal rights folks were booing because they didn't like that lion shot, but the only thing they all ended up doing was making the noise level of our stately City Park so high that you couldn't hear anyone or anything, no matter how right they were.

I guess Rockfeller agreed with me on the whole noise level, because before I knew it, he whipped out one of his guns, raised that thing over his head, and fired it into the air. People got really quiet really fast, but only for a minute. By the time the police got there, you could barely hear the sirens, people were shouting so loud.

Have I mentioned that it's really sad to see adults act like kids? Really. It makes for nothing to look forward to.

I know it's awful—and honestly a little embarrassing to admit—but Dad's gun was still in the house. Not the same one—the police had taken that first one away—but soon after Dad got back from the hospital, he figured out a way to get a second one from a friend, or a jackass dealer, or a lame-ass dealer who didn't do a background check. All I know is that one day as I was putting away folded laundry, I walked into Mom and Dad's room, and there Dad was, with his new gun on the floor and him opening up the lockbox.

"What the hell is that?" I asked, even though I knew perfectly well what the hell it was.

Dad didn't respond. He quickly put the gun in the lockbox, closed the door, and turned the key. Then he stood up and put the key in his pocket.

"It's nothing," Dad said.

"Fuck me," I said. I went straightaway and told Mom what I had seen, and when she tried to make Dad get rid of it, Dad started hollering about how that's his gun and she's going to get rid of it over his dead body. I guess Mom was in shock that he was hollering about something, period, which meant that he cared about something, and that could have been called an improvement. Most normal moms would have flown through the roof, put their foot down, maybe threatened to move out. My mom? In a tense conversation she asked her questions, then gave in and said that as long as it stays in the lockbox, it's fine.

Which, by the way, was not fine. I think Mom knew that too, but she also knew she had no spine to fight him, and maybe that's why for months afterward she hit her meds. In that way I guess she agrees with me: If you can't control it, tune it out. It was hard to explain to Mina, though, why Mom was sleeping right away after work, in plain daylight, and why we had to eat ham sandwiches with sweet chili sauce. Again.

During the days when Mom slept, I went into their room a couple times and tried to get into the box, but I couldn't find the key. I looked for that key everywhere. Every time I thought of that gun, I started to get panicky. One night I knew I'd have hives for the rest of my life if I kept caring about this shit, so I told myself that if Dad tries a second time, there's nothing we can do to stop him. That calmed me down, and I actually felt good for a moment or two. We humans like to think we can control everything, but life mostly steamrolls us over no matter what we do.

The one thing left that bothered me was that Mina had been doodling or whatever in her room and probably overheard Mom and Dad fighting about the gun. Sometimes I fantasized about what would happen if Mom would scream like a ninja and throw that gun out the window. Other times I fantasized that Dad would man up and decide that he didn't need a gun to make him feel better about himself, or safer, or that it wouldn't help him cope with the world's cesspool of disease. Still, other *other* times I fantasized that Mina and I would strike out by ourselves and leave my parents to fix their problems. If only they cared how much their messes ooze all over us.

Mom tries her best, given the circumstances, but she's got her anxiety to worry about, and Mina to worry about, and the finances to worry about, and Dad to worry about, including taking him to physical therapy and then to shrink therapy every couple days. That means she puts in extra hours at work to make up for the hours she's out of the office lugging Dad's ass around, which really means she only thinks about me when she needs to think about someone who doesn't need anything. It must suck for her, but it sucks for me, too. Still, I'm out there trying not to need anything at all.

Mom was making dinner when I got home.

"Hey, Mom," I said, slipping off my shoes in the middle of the kitchen floor.

"Hello, dear." Mom gave me a peck on the cheek, which she knows I don't like. "I saw Jello biking this afternoon, and I stopped the car to talk to him. He said you should call."

My eyebrows shot up. "Call?"

Mom sighed. "Okay, fine. Text. He said you should text him." She paused as she poured coconut milk into the pan. "But there's nothing wrong with getting on the phone and actually talking, you know."

"Yes, Mom."

At that point Dad called to us from his bedroom. "Ronney?"

"Yes, Dad," I called back.

"Linda?"

"I'm here too." Mom stirred spices into the milk.

"What do you want?" I shouted, annoyed.

"Are you home?"

I grit my teeth.

"Yes, honey," Mom said.

Silence, except for the coconut milk bubbling.

Mom shifted uncomfortably. "Oh," she said to me, "Sam's coming here tonight for dinner. Mina invited him over."

My sister was something else.

Jello didn't wait for me to text him—he texted me first.

I just saw on the news that the panther was spotted by the 7-11, get ready for Safari Trip Number Two.

I'm just about to eat dinner.

Eat fast.

Do you have meat?

Damn, Ronney, come on. Don't be lame.

No meat, no go.

You = Lame. I'm going to the store. Eat fast.

I got it the first time.

I had to admit, my pulse had jumped. What would we do when we saw the panther? I knew beyond a shadow of a doubt that Jello really hadn't thought anything through—that's just the kind of guy he is. So I needed to do that work for him: He was counting on me for that. I was getting all elaborate with the plans in my head, going through scenarios A through F, and maybe G, which meant that I was spacing out at dinner.

Sam looked at me. "So what do you think?" he asked.

I jumped a little. "What?"

Sam looked hurt.

"He said," Mina jumped in, giving me a pointed Mina look, "that if you wanted to see a picture that he made, he'd show it to you."

"Oh," I said, feeling warmth rise to my neck. "Sure, Sam. Let's see it."

Right there at the dinner table, Sam took a folded-up paper out of his pocket and handed it to me. I unfolded it, looked at the picture. The paper was covered in question marks.

I laughed as I passed it around. "Looks like you really like my jeans, kiddo."

Sam gave a small smile. "They were my jeans first."

When the picture came back to me, I looked at it more closely. I'd never seen anything like it. He'd drawn question marks, all right, but densely, so they were jamming into each other in all sizes and shapes and directions. It looked like the paper was screaming.

"Sam," Mom said, "that's a very nice picture. But why question marks?"

"Why not?" Sam asked.

"It makes sense to me," Dad said.

I threw Dad a look. That was the first thing he'd said all night. "It does?" I asked.

"Yes." Dad rubbed his chin thoughtfully with his good hand. I waited for him to say something more, but he didn't.

I caught a bruise on Sam's hand. It was an old bruise, but it made me wonder what other bruises were beneath his sleeve. I tore my eyes from his hand. "It's a cool picture," I said. "Could you do that to a T-shirt? I have a shirt you could paint up like that, if you'd like."

Sam looked adoringly at me. That kid would follow me anywhere, I just knew it.

The doorbell rang. We all looked at each other, and I swore to myself as I went to get the door. Jello couldn't let me finish my dinner. Couldn't freaking leave me alone when he had one of his ideas.

I opened the door, and what I saw made the air stop in my lungs.

It was George. She was standing on the porch in her fall coat with her hair down, dark jeans, and leather boots.

She was stunning.

She bit her lip. "Ronney, I'm sorry."

I stared.

Her eyes flicked away, then met mine nervously. "You were right. I was trying to make my parents happy. But I've really missed you, and I want to be friends again."

All words died in my throat. I just stared at her, my heart thumping wildly.

"And," she said, her eyes bright, "I want to go on the safari with you."

11

AT SCHOOL GEORGE AND I EXIST IN COMPLETELY different spheres. She belongs to the perfect valedictorian-contender crowd; I belong to the crowd that watches: the kind that doesn't really belong to a crowd at all, because once you belong to a crowd, you stop watching. But that's what I do—I watch people. Jello mixes with a whole bunch of crowds, but he hangs with me because I keep things real for him, whatever that means. And he agrees, I am his brains.

So George and I don't really hang out at school. I'm lucky she lives in my neighborhood, because if not, I'd maybe never see her, which I hadn't these last couple of weeks, anyway. But I was in her full presence as we headed to Jello's house—she's six months older than me, so she drives—and I was still shocked: George never admits she's wrong. Never. Not even when she knows she is. Honestly, I didn't think her beautiful lips would let her form the words "Ronney, I'm sorry." But it happened, it really happened, and I kept hearing those words over and over in my mind.

For the record, it was not a Thursday.

"I couldn't get what you said out of my mind," George was saying, twiddling her fingers on the steering wheel. "You're right: I am a pleaser. And I took a good, hard look at myself and decided that I don't want to do that anymore. I don't want to *be* that anymore."

"You keep saying that," I said.

Her eyebrows scrunched together. "That's the first time I said that," she said.

"Not that. The part about how I was right."

George blushed and tucked a strand of hair behind her ear. "Well, you were."

I gripped the door handle on the car so I wouldn't reach for her face and kiss her, driving or not.

"You're a good guy, Ronney," she said, "and what your dad did was awful, but you couldn't help that. And you help me a lot."

My head jerked a little in surprise. "I do?"

"Well, yeah. You remind me of what's important." She stopped at the red light and turned to me. "All my other friends care about is what their GPA is, or where they're applying to college. And you remind me that there's more to life than that. A lot more."

"I keep things real for you," I said, thinking of Jello.

She let me look into her hazel eyes. "Well, yes. And with you, I don't have to be per—" Her voice caught. She paused. "I can just be me."

We looked at each other until the light turned green, and she reluctantly turned back to the road. I could barely breathe, the air had turned so thick. Did this mean that she wanted to be more than friends?

"I still want us to be friends," she said, driving a steel spike into my stomach, "but I want us to be good friends. Like, *good* friends. You know what I mean?"

Yes, I thought. *You want to continue to torture me.* I shifted in my seat. "But why are you coming on this safari?" I asked. Something felt like it didn't quite fit, but I didn't know what it was.

George smiled. "Because I want to. It's a ludicrous idea—I'll give you that. But it's awesome. When will this chance ever come again?"

"And what would your parents do if they found out you're hanging out with me? Catching panthers?" I asked.

George pursed her lips as we pulled into Jello's driveway. "They'll just have to deal," she said.

God, that girl was hot.

Jello was ready for us by the time we dropped into the basement; he was packed and hopping up and down like a kid. Jello didn't even seem surprised that I'd brought George with me. Among other things, he'd packed his night goggles, three different cameras, three cans of mace (one for each of us), a couple flannel shirts, flashlights, portable flood lights, bug spray, a biological water filtration bottle, and a comb.

"A comb?" I asked.

Jello blushed. "For the pictures. In case, you know . . ."

"You need a touch-up," George finished. "For your head shot, when these go viral."

Jello looked at her and grinned.

George grinned back.

"And the meat?" I asked.

"Ah, yes, the meat," Jello said triumphantly. He whipped out a Styrofoam package from his backpack and threw it to me.

"Two pounds? That's it?" I asked.

"It was six dollars a pound," Jello whined.

I stared at him. "So what? How expensive is all your equipment you're carrying?"

"Oh. I hadn't thought of that," Jello said.

"Of course you hadn't," I said testily.

"I'm sure it'll be fine," George said, jumping in. "We probably won't even need it."

"Right," Jello said.

"So what's the latest on the panther?" I asked, pushing aside a strange feeling in my stomach. "That thing isn't going to hang around and wait for us to get there, you know."

"The last thing I heard was that it was behind the 7-Eleven," Jello said, "but if it's gone, we can track it."

"Sure we can," I said, totally unconvinced.

Jello adjusted a camera strap that was crossing his chest. "I took a tracking course with the Boy Scouts last summer, so we can get to the 7-Eleven and track the panther on foot."

"And I'm sure we'll be the only ones out there in the dark wilderness," I said, "since the whole state is out after these creatures. I paused. "And if it attacks us while we're on foot?" I asked.

Jello smiled. "R-Man, you worry too much, relax. We have the meat, right?" He patted his backpack.

George looked back and forth between Jello and me.

"Come on," I said begrudgingly, "before that thing gets any farther away."

Jello punched me happily on the arm. I didn't punch him back.

As George drove us to the 7-Eleven, she and Jello were talking excitedly about the different angles Jello could get of the panther. What if it was crouching? What if he could get a shot of it mid-jump and juxtapose that next to the picture of the squirrel? That's what George said. *Juxtapose.* They prattled happily all the way there. Me, I was trying to figure out if we could use the car as a tank, for refuge, if the thing attacked. Or if flashlights would stun it, like they do deer. Or how quickly I could reach for a can of mace. Or if two people could wrestle a panther off of someone.

I was right, though; there were all sorts of vehicles at the 7-Eleven. Fire trucks, county police cars, different government SUVs, and enough floodlights to make that whole area seem like noon in a desert.

We stopped maybe a half block away, and looked at the site.

I turned to Jello.

"Don't say it," he said as I was opening my mouth. "You were right."

I smiled smugly. That made for two people saying that in one day.

"So where do we head?" George said. "They just scared that poor panther away."

"What's the darkest place closest to here?" Jello asked.

"The fields," I said. "And ditches."

"So that's where we start," Jello said, pulling his night goggles onto his head.

We drove maybe a mile or two away into the countryside and parked the car along the side of the road. The air was different out here, earthy, smelling of autumn corn and cool breezes and night-time killer animals. The three of us were loaded down with Jello's gear and walked as quietly as we could along the gravel shoulder of the road, looking for the panther. I was about to say that we should get into the ditches because we're making too much noise, but then I thought better of it and shut up.

We were walking for about twenty minutes, Jello swinging his head—complete with night goggles—back and forth, scanning, when he said, "It's kind of hard to find a panther at night."

"Duh," I said.

"Shhh," George said. "We need to be quiet." She paused. "Maybe we should get into the ditches."

"Not necessary," I said, and readjusted Jello's backpack on my back. I glanced at George. "No offense."

No one pressed any further.

Word has it that it's hard to find a panther at night, but if you ever find yourself in that situation, you'll probably realize that it feels a lot like taking a night walk under a starry sky. With a hot girl. And your best friend. As we walked down that country road, I guess they agreed with me, because we started talking, panther or not.

"You ever wonder what's up there?" Jello peered up at the sky.

"Eternity," George said.

"Aliens," I said, "and government drones."

"You guys are so boring," Jello said. "What about different worlds? Like, places that have waterfalls of light and stuff like that?"

"Oooh, that's pretty," George said. "Waterfalls of light."

"Right," I said, ignoring a jealous pang in my gut. "That's where the aliens live."

Jello kicked at a stone on the road. "R-Man, why do you believe in aliens?" Jello asked. "I mean, you really believe in them."

"What's wrong with that?" I asked. "You believe in panthers waiting in line to have their pictures taken."

"I think," George said quickly, "that there has to be *something* out there, some kind of life form. The architecture of the universe has to be able to hold more than just us."

"*Architecture of the universe.* You're going to rule the world one day, George," I said.

"Well, it's true," George said uncomfortably.

"Which part?" Jello asked. I could hear the smile in his voice.

We walked along, keeping our eyes and ears peeled for crouching creatures. I started to relax as I hung back a little behind Jello and George. *We aren't going to find the panther,* I thought happily. *The thing's long gone. Jello's right. Sometimes I worry too much.*

That's when I saw it.

They were holding hands. Or rather, fingers. George's index finger was looped around Jello's index finger. Comfortably, like they'd done that before.

I stopped suddenly, and my shoes made a crunching sound against the gravel in an *I'm stopping suddenly* kind of way. George yanked her hand from Jello's, guilty as hell.

My stomach dropped. That *something* that was bothering me before now made perfect sense. "George, how did you find out that Jello and I were going out on a safari? That was pretty great timing, you know," I said accusingly.

George stuck her hands in her coat pockets. "Jello texted me."

I looked at Jello. "Really."

Jello shuffled his feet. "Yeah."

"You never texted her before," I said to Jello.

Jello looked away.

"And how often does this happen, all this texting? I had no idea you were so *close.*"

George threw her shoulders back. "Look, Ronney, you and I are not going out, okay? If Jello and I text each other, what's it to you?"

"What's it to me?" My voice pitched higher. "What's it to me? It's everything."

Silence.

In that silence a twig snapped.

"Why didn't I know about this?" I continued, glaring at Jello. "Huh? How long has this been going on?"

"Not that long," Jello responded.

"You don't have to answer him," George said. "It's none of his business." But her voice wobbled.

"It is too my business," I retorted. "He's my best friend."

"A couple weeks," Jello said glumly.

"What?!" I shouted. I turned and stalked away a good number of steps. Then I stalked back. I looked at George. "So you wanted to go on this stupid safari to be with your beloved Jello."

"Stop that," George said. "I told you, it sounded exciting."

"And you'd get to be with your beloved Jello," I repeated.

"Ronney," Jello said.

My chest was ripping up inside. "You know, you're right," I said. I turned to George. "It's none of my business. Neither of you are my business. None of your lives are my business. The only thing that's my business is me. Go have fun on your fucking safari."

Another twig snapped.

I started to walk down the road, toward town.

"Ronney, you're not going to walk all the way back," George called out.

"Watch me," I retorted.

George ran after me and grabbed my arm. "Come on. It's a good couple miles."

I yanked my arm away. "It's none of my business sitting in your car," I said.

"Ronney," she said tearfully.

Oh God. She was going to cry. I steeled myself and walked faster. "Go have your little fun, and good luck with the pictures. Jello, I hope you become rich and famous off of them and remember how you dicked over your best friend."

Jello ran after us. "Ronney," he called.

"What?" I said bitterly. I kept walking.

"I'm sorry, okay? I didn't know it was going to happen."

George started sniffling.

"You didn't say anything. Nothing," I said to Jello. "I'm standing here in the middle of corn fields because you wanted me to. Do you think there'd be any other reason why my ass would be out here? And look, you couldn't help getting all over her, right in front of me. Some friend you are."

Jello and George kept walking a little ways behind me. Jello's voice was strained. "I didn't know how to tell you about—"

I spun around. "Leave me the fuck alone," I said. I whipped off Jello's backpack and threw it into the space. "Both of you."

At that moment a flash of shadow sprinted from the fields and leaped into that same space between us. Its eyes glimmered in the moonlight as it took Jello's backpack in its mouth.

George screamed.

Jello screamed.

"The meat's inside," I said flatly.

The panther made off with the backpack and fled back into the fields. George was nearly hyperventilating. Jello wasn't much better.

I turned to George. "I'll take that ride home now."

We inched home in her car, and for the entire way George took loud, annoyingly deep breaths. Jello was in the front seat, looking like he wanted to put his arm around her, but he didn't.

That ride freaking took forever.

12

ONE OF THE NICE THINGS ABOUT WORKING ON
a house is that it's straightforward. Sure, stuff goes wrong when it
shouldn't—like the water heater, or the roof—but there's always
a logical explanation behind why it broke, and an equally logical explanation for how to fix it. The problems might not always
be simple, but they're always objective, and that's another nice
thing about houses. The refrigerator isn't going to break because
it doesn't like you anymore. The wood floor isn't going to buckle
because you hurt its feelings.

A house does not betray you.

My current project: the mold on the living room wall. Even
though Dad hadn't wanted to pay for the roofers to come back
and fix the leak from last year, that leak was causing the mold,
and I knew that wall needed to be taken care of. I mean, mold
is a big thing. The hard truth was that the whole wall needed to
come down, it was so rotten on the inside, but Dad really didn't

want me ripping out a wall. I don't know why, maybe he was feeling more insecure than usual. Anyway, there I was, taking out the mold on the surface. I used some bleach water and scrubbed down the wall, then painted over the area with a stain blocker, and then covered that over with a couple layers of paint. Presto: an unmoldy wall. Except if there's rotten stuff beneath.

Anyway, there I was, four days after the Panther Incident, putting on the stain blocker when the doorbell rang. It was Sam. He let himself in.

"Hey, twerp," I said cheerfully, putting down my brush.

Sam nodded. "What are you doing?" he asked.

"Taking out the mold."

"Can I help?" he asked.

Now, you have to understand that I work alone. That's how to get things done—you do it yourself. Besides, Dad never offered to help me, and come to think of it, Mom never did either. Of course, Mina always wanted to help, and of course I told her no.

"I don't need any help," I said. "But thanks."

Sam looked at the brush in my hand and the cans of stain blocker. "I can paint the stuff down by the floor," he said.

Now that was a thought. I hated bending to get down low. "Well," I said.

"And I learn fast," Sam added, playing with the zipper on his hoodie.

My phone buzzed. It was Jello. I deleted his text immediately without reading it. When I looked back at Sam, he was still waiting for me to answer. I took a deep breath: There was no use in me fuming over Jello when I was standing right in front of Sam. And anyway, there was something about Sam that made him look lost. Like a puppy that had wandered too far. Like he would have nowhere to go if I turned him away. My surge of anger melted away, and I realized that I did want some company.

"Aw, hell," I said. "Come on."

He was right; he did learn fast. In fact, he was a damn smart kid for someone who decided not to hand in his math homework. He did a good job with that crappy paintbrush he was working with, which was the only other one I had.

We worked mostly in silence, and he got down on the floor and did the low parts while I painted above him. It was pretty slick not having to bend down, and Sam did a nice job blending my strokes and his together after I showed him how to do it.

When we were done with the stain blocker and were waiting for it to dry, Sam said, "Nick and I did a lot of things together too."

"Really?" I said.

"Yeah. We painted the question marks on those jeans."

"Oh," I said, feeling like an ass for giving him shit over wanting them back.

"We did practical jokes together too. There was this one time that Nick and I got our cousin, bad," Sam said. He fiddled with the cuffs on his long-sleeve T-shirt. "We were sleeping over at his house, and when he was asleep, Nick and I put shaving cream on his hand."

"Really?" I said, going to the kitchen to make sandwiches for the both of us. "What for?"

"Well, he sleeps without a shirt on, right?" Sam hopped onto a chair.

"Okay."

"So we put shaving cream in his hand and then tickled his forehead, so he smacked himself with the shaving cream. Then we put more shaving cream in his hand and tickled his chest and arms." Sam started swinging his legs.

I grinned and grabbed some lunch meat from the refrigerator. "You didn't."

"It was awesome. There was shaving cream all over him before he woke up."

I snorted. He was tricky, for a runt.

"And then," Sam added, on a roll, "we knew he'd want to take a shower, so we replaced the liquid soap with pancake syrup."

"Nice," I said, chuckling.

"And we unscrewed the shower head and put Kool-Aid powder behind the filter. So when he turned on the water, Kool-Aid came raining down."

I groaned, but I was still laughing.

"It was great," Sam said excitedly.

"You and Nick sound like the perfect team," I said.

Sam got quiet.

I handed him his sandwich. We avoided looking at each other.

"He hasn't texted once since he left." Sam's voice was different. Smaller.

I didn't know what to say. "Maybe his phone died," I said lamely.

"He told me he'd text."

"How long has it been now?" I asked.

"Six months and five days," Sam said.

I whistled, then regretted it.

Sam didn't notice. His feet had stopped swinging by now. I took a bite of my sandwich, even though it didn't taste very good.

Sam looked up at me. "Will he text me?"

I paused. Do I lie and say that he'll text Sam one day? I really wanted to tell the kid the hard truth: His brother was probably slaughtered somewhere. Or that he was in Tahiti partying and had forgotten about Sam.

"I hope Nick texts you," I said finally. That was still the truth. I took another bite of my sandwich. It was starting to taste better. "Why'd he leave?" I asked.

Sam looked at the kitchen table. "He was drinking, and Dad and Mom found out."

I was confused. "That's why he decided to run away from home? That's a bit steep."

Sam shook his head. "He was drinking all the time. Sometimes he'd let me drink with him."

My eyebrows shot up. "Really. A bit young, don't you think?"

Sam sat up taller. "I'm ten, you know."

"Like I said, a bit young, don't you think?"

Sam grew quiet, and we both munched on our sandwiches. I reached for my second one.

"That was when we'd talk about a whole bunch of things."

Sam smiled. "Sometimes I'd get drunk and act all crazy."

A drunk ten-year-old. It was kind of funny, but for some reason I didn't laugh.

Sam saw me all serious, and he grew serious too. "When Dad and Mom found out, they were going to send Nick somewhere, and that's when he ran away."

"And you don't know where," I said.

"He told me he'd come back for me," Sam said. "He said he'd tell me where he's going."

Just then Dad walked into the kitchen. He looked at our paintbrushes and paint gear, and his lips twitched. I knew he wasn't going to say anything about them. He never talks about my repairs.

"Hey, Sam," he said, his good arm holding his bad arm.

"Still holding your arm, I see." I said.

Dad gave a one-shoulder shrug.

"It's not going to heal," I said pointedly.

"How's it going?" Dad asked Sam.

"Fine," Sam said, taking a bite of his sandwich.

"I'm just trying to help," I muttered.

"Did you hear they got another one?" Dad asked me. Those days, in Makersville, "another one" always meant one of the exotic animals. *They spotted another one. Another one killed Mr. So-and-so's dog.*

"Really?" I asked.

"The panther," Dad said.

My stomach flip-flopped.

Dad peered at me. "You know anything about it?"

I tried hard to keep a straight face. "No," I said. "Just thinking of stuff. Who got it?"

"The state warden," Dad said.

"At least it wasn't Rockfeller," I said. "I'm sick of seeing his ugly face everywhere."

"Word has it he was with the warden at the time," Dad said.

I groaned. "He'll take as much credit as they'll give him."

"Did they kill it?" Sam chirped up.

Dad paused. I looked at Dad. "Yes," Dad said finally. "They shot it."

"Why did you shoot yourself?" Sam asked.

Dad started coughing.

Sam waited.

I waited.

"I was going through a hard time," Dad said.

"I'll say," I said.

Dad coughed again. Then he went back to his room.

Not bad, kid. Not bad.

My second favorite memory of Dad was a couple years ago when I was thirteen and Dad was working on the car. He was in the garage, had the thing jacked up in the front with two jacks, and was lying on his back beneath the car. I remember staring at his legs as they stuck out, feeling kind of proud and kind of jealous, and I asked him what he was doing. He told me what he was fixing, but

I had no idea what that was, so I just said, "Oh," and stood there, like an idiot.

Finally, Dad scrunched his way out from beneath the car. His shirt and skin were all greasy, and he looked at me and said, "Want to see?"

Well of course I did, so there we were, the two of us beneath the car with our legs sticking out. The cement was cool beneath us even though it was wicked hot outside, and there Dad was, pointing out what goes to what, and where the problem was, and where the place is where you change the oil. Let me tell you, that was the coolest thing ever, to lie beneath that car with Dad, our faces just inches from all that metal and power, and him showing me what to do, part by part.

The conversation changed to girls, and how impossible they were, and Dad told me about his first girlfriend, Rita, which felt like a supersecret since I never thought about him with anyone except Mom. Anyway, this Rita kept making him stupid cards with love poetry on them and all that mushy stuff. Dad wanted to throw them away but he couldn't, because his parents might find them in the trash, and he wasn't supposed to be having girlfriends. So he kept all those cards in the safest place he could think of, which was in his math book, because God knows his parents would never look there. But then one day in math class, his teacher was walking by and saw all these cards sticking out of the book, and she thought he was passing notes or something, and she reached for the book and Dad tried to snatch it away from her, which only made the book go flying, and all these gross love cards with bad poetry came fluttering out, right in front of everyone. Dad spent the next while telling me about how he lived all that shit down—but he was laughing as he told me that story, as we were on our backs, beneath the car. He was laughing so hard I could tell he wanted to bring his hand up to wipe away the tears, but his hands were even grimier than mine, so he just lay there next to me and laughed and sniffled.

And though I was never planning on telling anyone, I ended up telling him about George, because I loved her even then.

We were out there for what seemed like five minutes, but all of a sudden Mom was shouting that it was time for dinner. Dad got out from under the car first and helped me up, and as we headed back to the house, we walked in perfect step with each other.

It was awesome.

Sam and I had finished our first coat of paint when Mom brought Mina home from flute lessons.

"Ron-Ron!" Mina cried as she ran at me. She hugged me before I could even turn around, which meant she hugged my back. That didn't seem to bother her. Also, she'd called me by my nickname in front of Sam again, but for some reason that didn't bother me, either.

"Hey there, kiddo," I said as I turned to face her, my brush dripping paint down my forearm.

"Whatcha doing?" Mina asked.

"We're fixing the wall," Sam announced. He put his brush down on the paint tray.

"Can I help?" Mina asked, hopping on one foot.

"Nope," I said. "And we're about done, anyway."

A foghorn went off in the distance.

"It looks nice, Ronney," Mom said, sticking her head into the living room.

"Thanks," I said. "Someone had to do it."

Mom disappeared, and I heard her in the kitchen shaking her pills out from her pill bottle. My jaw clenched.

"Please can I help? Pretty please?" Mina tugged at the sleeves of her orange shirt.

"Like I said, we're almost done," I said, putting down my paintbrush. "We need to wait for this coat to dry."

"Oh," Mina said. She started playing with one of her spiral curls, which she does when she gets shy, and then tinkered with the wads of key-chain toys on her backpack. After a while she poked around at our brushes, and I guess she was getting excited again, because she said, "Did you know that the last word in the dictionary is 'zyzzyva'? It's a kind of beetle."

"What are you doing still using dictionaries?" I asked.

"I like books," Mina said.

"Beetles are cool," Sam said.

"You're weird," I said to Mina. "And you're going to rule the world." Then I remembered that I had told George the same thing when we were looking for the panther, and my chest got tight. I forced that memory from my mind.

"I'm going to rule the world first," Sam said.

"Are not." Mina stuck out her tongue at Sam.

"Are too." Sam stuck out his tongue back.

Mina grabbed her orange bouncy ball from her pocket and gave it a good bounce so it hit the ceiling.

I was getting overdosed on fourth-grade-ness. "Okay, guys, painting fun is over. Sam, I'll clean up, okay? You and Mina can hang."

Sam and Mina ran down the hallway to Mina's bedroom, which was across the hall from mine. I guess I had left my door open, because I heard Sam shout, "Whoa!"

I found him in front of my doorway, looking into my bedroom.

"What's wrong?" I asked. I felt kind of pissed he was looking at my shit.

Sam pointed. "The poster. You put up Nick's poster on your wall." Sam grinned at me.

"What?" I asked, trying to play innocent. Then I looked away, briefly. "My wall needed a poster," I muttered.

Sam's face was one huge beacon of joy.

13

THE NEXT EVENING MOM AND I WERE IN THE car, headed to the store to get her a new pair of jeans. At first I had told her I was busy, but she kept nagging me to go with her until I said I'd go. She needed someone to tell her if the jeans looked right, she said. *That's Dad's job*, I wanted to say, but then I realized I'd rip a hole in her chest by saying that, and I wasn't feeling up for doing that.

We were approaching a stop sign, when out of nowhere a monkey came sauntering along and started picking at some grass in the median. Mom slowed to a stop. "They didn't say anything about a monkey," she said as she picked up her cell.

"Mom, don't call," I said.

"That monkey could get hurt."

"It probably likes being free," I said.

She paused, then put her phone down. We drove in silence the rest of the way until she pulled into the parking lot. That's when my phone buzzed—it was another text from Jello—but I mumbled something and turned off my phone.

As I was sliding the phone back into my pocket, the radio came on and started talking all rapid-fire about how the cheetah had just attacked some kid in town and was gorging on the kid's entrails when something scared it away. Of course, the authorities were out looking for it even harder now that there was all this screaming going on. My first thought was *Maybe it got Jello,* and I got all sweaty and nervous for a moment, and I realized that I wasn't as mad at him as I thought I was. Then the announcer mentioned the part of town the kid was from, and it couldn't have been Jello, and the bitter part of me completed that thought: *But maybe it should have been.*

I'm not the jealous type. Really. Jealous types get pissed when they don't get something they think they deserve, and I see no reason to expect I'm going to get all this great free shit falling from the sky. But you see, George has been my friend for years, and it just seems like the most natural, plausible thing in the whole world for her to fall in love with me. We do all kinds of stuff together outside of school. I make her laugh. Once, when she was trying to teach me how to play the guitar, I made her laugh so hard she peed her pants. She literally peed her pants. And I was there helping her clean up the floor. What more do you freaking want? I mean, if I were to come to you and say, *Hi, my name's Ronney and I'll help you clean your piss off the floor, but I just want you to love me,* don't you think you would?

Maybe because I helped her clean up the floor, I thought she'd see me as better-than-friend material. I don't know. Or maybe because I held her when her last boyfriend dicked her over. Or I listened to her go on and on about colleges and grade point averages when she knows I don't care about them. Or that I tell her I don't care if she's perfect, she's great the way she is, which is absolutely true. I know I can't do anything to make her love me, but God, I just wish she would.

They couldn't even tell me. That's one of the things that ripped me apart. I mean, it's not like I would've been celebrating, but at least they would've been real about it. And goddammit, they know that I hate fake people, and nothing's faker than your closest friends lying to your face and pretending they're not. The fact that George, the girl I loved, and Jello, my best friend who had once saved my life, were all over each other made me want to go and find that cheetah and shoot it myself. Maybe that's what Rockfeller was feeling when he took down that lion.

When we got to the store, I tried to hide in the electronics section, but Mom dragged me to the women's department, where she sat me down and made me give her my opinion on which pair of jeans looked best. Gag me. If I had to do this for George, it would be a completely different story. But my *mom*? So I told her which pair I liked best, which was a complete and utter lie, since they all freaking looked the same to me. What the hell was she talking about, which one looked better? They were all the same: They were blue, and jeans, and she could zip the goddamn zipper up on each one, so what difference did it make?

As Mom was trying them on, it did give me time to think about Dad. He hadn't always been depressed, and I'm sure in the past there were at least a couple times when he was sitting in the chair I was sitting in, looking at Mom's various jeans, and lying through his teeth. I don't know, maybe he even liked it. But those times were long gone, and it must have sucked for Mom to know that.

Really suck.

The pair of jeans Mom wanted wasn't on sale—in fact, they were the most expensive ones—so she ended up not getting them after all. She was really bummed about it, like a pair of jeans actually mattered, and I wanted to say, *Hey, it's a Thursday, of course they're too expensive*, but she doesn't believe in Thursdays like I do; she makes weird comments when I bring Thursdays up.

"Maybe they'll go on sale," Mom said cheerfully as we were driving back home.

"Maybe not," I said.

Mom didn't hear me. "I could hide that pair of jeans in the store so no one will buy it in the meantime."

"Well," I said, "since they're so great, they'll probably never go on sale and they'll sell out and you'll never get them, period."

Mom swerved to the side of the road, and I grabbed for the handle in the door. The tires screeched long and hard.

Mom looked at me. "Stop it."

I stared at her. "What?"

"I'm sick of you acting like you know everything and don't care about anyone."

How I don't care about anyone. Isn't that what George said, I'm cold? "Is this a girl thing or what?" I said. "I was just saying—"

"I highly doubt that only females want decent human beings to deal with, Ronney. Or tell me, do you enjoy dealing with jerks?"

My mind immediately went to Jello and George. I grimaced.

"I'm sick of your attitude," she continued. "I only wanted someone, anyone, to go shopping for jeans with me—"

Then, to my horror, she started crying. Hard. I guess she had been thinking about Dad all along, even more than I had. Maybe she was lonely—I mean, you have to be lonely to ask your son to shop for jeans with you. That thought made me feel like a total dickwad. I wanted to say something nice to make her feel better, but I didn't know what I could possibly say and I didn't want to make things worse, so I just sat there.

At that moment the radio announcer came on saying the cheetah was still on the loose and last spotted on the west side of town, just where we were headed. They got the crying family on the radio and asked lame-ass questions like how do you feel now that your son has been killed by a cheetah and shit like that. Mom took a couple deep breaths, and with the announcer going on and on about the cheetah, she drove us home. She even started humming, which is what some relaxation guru she'd watched on TV said helps calm you down, and which she only does when she's really pissed and trying to be nice at the same time. I looked out the window and tried not to hear the radio announcer or the humming.

I don't know why she doesn't believe in Thursdays. The proof is freaking everywhere.

It had been a Thursday two years ago when Dad plunked a gun down on the kitchen table. At dinner. He didn't even say much, just, "Look what I got today."

Mom put down her fork. Mina watched Mom put down her fork and then put down her own fork.

It was a gun: black, compact, and powerful. It had a four-inch barrel and roughened texture for the handle. The safety was on the side.

"Whoa," I said. "That's cool."

"Roger," Mom said. "What is this all about?" Her voice trembled a little.

"I've been thinking of getting one for a long time," he said. He rubbed his nose.

"For what?" Mom said.

"Protection."

Mom didn't move. "Against what?"

Dad mumbled something.

"Against what?" Mom repeated.

Dad shrugged. "You don't get it."

Mom stared at the gun, silent. Her eyebrows drew together.

"Are you going hunting?" Mina asked. This was a couple years ago, so she was eight. "Are you going to shoot a bear?"

"It's not a hunting gun," Dad said.

"Then what are you going to shoot?" Mina asked.

"Yes, Roger, what?" Mom asked.

"He said it's for protection," I said. "What's wrong with that?"

"Can I see it?" Mina said.

"Sure," Dad said, and handed it to Mina.

"Roger," Mom said, and her voice was hard.

"What?" Dad said, taking a bite. He swallowed. "It isn't loaded."

"It's always loaded," Mom said. "I thought they taught you that."

"Bam," Mina said, pointing the gun at the food on our table and mock shooting it. She looked at Dad for approval. "Bam, bam."

Dad smiled and nodded.

Then Mina pointed the gun at Dad. "Bam."

"Roger!" Mom said. She snatched the gun from Mina's hands, slammed it on the table, and left the room.

Mina's eyes grew big and watery. "Dad?" she said in a small voice.

"Don't point it at people, honey," Dad said gamely.

Now, I have nothing against guns: They can be pretty great if you know how to handle them. But for some reason, seeing Mina shoot that gun at Dad made my stomach churn and the room go heavy. The resentment lasted for days.

With the killing of that kid, the gun rights folks in City Park went all apeshit at the gun control folks and animal rights folks, howling that that cheetah should have been shot a long time ago, and if it had, the kid would still be alive. I don't really know what happened since I wasn't there, but I heard that Rockfeller was calling for everyone to open carry their guns, and if they didn't have a gun, to get one any way that they could; we had to stop waiting for the government to do something that we as individuals can do ourselves. That got the gun rights folks all pumped up, and they started whipping out their rifles and handguns and shit, and then the gun control folks started messing with the gun rights folks—bottom line, two people got shot by accident, one seriously, and were whisked off to the hospital.

But Rockfeller was still on a roll, and the gun rights folks decided to disperse from City Park and go looking for the cheetah, the tiger, the cougar, the python, maybe the hyena, and the camel. That was a couple days ago, and we had to see even more of Rockfeller's ugly face as a result. I have to admit, it was kind of strange in the mornings to see grown-ups with rifles and ammo and gear as they drove their kids to school. The gun control people protested that folks were selling their extra guns to people like they were candy, and that people were carrying guns without a license; the mayor replied that a license can take sixty days, and he didn't seem bothered by all the guns, or maybe he was just too chickenshit to put a stop to it. Either way, there we were with the "blind eye" thing again, and that was that.

All this time, I wasn't talking to Jello. Or George. One day—precisely a week after the panther incident—Jello texted me. I figured I would look at it since it was the third time he had texted me, and that I would try to be nice.

Hey, Ronney.

Fuck you.

Come on, R-Man.

Fuck you, twice, rolled through a pile of shit. A pile of filthy, fucking, stinking shit.

I'm still your friend. I should've told you, okay?

Um, yeah, you should have. Exactly how do you define "friend"? Let me share with you a little story as an example, based on personal experience: Friend #1 goes behind Friend #2's back, secretly dates the girl Friend #2 likes, chooses not to say anything, and in fact hides all evidence until one day Friend #2 happens to find out by accident. Friend #1 then expects Friend #2 to say oh yeah, we're friends, it's cool. No big deal.

Jello didn't respond.

Well, it's not cool. None of it is. Am I supposed to be okay with this? Fuck you.

He didn't text back, and I was grateful he didn't—I mean, would Jello's trying to be my friend three times be the same as asking me for something three times? And if it was, what would he be asking of me, and would I have to do it? Luckily for me, it wasn't a Thursday, he only texted what he did, and I didn't have to deal with him after that.

• • •

It turned out that Sam was eager for anything I put him to, including taking out the garbage. I mean, really? Was life at home so bad that he'd be happy to take out the trash? Maybe it was, because he was over at our house a lot, and our garbage cans were pretty empty. At some point Mom called his mom, and they talked for a while, and when she hung up, she had a confused look on her face. *What did his mom say?* I asked. *Oh, nothing much,* Mom said, but I knew it was a lie, and also that I wouldn't get anything out of her.

So we had another kid at our house. For a ten-year-old, he was pretty cool, and smart, given that he didn't turn in his homework. One day, while Mina was doing her social studies lessons, Sam was playing with her bouncy ball and said to me, "How come you don't do homework?"

My face got hot. "Why don't you?"

Sam shrugged. "It's stupid."

"Well, there you go," I said. "I have too many other things to do."

Sam looked at me and nodded. "Like the living room," he said.

Mina put down her pen. "But I'm going to rule the world," she said.

"That's right," I said. "Because rulers of the world do their homework."

Mina's look got wobbly. "But then what about you, Ron-Ron?"

"What about me?" I said.

"I want you to rule the world with me."

"Someone has to make sure the living rooms don't have mold," I said.

"Yeah," Sam said.

That seemed to satisfy Mina, because she skipped over to Mom, who was heading out to run an errand. Sam and I went outside, watched them leave, and sat on the front porch. I zipped up my hoodie; the sun was warm, but the air was cool. Sam zipped up his hoodie too and shoved his hands in his pockets. I had to admit, it was pretty nice just hanging with him on the porch.

A car drove by with a dad and mom and some kids in the back, and the mom was holding a rifle. A fucking rifle.

"It looks like we're all on safaris now," I muttered.

Sam watched them with me. "Everyone is so afraid."

"Bingo," I said. I paused. "Why are you so afraid of being at home?"

Sam struck his heel against the step of our stoop. "I'm not afraid."

Silence.

Sam looked away. Squirmed. "It's different with Nick gone."

I looked at Sam's arms. The bruises were still there, yellowed and faded. "And the bruises?"

Sam blushed. "I got mad."

"Being mad does not give one bruises," I said.

"Yes it does."

"No it doesn't."

Sam hesitated. "I was shouting at Dad and Mom. About Nick. About how he ran away because of them. And how I'm going to run away too." He paused. "That's when I hit Dad. And that's when Dad grabbed me." He paused. "It didn't hurt much."

"Huh." Another car drove by, this time without someone holding a rifle in the front seat. "Does this happen a lot?"

Sam grimaced. "No, this was the first time. But they were throwing away more of Nick's stuff, and I got really mad."

It had to suck to see your parents throwing away your brother's shit. I couldn't blame him for being angry.

A cool breeze picked up. Sam struck his heel against the step again. "I've been checking my e-mail a lot," he said.

"I bet you have."

A gun went off in the distance.

Sam looked at me. "Why hasn't he e-mailed me?"

"No texts?"

Sam shook his head. "Ronney?" His fists went deep into his hoodie pockets.

"Yeah."

"Help me find Nick."

I stretched open my arms. "I can't, Sam. Where would I even start?"

"Please?"

I winced. "I'm telling you, I don't go looking for missing people."

Sam's eyes started to water, and he looked away angrily and swiped his eyes with the back of his hand. "No one else can help me," he whispered.

I sighed inside. That was the third time. The third goddamn

fucking time. How was I supposed to know how to help him? I work on houses to stay out of problems like this. But as Sam sat with me on my front porch, he sure looked like one of those poor helpless kids that the world didn't give a shit about. Maybe because I knew how tough this kid was, or maybe because he kind of reminded me of myself, or maybe because it was a Tuesday and I feel nicer, in general, on Tuesdays, I found myself giving a shit. A small shit, but a shit.

"Yeah, fine, let's do it," I said. "You lucky bastard."

14

I WASN'T EXACTLY TELLING THE TRUTH WHEN I told Sam I don't go looking for missing people, because I went out looking for Mina when she ran away from home after Dad shot himself. I wish I could say she ran away like a lot of other kids do when they decide they're going on an adventure or something like that. Then running away would have a bit of . . . fun . . . to it. But not with Mina, and not with my family.

So I guess I do go looking for missing people. However, with Nick, it was worse: I wouldn't even know where to start. That's what I was thinking as I watched Sam walk home.

The thing was, I had promised to help find Nick, so I needed to start somewhere. Which was bullshit. Where do you go to start looking for someone who's been gone for six months? For all I know, he'd been eaten already. I know it sounds cruel, but a lot of crazy-ass shit can happen when you run away from home, things you had no idea could ever happen. Homes are funny like that: In some ways they shield you from the world, and in other ways they leave you more exposed than you ever want to be.

That's what I was thinking about when Mina and Mom came home from their errand. Mom was putting away her jacket when she said, "I'm supposed to tell you that George wants you to text her." Mom's lips turned up slightly. "She really likes to write with smiley faces."

My blood pressure spiked. "What? She texted you? How did she get your phone number?"

Mom looked at me strangely. "Remember when she babysat for Mina a year ago—I had given her my number. I guess she never deleted it. Why? Is something wrong?"

Mina didn't notice that I'd gone all tense, or maybe she pretended not to notice. If that was the case—the latter, I mean—then she was getting just as good as the rest of us at pretending not to notice shit.

Instead, she tugged on my shirt. "Ron-Ron," she said. "Guess what?"

"What?" I asked, trying to cool down.

"Guess." She boinged a black spiral curl of hers that was dangling by her face.

"You have a new pet baby hippopotamus," I said, waving my hand in the air.

She grinned. "No."

"You got all As on your progress report."

"Well, yes, but that's not it."

"You did five handstands."

"No."

I couldn't help it. I smiled a little. "You flew to the moon and back."

She tugged on my shirt again. "You're not trying, Ronney."

I shrugged. "So tell me."

"I gave my bouncy ball to Sam," she announced.

My jaw dropped. "Really?"

Mina nodded bigger than necessary. "When Mom and I were coming home, Sam was walking on the sidewalk. We slowed down, and he was so happy to see us that he waved us down. Mom stopped the car and he opened the door and twirled me around on the street." She giggled.

I was stunned. "Seriously?"

Mina nodded. "He was so happy, and I wanted to make him even happier. So I gave him my bouncy ball. He twirled me around for a while more until I started getting dizzy and Mom told me to get back in the car."

My jaw would have dislodged if possible. "He was dancing? Sam?"

Mina nodded again, all wide-eyed. "Yup. For real."

Mom was smiling with her eyes. "It was really cute. I was going to give him a ride home, but he said that he was just a couple of blocks away."

Sam was dancing. Probably because I'd said I'd help him. What would he do if I let him down?

"Ronney? Mina?" That was Dad, from his bedroom.

"Yes, Dad," we called back, almost in unison.

"Linda?"

"We're home, honey," Mom said. "What do you want?"

Silence.

Dad shuffled out from their bedroom. He was still in his pajamas, even though it was late in the afternoon.

"Hi, Daddy," Mina said cheerfully, and gave him a hug around his waist. He didn't touch her.

He did that all the time, but it didn't stop me from getting pissed off. "What's wrong?" I asked him. "Did the computer break?"

Mina's arms fell, and she came and stood by my side. I put a hand on her shoulder, and she leaned into me.

"How was your day, dear?" Mom asked.

Dad ignored us and went to the refrigerator. He opened the door and stared at its contents.

"Roger, do you want something?" Mom asked.

Dad shut the door. "No."

"Are you sure?" Mom asked.

"The only thing Dad's sure about," I said, "is that he hates his life."

"Enough, Ronney," Mom said pleasantly. "Your dad has been going through a hard time."

"I know, he's sensitive," I said. "We've been through that."

"I'm sensitive too," Mina chimed in, looking back and forth at us.

"Yeah, what about the rest of us?" I asked Mom. "We might be just as sensitive, but we don't get any of the perks."

"They're not perks," Dad said, almost mumbling.

"Checking out on being a dad is certainly a perk," I said.

"Maybe some of that curry," Dad said to Mom.

Mom went to the refrigerator to get the leftovers. As she was opening the refrigerator door, the doorbell rang. Mina bounded to get it.

It was Sam. Again.

"Hey, kiddo," I said, a little confused. He'd just left.

"Can I eat dinner with you guys tonight?" he asked. His face was all pinched.

My stomach did a flip-flop. Something had happened.

"Sure he can," Mina said. "Right, Mom?"

"Right," Mom said. "As long as he calls his parents."

Sam came into the house and I gave him a high five, and that alone seemed to perk him up. Freaking crazy, all the little things that matter.

Sam looked at Dad. "Why are you still in your pajamas?" Sam asked.

I snorted. I was liking this kid more and more.

Dad hesitated. "It was a long day," he said.

"Oh," Sam said, pulling up a kitchen chair. "What did you do?"

Dad shifted uncomfortably. "I was online," he said, as if that explained everything.

Sam looked at him.

Mom put the curry in the microwave, but I knew she was listening.

Sam kept looking at him.

"I might have found some new clients. . . ." Dad trailed off.

Sam kept waiting.

Mom pushed the start button on the microwave.

Mina looked at Dad.

I looked at Dad.

Dad swallowed. "I . . ."

And to my shock, Dad started to cry.

For the record, dads don't cry. That's a universal rule from the ancient caveman to today: Dads don't cry. But my dad was crying as he sat down at the kitchen table, as his shoulders shook and he made these weird crying noises I'd never heard before, and as Mina crawled into his lap and threw her arms around his neck, saying "Daddy, Daddy, it's okay, Daddy." Mom stayed where she was, watching the curry heat in the microwave, as if this whole scene wasn't happening. For some reason, I was immediately pissed at everyone.

Except Sam. I turned my head away and took a deep breath. "You sure you want to eat here?" I tried not to show how shaken I was.

"It smells good," Sam said.

"Well, okay," I said.

It turned out that we all ate curry, right then, even though it was early for dinner. Call it an impromptu meal, I suppose. Maybe

Mom didn't want Dad to eat alone again, especially with him crying. Or maybe she wanted us to eat together for Sam. Whatever it was, she reheated the rice, and we sat down and ate.

And I have to hand it to him, Sam ate everything we gave him, even though it was a curry casserole with meats, vegetables, and chicken feet. Most people are idiots when it comes to eating and don't know how stupid they look throwing out perfectly good food. But Sam, he was a sport. We had to show him how to eat the chicken feet, but once he caught on, he ate it all. Even said he liked it.

I smiled when he said that.

After we were done eating, Sam was going to walk home and said to me, "Want to come with?" And though I didn't want to, I put on my shoes. Mina had to study her spelling words, thank God, and didn't ask if she could come with us. I shouted to Mom that we'd watch out for the tiger. And the cougar. And maybe the hyena.

It was one of my favorite kinds of nights: The air had a crispness that goes down your lungs like a cold glass of water. I zipped up my hoodie, and Sam did too. We walked in silence, and I couldn't help but remember that pinched look on Sam's face when he first came over. Clearly, the kid wanted to talk. A part of me didn't want to ask what was wrong. That part of me was saying, *His shit is none of my business. I don't get messed up with other people's problems. I have enough problems of my own.* And while all of that was true, another part of me couldn't forget how my stomach fell when I saw him standing in our doorway, his face tight, like he wanted to cry. My stomach freaking did somersaults. I couldn't remember the last time that happened. Then, another thought: If his shit is none of my business, why the hell did I tell him I'd help search for his brother? I tried to think of the precise moment Sam wormed his way into my crappy life, and I realized I couldn't remember. Who knows, maybe it was when I was feeling pity for him, or I was having a good day, or maybe when he kept coming back after I smacked him with that tree limb. Whatever it was, here he was, waiting for me to ask him what was wrong. As if I cared.

But then, I did care. I had to admit it. I was worried about him. And I liked that Lennon poster on my wall.

"Goddammit," I said to myself.

"What?" Sam said, confused.

"Nothing, kiddo," I said. I paused and steeled myself. "So, what's up?" Asking this question was like pulling teeth. It physically *hurt*.

Sam looked away. "What do you mean?"

"Why'd you eat dinner at our house?"

Sam pulled up the hood on his hoodie. "My dad was mad."

"Oh, you beat him up again?"

Sam shook his head. "No, a kid at school."

"You beat up a kid?"

Sam nodded and kicked at a stone on the sidewalk. "The principal called my dad."

I stopped. "Way to go. Now everyone's pissed at you."

Sam stopped. "You too?" he asked in a small voice.

"Okay, everyone except me," I said begrudgingly.

Sam relaxed.

A foghorn went off in the distance.

"But why the fight?" I asked.

"It was with a classmate of mine. Ben. He was telling me that Nick would never come home." Sam's voice wobbled. "He said Nick was a drunk loser. So I hit him."

"Where?" I asked.

"First in the stomach. Then in the face."

I whistled. "Did he bleed?"

"Yeah. He got a cut on his cheek by his eye."

I smiled faintly. "Not bad."

Sam took his hands out of his hoodie and spread his fingers open. His right hand was swollen, all right.

This was why I gave a shit about this kid, I thought. Precisely this. Sam's a fighter in the realest sense of the word. "How big was the other kid?" I asked.

"Big. Bigger than me by this much," Sam said, lifting his hand over his head about four inches.

"And you won," I said.

"Yup." He took out Mina's bouncy ball and bounced it a couple times.

Gunshots went off. A squirrel ran halfway down a tree, looked at us, then ran back up and disappeared into the leaves.

"I once beat up a kid larger than me," I said.

"Really?" Sam's eyes were bright.

"Yeah, I was about as old as you," I said. I wasn't planning on telling this story, but I was stuck now, and a part of me said *why the hell not.* "He picked on me every day. You know, taunting, pushing me around, that kind of shit. He was big and he knew it, and all the kids were afraid of him."

"Were you?" Sam asked.

"No . . . well, okay, a little," I admitted. "But I wasn't going to let that stop me from getting in his face." I smirked. "His name wasn't Jack, but that's what I called him, because it went well with his last name."

"What do you mean?"

"Ass."

Sam laughed.

"One day, we were hanging outside before school, and Jack comes up to me and starts pushing me around, calling me names and shit," I said. "And I started saying stuff like, 'Oh, sorry, *Jack*,' and 'You better leave me alone, *Jack*,' but that didn't seem to work. Then he got the idea that punching me would be a lot more enjoyable, and I was sick of it. So I hit him with a brick."

Sam's eyes grew huge. "Really?" he asked.

I was surprised at how much I enjoyed telling the story. "Yeah, I launched it at him and he turned away from it, but not before one of the edges caught him on the arm and gave him a huge gash. He bled everywhere, needed stitches. I got a long-ass suspension for it. His parents threatened a lawsuit and said they were going to call the police, and I got months' worth of lectures that I could have killed him. It was bullshit, but let me tell you, Jack left me alone."

"What an ass," Sam said.

"Exactly," I said. As Sam grinned at me, and as I was shaking my head, a spot in my chest relaxed. I had never noticed it was tight, but now here it was relaxing, and it felt damn good. Right then, Dad didn't matter, and neither did crazy animals or Jello or George or even Mina. It just felt damn good to be walking with Sam and telling him my Jack Ass story. It was a little thing, but it mattered.

We walked in unison to the front door of his house. It was a normal, two-story house with a mowed lawn and ceramic statue of a gnome, and the lights were on. Sam was opening the front door when it swung open from the inside. His dad looked at us. He was pale and balding and had combed his hair over the balding spot in the way I hated. He sized me up in the way I hated too. "So this is Ronney," he said, hooking a thumb around the belt loop of his dress pants.

"Yeah," Sam said, looking down. I swear to God, that kid lost five inches right in front of me.

I met Sam's dad's eyes. "Just walking him home," I said. "There are some big animals still out there, you know."

Sam's dad laughed louder than he needed to as Sam reluctantly stepped into the house. He put his hand on Sam's shoulder. "They're probably busy stalking someone right now."

"Perhaps," I said.

Sam squirmed under his dad's grip. His dad removed his hand and peered at me hard. As he did, my skin actually *felt* darker than his—squarely on the other side of the color spectrum.

"What are you?" he asked, almost accusingly.

"Why did you just call me a 'what'?" I asked back.

"No, I—" He paused. "You're not from around here."

"I was born in this town. I completely belong here." I looked back at him just as hard.

A gunshot in the distance.

His eyes flicked away. Then they narrowed. "I mean, where are your parents from?"

"You don't see me asking you where your parents are from. Don't you think it's strange that you want to know my genealogy?"

"I'm just curious. What countries?"

"Does it matter?"

"No, like I said, I'm just—"

I smirked. "You mean, what's my race?"

His lips twitched. "Yeah."

"I don't tell that to strangers."

Sam's dad looked away, and when his eyes met mine again, they were like steel blades. "So is it true, then, Sam's been helping you and your dad with your living room wall?"

"No," I said, smiling, "Sam and I did it ourselves."

"Right," his dad said, totally unconvinced.

At that moment I despised the man.

"Sam's a good worker for his age," I continued.

"You're a bit young to be doing repairs yourself, aren't you?" he asked, pulling at the cuffs of his white business shirt.

"'Young' is relative," I said.

"You're what, sixteen? Seventeen?" He used his hand to smooth over the hair on his bald spot.

"Fifteen," I said. My jaw clenched.

"Why, you're a baby," he said.

"Ronney got the mold off the living room wall," Sam piped in. "And we resealed and repainted it all ourselves."

"I'm sure," his dad said.

I smiled again. "I could give you some pointers, if you like."

His dad gave me a hard look. "Well, have a good walk back," he said. "And watch out for the animals."

"Don't worry," I said. "I'm sure they're busy."

I swear to God, I wanted to hit something on the way home. In fact, I ended up doing just that: I punched a tree and got my hand all bloody. It didn't matter—it actually felt kind of good, and for a moment it took my mind off of how much of an ass Sam's dad was, how much I hate asses, and how they all need to be taken down a notch. It didn't take a genius to see why Nick ran away, or why Sam had steel balls: You do what you have to do, and you grow what you have to grow. In a strange way, I felt that I understood Sam better than anyone and that I was looking at a ten-year-old version of myself. Before I knew it, I was swearing that I was going to help Sam find his brother, even if it killed me.

15

THEY FOUND THE CHEETAH THE NEXT MORNING,
roaming through City Park. I guess the folks over there were
getting lazy with their trash and also lazy with the electric fence;
nevertheless, that cheetah must have been hungry as hell to ven-
ture where all those people were. It attacked this woman, and as
she was screaming, five guys came out with their guns blazing.
Two of the people had semiautomatics and pumped that cheetah
through.

So the cheetah was dead. And even though this happened
right in front of the gun control advocates, it was obvious that
guns saved that woman's life, so they were pretty quiet about it.
Although they did mutter that forty-four bullets for one cheetah
was a bit much.

That very same day they found the hyena: I guess it hadn't
turned into a zombie hyena after all and instead had gotten
pretty sick from eating the bodies. The hyena had staggered over

to the senior center, where there was a hose running on the grass. The hyena was drinking water when Silvia, the oldest member and who was progressing with Alzheimer's, thought it was her dog come back from the grave, and she started feeding it popcorn and talking to it. It wasn't long before the hyena died right in front of her, and she, distraught, interrupted Bingo Time shouting that her dog was dead, and of course no one listened to her—the only way they finally did was when she took a scissors, cut a tuft off of the hyena's fur, and showed it to the group.

The next day the cougar made its appearance along the side of the road; somebody got out of their car and started shooting at it and killed it, but not before accidentally shooting a car that was passing by, including a kid who was sitting in the front seat, killing her immediately.

Everyone in town came out to go to the girl's funeral and bring over scalloped potatoes and ham and green bean casseroles. The girl's family was shaking people's hands as folks arrived; since the girl's father was one of the leaders of the gun rights group, a whole bunch of people from the organization showed up too, from several towns over.

For the eulogy, the girl's father went up to the podium to talk but couldn't—he just stood there, ashen faced, looking down at his notes, his hands gripping the sides of the podium. Every time that it looked like he would say something, he would lower his head again, and finally he ended up covering his face with his hand. A full minute passed by, and then Rockfeller stood up and said that while the girl's death was tragic, we should remember also the bravery of the five people who killed the cheetah and the man who killed the cougar, whose courage and actions would prevent other children from dying such needless deaths. That was when a group of gun control people shouted that it was because of guns that the girl was needlessly dead and everyone was at the funeral in the first place. Rockfeller waved his hands to quiet them down, but it was too late—the fighting had started—and the funeral wrapped up early. That whole time, the girl's father was still there at the podium, silent, his hand covering his face.

Since the whole town was there, of course George and Jello were there too, with their families, and they took up a whole god-damn pew. I got there late and sat a couple rows behind them, so they didn't see me as they held hands, or as Jello rubbed George's back when we all stood and said prayers. They looked so comfortable together, like they were really happy, even at a fucking funeral. The only thing I could do was stare at them and imagine that it was me in Jello's place, and what it would feel like to have my arm around her shoulders, her navy blue dress beneath my fingers, and what it would feel like, her lips on mine. Then I got pissed, and then I wanted to run out of there and never come back, and then I wanted the earth to swallow me up and for me to never return to this shitty hellhole, because whatever shitty hellhole was at the middle of the earth, it was better than the shitty hellhole it was watching Jello and George together. And it was as pleasant as dog vomit when they saw me as the congregation was filing out, and how almost faster than I could blink, Jello took his arm from George's shoulder, and they both turned into cardboard right in front of me.

So the only animals left were the tiger, the python, and the camel. There almost came a sense of normalcy to Makersville, although there were whispers that if that tiger had eluded folks for so long, it must be one cunning creature, maybe even superhuman, which goes to show you how lame-ass stupid people can be, since a cat can't be superhuman—it would be supercat—but that's what people said, and no one questioned it.

Mina did not hold up well with all this news. Our TV was still unplugged, but everyone, everywhere, was talking endlessly about the killing of the girl, who ended up being in the class behind Mina's, and if the person would be prosecuted, if at all, since it was in self-defense and he had been aiming for the cougar. They also talked about the downing of the cheetah, and how much blood there was, and what kind of bullets were used: Everyone talked about all of this, from the schoolkids to their parents to the grocer. Mina grew quiet and more than once crept into my bed to sleep with me. She didn't cry, and she didn't want to talk about it either. She'd just shake her head and make a little mewling sound at the back of her throat until I stopped asking questions.

It didn't help that some nearby farmers had started reporting that their cows had been mauled to death, their throats and intestines ripped out, legs and whatever strewn across the field. People went out en masse, of course, but they couldn't find any trace of the tiger. With those cows taken down, though, I'm sure that tiger had a full belly and lots of energy to play hide-and-seek.

There were more guns now in Makersville than ever. People who owned a gun went out and bought another one—more tiger-worthy, I suppose—and people who hadn't ever owned a gun got one for when they took their kids to school. The gun control folks, recognizing defeat when they saw it, packed up their RVs in City Park and went home, and the animal rights activists did the same thing. Almost all their animals were dead, anyway.

I was worried about Mina. I grew even more worried when I saw that she wasn't studying her spelling words anymore. That was when I talked with Mom.

"I think it's fine for Mina to take a break from studying so hard," Mom said, leafing through her magazine.

"I don't," I said.

"She's just a kid," Mom said.

"This is Mina we're talking about," I said.

"I'll talk with her," Mom said.

Mina shook her head and didn't say anything to Mom, but she did crawl into my bed that night.

As worried as I was about Mina, I didn't have too much time to spend with her because I had started looking for Nick. Sam sent me a picture of him, and I started going to every liquor store in Makersville, showing shop owners Nick's picture and asking if they'd seen him. Which they hadn't. This was no easy feat for me either, because it's not like a bunch of liquor store owners would take kindly to a fifteen-year-old kid like me walking into a place with tons of booze. A number of them ran me out of the store before I could even open my mouth.

Then Sam told me that Nick really liked sports, and maybe he went to parks around town, so we did the same thing at all the parks in Makersville and ended up at the largest one, Rogers Park.

There was a woman watching her little kid on the jungle gym. I went up to her. "Excuse me," I said politely.

She looked at me warily, her eyes scanning my face, my dark skin. She leaned away. "Yes?" she responded.

I held out my phone with Nick's picture on it. "I'm looking for a missing guy. Nick Caldwell. Have you seen or heard of him?"

She didn't even look at my phone. A hand went to clutch her purse, and she called her kid over to her as they walked away.

I tried not to roll my eyes.

None of the other moms with strollers had seen him either, but at least they weren't as jackwad-y.

"He's gotta need money," I said as we sat on the swings. I took a swig from a can of soda I'd bought and passed it to Sam.

"He took some of Dad's money when he left," Sam said, taking a swig too.

"How much?"

Sam passed the can back to me, twisted his swing up a couple times, then let it unravel. "He told me a couple hundred."

"But that was over six months ago," I said. "He has to be running out."

"Maybe he got a job," Sam said.

"Maybe he's stealing it," I said.

Sam's eyes grew wide. Then he recovered. "Nick wouldn't do that."

I snorted. "If you're hungry, you're hungry. Or in Nick's case, thirsty."

Regardless, we went to all eighteen fast food restaurants in town and asked about Nick. No one had seen him.

At some point during the afternoon I could have sworn that George's car was trailing behind us. I got so curious that I told Sam to stay put and started biking toward it; that's when the car quickly pulled a right-hand turn, and I caught a glimpse of George's beautiful hair. I gripped my bike handles and raced after her like a beast. The great thing was that she needed to stop for the stop signs, and she totally saw that I wasn't giving up. In fact, I was maybe fifty feet from catching up to her when a train slowly rolled through town; she gunned the car and hopped over the tracks right before the railroad arms went down, leaving me panting and my shirt wet with sweat. I was both pissed and pleased: Here she is, so guilty that she's following me. Good. Let her be guilty. *But I guess that means I matter to her*, I thought. *A lot.*

Anyway, it took Sam and me two days to go to every park and fast food restaurant in town. On the second evening, after visiting our last burger joint, we went back to my place and collapsed on the front porch.

"I don't know, Sam," I said.

Sam didn't look at me.

A foghorn went off in the distance.

"He might not have even stayed in town," I said.

Sam's skinny face somehow looked smaller.

I went silent. I felt awful, but what could I do? Snap my fingers and make him come back? Put a Batman light in the night sky asking Nick to kindly come home? What could I possibly do?

Sam placed his elbows on his knees. "We'll just have to ask around in Algoma."

Algoma was the next town over, about five miles away.

I sighed. "Sam, who's to say that he went to Algoma? He could have gone to Pickett instead."

"Then we'll try there next."

"That's not my point," I said. I was frustrated and tired and yet couldn't help but admire him. "He could have gone to Utah. Alaska. Florida." I waved my arm. "Anywhere."

Sam nodded mournfully. "That's what the police said."

I paused. "And the police have given up?"

Sam nodded again.

I fought a sudden, strange urge to give Sam a hug. Instead, I picked at the laces on my shoes. "I don't know, Sam," I said again.

Sam sighed. "I know."

• • •

With all this running around looking for Nick, Dad noticed I was gone more.

"Where have you been?!" Dad said. He came right up to me as soon as I came inside and started raiding the refrigerator. Dad's face was flushed and he was in his pajamas, which he'd probably worn all day. I ignored him as I pulled out some cold pizza. Damn, my feet were sore.

"It's nine o'clock at night!" Dad ran his hand through his hair.

I didn't have the energy to say much at that point, so I just grunted. It sucked that I hadn't had money with me and that Sam and I had to smell those burgers and fries all day long. I stuffed the pizza into my mouth.

"It's not that late," I said with my mouth full.

"Where'd you go?" Dad said, his voice still tense. Twice through the hair.

"Out," I said. I took another bite. God, I was hungry. I was worried about Sam, too. And Mina. Maybe that's why I added, "Sam and I are asking around for Nick."

Dad did a double take. "His brother?" he asked. I guess that somehow calmed him down, because his shoulders relaxed.

I shoved another bite of pizza into my mouth and nodded.

"Any luck?"

"Not yet."

"Nick could be anywhere," Dad said.

I slumped into the chair at the kitchen table. "That's exactly what I told Sam," I said, propping my head up with my hand. I let out a long, slow breath. "But nothing can replace a missing person, you know?"

That question hung in the air. Then Dad silently turned and went back to his room.

Later that night I saw that George had texted me. My breath caught. Then I got mad at myself for caring so much.

Ronney, listen to me.

Are you still with Jello?

Ronney, I'm still your friend.

One hell of a friend, I'd say. You should join the CIA with the way you lie to people. And stalk them.

I didn't know how to tell you.

You'd make good money.

You want to go for coffee tomorrow after school?

Are you asking me because you want to or because you want to feel less guilty?

No response. Then ten minutes later my phone buzzed again.

Hey, R-Man.

What the fuck is this? How lucky am I that you two are taking a break from making out to text me! Very sweet to be remembered.

You're being a dick. Listen to us.

I'M being a dick? Well now, if you want to talk about dicks . . . Some dicks are prettier than others. I wouldn't try out for any beauty contests right now if I were you.

Ronney.

Go blow yourself, Jello. Or get some help from a particular CIA operative. There are some good ones out there, I hear.

I turned off my phone and felt like a jerk, especially if I had made George cry just then, but she had Jello's shoulder to cry on. Who knows, they were probably together right now, talking about me, and she was crying, and he was holding her and had her tears on his fingertips—

I slammed my pillow onto my bed. The John Lennon poster looked back at me. It was a chill poster, Lennon looking right into the camera, right at you, and it seemed like whatever you had that was going on, he got it, he really did. Somehow he got that Jello and George had dicked me over, and he got that Nick was out there somewhere.

Nick.

"Hey, John," I said to the poster. I put the pillow down.

Lennon looked back.

"So, do you know where he is?" I asked. "Because I got a kid who really wants his brother."

Lennon looked back.

"Couldn't you give me a hint?" I asked. I peered into Lennon's face. It was a calm, serene face—knowing. Like the guy had a shitload of secrets. "Well, any time you want to tell me, go ahead," I said. "I'm not going to stop you."

Lennon looked back.

I sighed and crawled into bed. I still had on my jeans, and I was tired, even though it was early. It had taken a lot of energy to be hopeful for Sam, more energy than I thought it would take; there were so many things that we just didn't know. For a moment I really wished I had those jeans I'd bought—Nick's jeans, with all the question marks. I'd bunch those jeans up into a ball and use it as my pillow. Sleeping on questions, literally. Then I thought, Nick was a freaking genius for painting those jeans like that. Because that's what life is: One big-ass question mark. Or rather, a tangled mess of them.

I was happy when I was Sam's age. Not really happy, mind you, but when I think back on those times, it wasn't bad. Mom was still taking her pills back then, but Dad was different. He worked on the car a lot, and he belonged to this bowling league, which he went to every Saturday. He would take me with him and give me money to buy three loads of fries to eat while I waited for him to finish bowling. That was pretty sweet, eating three loads of fries. I got to watch Dad bowl, which isn't as lame as it sounds, because he was pretty good, and whenever he had this string of strikes going, he would pump his fist, and even the guys competing against him would pat him on the back or nod respectfully or whatever. And I would watch Dad turn into a different person out there—fucking chill—getting strike after strike, and I would pile my three loads of fries into one big french-fry hill, drench them with ketchup, and eat them with ketchup-y hands, watching my dad, proud as hell.

Mom said, later, that there were signs of his depression all along, but when I pressed her on it, she didn't give me any details. Still, there's a difference between being able to cover up for your depression and the depression exploding in your face—and everyone else's. I know that the doctors told us that depression just *is* and not to think about what started it all, but they're jackwads: It's impossible not to think that something made everything change, not to look for something to blame, which is exactly what I thought about for countless nights. It could have been that he left the job he'd had for ten years and realized that working for himself takes more balls than he had. It could have been that he blamed himself for Mom taking her pills. It could have been because he turned forty and was wondering bigger things, like how can life just be about fixing cars and going bowling and having a family, and isn't there something more out there, something that he wasn't lining up to get. Anyway, if there were cracks in his great windowpane of life, he certainly didn't show it—or at least Mom covered up for it—until one day he woke up and the whole thing came shattering on him in a million irreparable pieces. And I don't know, maybe I myself had turned a blind eye to Dad's "bad days" because I didn't want to see reality either. Maybe it was my fault.

Once, about two years ago now, he stayed in bed for a week straight. At first Mom said he had the flu. She was constantly in and out of their bedroom, tiptoeing around the house. On the fourth day, though, I ran into him in the hallway, and I knew this was no virus. His eyes were flat, and he walked like each step was a million pounds, each blink of the eye painful. I was confused: What had happened to him? Where had Dad gone? How could I fix this?

Mina, of course, tried to cheer him up, but it was like hugging a brick wall. That didn't stop her from trying, and she got really good at hugging brick walls. I tried too. I asked if he wanted to go bowling or if he could help me repair the lawn mower. But each time he barely gave us a word, as if making a sound would take up all his energy.

In the beginning I really worried about him—I stayed up late into the night thinking about what could make him better, what could make him worse, and I got a lot of detentions for being late to my first-period class because I'd gotten shit sleep worrying about him all night long. I'd try to talk with him, but he'd give me one-word answers, or no-word answers, or lock the bedroom door so I couldn't talk to him, period. I know people say that the heart heals, but those people are assholes because they never mention the scars.

So anyway, I watched Dad wander around the house, neglect things that he'd always done—putting winterizing putty on the windows in the fall, mowing the lawn, spreading the mulch. One day about a year later, the bone-awful truth hit me: The Dad I knew—my bowling dad, my car-fixing dad—was gone for good. It was like he had died, right in front of us. A dead living person.

I have to admit, though, there were nights when I snuck out of the house, crawled under the car in the garage, and lay down under one side, leaving room for a make-believe dad beside me. As I stared up at all that metal and power, it felt like that entire car was pressing down on my chest. Every single time I wanted to cry, I tried to cry, but I couldn't.

The next day was a Thursday, which sucked. I have a Thursday routine that's different from my other-day routines. On any normal non-Thursday, I get up, spend some time on the can until Mom starts yelling, brush my teeth, dig around in my bedroom for my clothes, flop back into my bed for as long as possible, then finally finish getting dressed. I go into the kitchen, pour myself some cereal, and if I'm in a good mood, I dick around with Mina— maybe fling some cereal at her—and let her give me a good-morning hug, which she always gives me, wet cereal or not. That always cracks me up. If I'm not in a good mood, I take my cereal and eat in the living room.

Anyway, on Thursdays things are different. When I wake up, I spend at least ten minutes in bed debating if I should stay in bed, and if I'd be like Dad if I do. Deciding that I will be, I get out of bed, go into the bathroom, and use my special Thursday toothbrush. I also use my Thursday tube of toothpaste and wear a special pair of jeans. They look like normal jeans, but they're a little cleaner—a little newer—because I only wear them on Thursdays. I always outgrow them and have to get new ones, but I really like my most recent ones: The first day I wore them, I won my bike from my school's raffle fund-raiser, then afterward some random-ass dude in line in front of me paid for my vanilla custard cone, and later that same day George gave me a kiss on the cheek for saying something witty. That's the word she used: "witty." So those are the jeans I wear on Thursdays, and I used to wear them exclusively, every Thursday, until I found those question-mark blue jeans at the secondhand store, and I started alternating the two pairs of jeans because I figured that jeans with a bunch of questions on them had to protect me from something. But then I gave that pair to Sam, so now I'm back to one. Which is cool.

On Thursdays I don't eat breakfast. That minimizes the chances of things going wrong. Nothing to spill, no empty cereal boxes that I think still have cereal in them. I just sit in the living room and wait for Mina to be ready to go to school; then I take her to her bus stop. I make sure to give her a hug on Thursdays. She knows this and squeezes me extra hard.

I look both ways, twice, before crossing every street.

I always make sure I have at least a dollar in change in my pocket, because you never know when some sort of emergency will pop up.

Most importantly, I make sure to put my lucky medallion in my pocket. It's a cool thing, with this king or something on it, and it's in this language I've never seen. I found it one day some years ago now, and it was sitting on the ground by the cemetery's cast-iron fence, like someone knew I was going to be walking by and dropped it there for me. It looked so odd, this gold medal-lion—okay, so it's probably not really gold, but it looks gold—sitting there in the grass. When I took it, I could tell it was meant for me. I don't know how I knew, I just did. Later that night, in my bedroom, I put the medallion on my nightstand. I couldn't get over the feeling that someone had left it for me, and damn, did that make me feel great. And if I was remembered, I'd better take good care of it, right? So I keep it on my nightstand all the time, except for Thursdays, which is when it goes into my pocket with my loose change, and no one knows the difference except for me.

That Thursday morning the phone rang, which was strange, being so early in the day. Mina was eating her breakfast, and Mom had already left for work. Dad wouldn't get the phone, of course, so I picked it up. I wasn't feeling good about a phone ringing so early in the day.

"Hello?" I said, jingling the coins in my pocket.

"Hello?" said the other voice. It was a guy.

"Yes?" I said testily.

"Are you Ronney?" the guy said.

"Yeah," I said. "Who is this?"

"Hey, Ronney," the guy said, his voice relaxing a bit. "This is Nick."

16

"WHOA," I SAID. "FOR REAL?"

"Yeah," Nick said. His voice was deeper than mine. A little thicker, too.

My brain was spinning. "How'd you get my number?" I asked.

"When you go looking for someone all across town, word gets out," Nick said. He sounded guilty.

I didn't know what to say, so I stated the obvious. "Sam's been hanging out with me."

"I know." Nick gave a little laugh. "That kid is truly amazing."

I held the phone, quiet for a moment. *That's something I would say*, I thought. I cleared my throat. "You got that right—he's amazing." I paused. "He's been trying to buy all your shit back from the secondhand store."

"Really? They threw my stuff out already?"

"Yeah, and Sam's been in there, getting back what he can. He thought you left him a message on that Lennon poster."

Nick sighed. "That was the plan." I heard him take a drink of something, and I realized his speech was a little slurred. What was this, a drunk dial early in the morning?

"So, where are you?" I asked, feeling more ballsy. I was sick of the chitchat.

"Doesn't everyone want to know." Nick gave a little laugh.

The way he said that sent my temperature soaring. I gritted my teeth. "You know, the kid needs you."

"He's better off by himself."

"Is that what I should tell him you said? Nick said you're better off by yourself?"

"No, no," Nick said quickly. He took another sip. "That's just between you and me."

This whole conversation was quickly heading south. Sam had been idolizing his brother, who was a drunken dickwad. He was just too young to know it—or too desperate to acknowledge it.

"I met your dad the other night," I said.

"Oh, you did?" Nick's words were measured.

"He's an ass."

Nick snorted. "You got that right."

"And you're an ass for leaving Sam alone with him," I said.

Silence.

"Score one for Ronney," I said, smirking.

"Mom's all right," Nick said, recovering. "She's just . . . weak."

"Like I said, you're an ass for leaving Sam alone with him."

"You're real smart," Nick said sharply. "When I see Sam next, he's going to sound like a jerk. A smart jerk, but a jerk."

"And when are you going to see Sam next?" I prompted.

"I just . . . have some things to finish here," Nick said.

"Like your couple of kegs."

"Shut up," Nick said. "You have no idea what's going on."

"You're right, I don't," I said. "And you have every idea what's going on with Sam, and you don't give a fuck." I gripped the phone. "Way to go, hero."

"Tell Sam . . . to take care of himself," Nick said tightly.

"Why don't you? I could get him on the phone, you know."

"That's no—"

"Or does being weak run in the family?" I asked.

"Fuck you," Nick said.

"Fuck you," I said back.

I don't know who hung up first.

At first I was afraid Mina had overheard the conversation, but when I checked on her in the kitchen, she was still talking to her cereal. Mina talks to her cereal every morning; she asks it if it likes swimming in its swimming pool, if it wants to swim underwater. Then she moves it around in her bowl, pretending that it's doing the backstroke. Then she eats it.

"Don't you think that's mean?" I say when I see her eating the food she was talking with.

"It's meant to be eaten," she replies, as if I was stupid.

Anyway, she was talking with her various cereal bits, which calmed me down; at the very least, she wouldn't be running and texting Sam that I'd told his beloved brother to fuck off.

My stomach lurched a little. What do I tell Sam?

"I'm done, Ron-Ron," Mina said, putting her bowl in the dishwasher. She was so good to Mom like that; I just leave my dishes on the table.

"Got your backpack?" I asked.

"Yup," she said.

She skipped next to me as I walked her to the bus stop, and all the while I was thinking about Sam. Do I tell him we don't need to look for his brother because his brother doesn't want to be found? That he doesn't give a shit about what Sam's going through? That he's too drunk to be of help, anyway? Or do I pretend the call never happened, maybe even continue looking for him?

I had a headache. I sighed and rubbed the base of my skull with my hand.

"The bus is coming," Mina announced.

I gave her my usual Thursday hug, tight as hell.

"You behave," I said, tousling her hair.

"You too." She grinned at me. Then, right before she hopped onto the bus, she turned back to me and called out, "But, Ron-Ron, you wouldn't make a good politician."

I stared at the bus as it sped away.

I didn't have to worry about Mina telling Sam about the phone call, because she ended up texting me when her school went into lockdown later that day. Three guys were in the parking lot of her elementary school, and they started arguing about something; one brought out his semiautomatic gun, the other two did too, and the three of them started running through the playground shooting at each other like it was some Western show, except with semiautomatics. Once the gunshots started, the school's alarms shrieked, and all the teachers started the lockdown procedures: Close and lock the doors. Barricade them. Kids in the closet. I was in geometry when I got her first text.

Help me Ronney, there are guns.

Where?

Outside, and I'm in the closet and I think I peed my pants.

It's okay. Calm down. Is the teacher with you?

Yes, she is, but I'm scaredscaredscared

Calm down. What's your spelling list this week?

It's a stupid list, so I'm studying the word tessellation instead.

Good girl. Spell it again. And go through your other words.

On my modified list?

Yes. And I'm coming.

That was wen the geometry teacher called my ass out for texting in class. I stood up, told him to go fuck himself, picked up my bag, and left. I raced on my bike to Mina's school, and there were tons of police cars and fire trucks and TV news people and parents on the sidewalks and big sisters coming to pick up their siblings. Mina and I were still texting spelling words back and forth, one maybe every thirty seconds, steadier than a heartbeat. In the end the police shot two of the three guys because they turned their guns on the police, one of them surrendered with his hands up, and then they were all loaded into vehicles and hauled away. Maybe ten minutes later, hundreds of crying kids came running out of the school, running to hundreds of crying parents.

I don't know who started it, but at one point a kid took out a foghorn and blasted it long and hard. People flinched, and a number of folks bent over and brought their hands to their ears. Some adults rushed over to try to make the kid put it away, but then another kid sounded a foghorn, and another kid, and another. And then they raised their foghorns to the sky, arm after arm extended, so many little hands pressing those little buttons, those foghorns sounding out cries that you could hear for miles. The adults couldn't look at each other, didn't do anything except look ashamed, like this crappy world was the best world they could give us.

Throughout it all, Mina barely said a word. I didn't know what to think about that. She did want me to carry her home, though, which sucked because she was heavy, she had peed her pants, and I had to leave my bike at her school to do so. Since it was a Thursday, it would be stolen, but she wouldn't walk, even when I asked her nicely. So I left my bike there and carried her wet ass all the way home.

We were almost at our door when I remembered that Mina and

Sam were in the same class. "Where was Sam?" I asked her as I put her down. My back hurt like hell.

Mina shook her head.

"What does that mean?" I asked, alarmed.

"He wasn't at school today," she said.

"Thank God," I muttered.

Mina didn't say anything at all.

Two days later there was another shooting, this time at Mike's Place, which is a bar in town. I guess the guys were drunk and they started fighting. One of them was hit in the chest; he died on the way to the hospital. It was on the news, which I watched when Mina wasn't in the house. I unplugged the TV before she got home, but she must have known, because she went straight to my bed and crawled in, even though it was plain in the afternoon. She wanted me to lie in bed with her. So I did, and I held her.

"Why is everyone shooting each other?" she whispered, laying her head on my chest.

"I don't know," I said.

"Why does everyone have guns?"

"For protection. You know that." I smoothed her hair from her face, and I could feel my shirt getting wet.

"Then why is everyone getting hurt? We're not protected then, right?"

"I don't know."

"I'm scared, Ron-Ron."

"I know."

"I don't want to be alone," she said softly.

I asked her what she meant by that since she has me, but that was all she said about it.

I thought she had maybe even forgotten about the shooting at school until a couple nights later she and Mom came back from the store with all these bags of new clothes in their hands. Mina came walking into the house with blue jeans on. And a white T-shirt.

"What the hell?" I asked.

Mina looked at Mom.

"Mina doesn't want to wear orange anymore," Mom said, as if this explained everything. "She changed out of her old clothes right there in the store."

"This must have cost a fortune," I said.

"It'll be okay," Mom said.

"How do I look, Ron-Ron?" Mina asked. But she didn't twirl around, like I expected her to. Instead, she just stood there and looked at me.

I stood up and left the room.

Mom kept saying how nice it was now that Mina's orange phase was over, and she said it so many times I wanted to punch a hole in the wall. I didn't put Mina on the school bus anymore; Mom made sure to drive her to school, which meant she dropped Mina off super early. I didn't like that Mina was hanging around school for over an hour every day before classes, but driving Mina to school calmed Mom down. So every day Mina left in blue jeans and a non-orange T-shirt. Every time she hugged me and got into Mom's car, my chest clenched from not seeing that flash of orange; another part of me was pissed at Mom for being so nonchalant about it. The only good thing was that none of the kids at Mina's school were allowed to play outside for a month after the shooting, which helped calm *me* down, but still it was weird thinking about romp-and-polly Mina being stuck indoors, caged up.

I was shrugging on my backpack and about to head to school myself, when the doorbell rang. It was before eight o'clock in the morning. Weird. I opened the door.

It was Jello.

My blood pressure shot through the ceiling.

I stared at him. He was the same Jello: nice jeans, T-shirt hanging just right. Hair combed for the girls.

Or, more correctly, for the girl.

"What do you want?" I asked.

"Punch me," Jello said.

"What?" I said.

"Punch me," he said, and he opened his arms a little. "You know you want to."

"You're crazy," I said, but even as I said that, my hands started tingling. "I've never punched you in my life."

"You punch me all the time," Jello countered. "Do it."

"Socking you off of your computer chair doesn't count," I said.

"Punch me," Jello said again.

I paused. Dad was asleep in his bedroom. He'd never know. No cars were passing by; we lived at the quiet end of the neighborhood, and the neighbors had all gone to work by now.

"I'm seeing George," Jello announced.

"No shit," I said. My jaw clenched.

"Come on, hit me," Jello said.

It would feel great to beat the shit out of him. To see him double over, wheezing. I stepped outside, and Jello countered a step back. But still, I couldn't hit Jello. Not for real.

"She's great," Jello said.

"Stop it," I said. My forearms tightened.

"She's an amazing kisser," Jello said.

Without thinking, I lunged at him, pummeling him with my fists, in the stomach, in the legs, the arms, the chest, anywhere I could reach. I connected with his jaw and grunted as pain shot up my hand. Jello staggered and fell over on our lawn; I could tell that he wanted to curl into a ball, instinctively, and was just barely willing himself not to, so he looked like the letter C on the grass.

I grabbed him by the shoulders and banged his head into the dirt. "You're an asshole," I shouted, my voice nearly breaking.

"I know," Jello said thickly. I punched him in the stomach, and he crumpled around my fist.

"When did you even have time to hang with her?"

"We started sharing a lot of the same classes," he said, wheezing. "She was my AP Chemistry lab partner. We were working on our labs all the time, sometimes late into the night. I didn't realize we shared so many things in common. We both like thermody-namics. What are the chances of that . . . ?" He trailed off.

"Did you ask her out or did she ask you out?" I leaned my hands into his shoulders until he winced.

"No one did. It just happened. And trust me, we tried not to . . . you know . . . We both knew how you felt. But things kept happening."

I spit onto the ground just inches from his face. "Like what?"

Jello winced. "You know, things."

My neck tightened. "Things?"

"I told you, she's a good kisser."

I punched him again.

"Do you take her to Standee's Ice Cream?" I asked.

"Yeah," Jello gasped.

I punched him in the side.

"You went behind my back," I said.

"I know," he panted. "We talked about you all the time, what we were going to do, if we were going to tell you."

"If?!" My voice got tight, and I punched him in the face, just under the cheekbone. His skin split and blood ran out. He gasped and gave a guttural moan of pain. My hand was instantly numb.

"And yeah, we did talk about maybe never telling you," Jello continued, panting hard. "But then George would start crying, kept saying that we had to tell you, and soon. And she was right. But we didn't know how."

"Well good thing I found out by mistake so you didn't have to figure out the answer to that question," I said as I punched him in the stomach again. Jello curled up tight, despite himself, and rocked to the side so his back was to me.

"I love her," I said, and my chest burst.

"I know."

"You're a fucker." My voice pinched up.

"Yes, I am," Jello whispered.

I sat back on my haunches and wiped my face while Jello lay in the grass, panting. A light wind picked up. "I always wanted to take her to Standee's," I said.

"The chocolate chip cookie twist is good," Jello said.

"That's what I would have gotten her," I said.

"She liked it."

"Finished it all?" I asked.

"Yeah."

I massaged my right hand. I still couldn't feel it. The trees' leaves rustled.

"So she's great?" I asked. My voice was soft.

Jello smiled in a way I'd never seen before, until he remembered I was there. Then the smile disappeared as he nodded. "Except it's hard dating a perfectionist," he said. "She gets upset when I mess up."

I snorted. "That must happen pretty often."

Jello didn't respond.

I flexed my fingers, wincing. I was going to be late for my Western Civ class if I didn't leave soon.

"You know, I've given up on the cat safari," he said with a curious tone in his voice.

"Really?"

"Yeah. Going out into the who knows where is dangerous, you know? We're too exposed. Anything can happen."

My eyebrows lifted. I didn't know what to say.

"Anyway," Jello said, "I think I have a better subject. A different kind of safari."

My hands clenched into fists. "I don't want to hear about George," I said.

"Her?" Jello made to shake his head but winced. "No. Not her. It."

"It?" I repeated.

"It," Jello said proudly. "The python. It's in my garage."

17

JELLO REALLY WANTED TO MAKE IT TO CLASS, so at that point he went to school, and I went back into the house. My Western Civ class was fine and all, but I was too jacked up to sit in a desk all day and pretend I was thinking about Thucydides. I mean, I just beat the shit out of my friend because he wanted me to, and he had a python in his garage. To calm down, I went online and learned the difference between ground faults and short circuits. While I was on the computer and eating cereal, Dad came out of his room.

"Ronney?"

"Yes." I stuck another spoonful into my mouth, feeling happier than I had in a long time.

"Why are you still home?" he asked, rubbing his face.

I swallowed. "Could you call in for me?"

He looked at me blankly, like I just spoke in Aramaic. "I didn't call in for you," he said.

"Could you?" I repeated.

"No," he said.

That was the first time he'd said no. "Excuse me?" I asked.

"No," he repeated.

A strange feeling popped up inside of me when he said that, but it was so terrifying a feeling that I pushed it right back down. "Oh, so your shrink finally decided to see you?" I snapped.

"Perhaps," he said.

I shrugged like it didn't matter, took my bowl of cereal and started eating it standing up. He was still in pajamas, like always, but something had shifted. I didn't like it; it made me feel off center, and that terrifying feeling from before still remained. I needed to stop thinking about it; maybe that's why I added, "I just beat Jello up in our front yard."

Dad's eyes grew big. "Where is he?"

"Now? In school." I snorted. "He looks like shit. They'll send him to the nurse's, first thing."

"Was it that bad?"

"Bad enough to have a cut on his face, blood coming out all over, and multiple gut punches." Dad stared. I shrugged. "He wanted me to hit him."

Dad cocked his head, then looked at my hand, which was all swollen.

I flexed my hand, even though it hurt like a bitch, and shrugged again. "It wasn't a big deal."

"Jello was a pretty good friend," Dad said.

"Is."

"What?"

"Jello is a pretty good friend," I said.

"That you beat up."

"Like I said, he wanted me to." I shook my head and glanced back at the screen. "You wouldn't get it."

Dad stood there holding his arm, even though he wasn't supposed to anymore with his physical therapy. "So things are cool with you now," he said. It wasn't a question. The corners of Dad's lips pulled up slightly.

My throat tightened. Dad had figured out this whole fight thing without me telling him. He got it. Even though he was standing across the living room, it was as if he were in my face, way too close, trying to be buddy-buddy with me. And he had no right to be.

"Yeah, well, get your shit out of my business," I said.

The slight smile disappeared. "You should go to school," he said.

"And you should get a job," I said.

"And you should get your grades up," Dad said. "Or do you want to flunk out this year?"

"You have no right to tell me what I should be doing," I said. "May I remind you that you shouldn't have put a gun to your head?" I put a hand to my cheek. "Oh dear, I remember now. You *didn't* put a gun to your head. That's why you fucked up your shoulder."

Dad ran his hand through his hair.

"And you should do your arm exercises; I haven't seen you doing them lately. Or maybe you always want to hold your arm like a loser," I said, feeling the venom building in my throat.

"I am doing them," Dad said, walking back to his bedroom.

"Like hell you are."

"I don't always have the time." He retreated farther down the hallway.

"Go ahead, run away. Do what you—"

Dad closed his door.

I slammed my bowl of cereal into the sink and left.

Outside, helicopters thrummed the sky above me, and some cop sirens went off in the distance. I shook my head, not caring about any of it. I just couldn't believe that Dad had told me *no*—I mean, what was wrong with him? He always called in for me. That was the deal, and he just broke it. What an asshole.

On top of that, I couldn't believe that Dad had really understood what had happened between Jello and me; I didn't have to spell it out for him. That was so weird. I shook my head and kicked a stone on the sidewalk. But who knows, maybe he had beaten up his best friend too when he was my age. Maybe over a girl.

If Dad understands what happened, then he might understand more than I give him credit for, I thought. *But then why doesn't he understand that retreating to his room like a loser is chickenshit crap?* I stuffed my hands into my pockets. *Why doesn't he understand the extra work he gives to Mom by being MIA? Why doesn't he understand that Mina would give anything to be his little girl again?* It just didn't make sense that you can get one part and not the rest, how you could be a solid, living dad one moment and a ghost the next. I mean, really: What was I supposed to do with a dad like that?

Since my bike had unsurprisingly been stolen the Thursday I picked Mina up from school, I needed to buy a bike. By the time I got to there, my feet were tired, but in a good sort of way. I had just enough cash saved up from doing lawn work at the Goupells', our neighbors, and paid for a mountain bike that had a bigger frame than my old one. Allen, the owner, chitchatted with me for a little bit about the tiger, and then he assured me that I'd grow into the larger bike, which was cool. I tooled around town for a couple hours until Mina's classes got out, then I went to go pick her and Sam up. I forgot to buy a lock, so I had to wheel the bike around with me, which wasn't all that bad since it looked pretty slick.

Mina's face lit up when she saw me. "Ron-Ron!" she cried, and flung her non-orange self into my arms.

I tousled her hair. "Hey, kiddo," I said.

"Mom's not picking me up?" she asked.

I smiled. "I already texted her—I came to walk you home and to see how Sam's doing."

Mina perked up even more, believe it or not. "Sam's great," she said. Her hands instinctively grabbed the key-chain toys on her backpack. "And I'm sure he'd want to walk with us."

Which was totally true—he did. So there I was, with two

perked-up kids, walking along the tree-lined street of Makersville, Indiana. I don't know if Mina is that much of a genius or if I got lucky, but the moment we got home, she said she needed to do her math homework and wanted to start right then, leaving Sam and me alone, but not before telling me that the garbage disposal had broken. I promised her I'd get around to it, and then Sam and I grabbed a bag of chips and sat on the front porch, watching the clouds pass in the sky. I fidgeted while I tried to figure out what I was going to tell Sam about Nick—knowing what I did about Nick felt about as great as a nail in my eyeball.

Believe me, I did entertain the thought of lying about Nick— *Why, sure I talked with Nick, and boy did he want to come home!*—but every time I thought about that, I felt like pure crap. I mean, if you're going to live and walk on this planet, you'd better as hell be real about it. The last thing this world needs is one more fake person with fake shit spewing out of their mouth. Besides, if the truth's the truth, then Sam had better get used to facing hard facts, like I did when I was his age.

I played with my shoelaces. "So, what happened in school today?" I asked.

"We learned about parallelograms," Sam said.

My eyebrows shot up. "Not bad."

Sam shook his head, grabbed a handful of chips from the bag I was holding, and stuffed them into his mouth. "Not good," he said, but the words weren't the clearest.

"What do you mean?"

"I mean," Sam said, swallowing, "who cares about parallelograms? How will that help me in life?"

"It won't."

"Exactly," Sam said, being all indignant about it.

I picked some mud off my shoes. "So what *will* help you?" I asked. I swatted at a mosquito.

"In life?" Sam cocked his head.

"You said it."

"Well—" He paused, thinking. "I want to find Nick."

My stomach tightened into a fist. Of course Sam would say that. "Look," I said, "about that . . ."

Sam suddenly became alert. Very alert. "What? What happened?"

"Well . . ."

Hope flashed across his face. "You found him?"

I yanked at my shoelace. "Not exactly," I said.

Sam leaned into me. "What do you mean?"

"He called me."

"How did he get your number?"

"When you go looking for someone all across town, word gets out. I guess."

"How is he? Where is he?" Sam asked excitedly. He stood up. He would have crawled under my skin if I could have let him.

"I don't know."

"But—"

The unspoken question hung in the air. Sam's eyebrows knit

together as he looked at me with huge eyes. I looked away so I didn't have to see the confusion on Sam's face. "From the way he was talking, though, he sounded pretty good," I said.

"What is he doing?" Sam asked.

"Drinking," I said.

The sudden look of dejection in Sam's eyes almost killed me. I regretted opening my mouth. "Look, Sam—"

"He's not coming home, is he?"

"Well, it's not that Nick doesn't *want* to, but—"

Sam took a step down our front porch and turned away from me. "I don't want to hear any more," he said quietly.

"He was concerned about you."

Sam clenched his fists. "I said, I don't want to hear any more."

"He said that—"

Sam ripped the bag of chips from my hands, stomped on it with one foot, then twisted it up and whacked it against the front porch post. Twice.

"Okay," I said quietly.

Sam ran down our porch steps, crossed over to the oak tree, and kicked it a couple times. There really wasn't anything to say. I had just told him his brother was a drunken dickwad who didn't want to rescue Sam; how the hell do you follow up on that?

A police car whizzed by on our street.

After a while Sam came back and sat with me again on the porch stairs. He untwisted the potato chip bag and started eating the crumbs with pinched fingers. He ate that damn bag of chips so intently it was like his entire life depended on it.

My chest hurt, watching him. "Hey," I said.

Sam licked his fingers.

A helicopter hovered in the sky.

"At least we know he's okay."

Sam kept eating.

"And we can stop looking for him."

Sam shook his head. "I don't want to talk about it." We sat there in silence for a long time, with the only sound being the helicopter and Sam eating chips, until Jello came strolling up the driveway. Okay, not really strolling. He rolled up onto our lawn with his bike, then flung it aside and ran up to us. The nurse had done a good job cleaning up his face, but he still looked awful.

"Well, are you ready?" Jello asked. "Man, I couldn't concentrate in class all day."

My stomach churned.

"What happened to your face?" Sam asked. "And ready for what?"

Jello was hopping with excitement. "This photo shoot is going to be great."

I fidgeted on the porch step. "When'd you find it?" I asked.

"Find what?" Sam asked.

"Yesterday. In my backyard, sunning, of all things," Jello said. "And I've been dying to tell you ever since."

"What was sunning?" Sam asked. He put down the bag of chips.

"How'd you capture it?" I was curious, despite myself.

Jello shrugged. "A box. And a shovel. I put the box over it, slid the shovel underneath, and *sloop!*—turned the box over and that was that. Captured."

Sam stood up. "What did you capture?" he asked loudly, crossing his arms over his chest.

Jello looked at Sam for the first time. "Who's he?"

"Nick Caldwell's younger brother," I said. "He hangs here sometimes."

Jello nodded approvingly. "Good. We'll need two people for the photo shoot anyway—you're both in?"

"Sweet Jesus," I muttered.

"Photo shoot of what?" Sam asked.

"I need two people to hold the python," Jello said.

Sam's face lit up.

"You're a freaking crazy freak," I said.

"That's cool," Sam said.

Jello smiled at Sam. "I need two people to hold the python while I shoot it. Right now it's in a box, and it's all curled up—you can't get any sense of its size when it's like that. So I need two people to hold it out. It's big, you know."

"I'm sure," I said.

"It is," Jello insisted.

"I absolutely believe you," I said.

Jello turned to Sam. "At first I was thinking that we could curl the python around Ronney—you know, loop it around him to let people see how big it is—but holding it out with two people is much better."

"Much better," I repeated. "Especially since a python looping itself around an animal means it's killing it."

"Right," Jello said. "So we'll have each of you take an end of the python, and there's going to be some great pics. I just know it."

I turned to Sam. "We'll flip for it," I said. "Heads or tails?" I gave Jello a look. "You do realize that you're asking us to hold a living, pissed-off python."

"I didn't say it's pissed off," Jello said.

"That's because you don't speak python," I replied. "I'm sure the python is completely happy being in that dark box right now, tame as a sleeping dog."

"Huh." Jello paused. "I have some leather gloves you guys could use. I've heard that a lot of animal bites don't go through leather."

"You're so right—of course cows have hides of steel. That's why that tiger hasn't killed any of the cows. In fact, I don't think anyone has ever killed a cow. They're indestructible."

"Shut up, Ronney. You know what I mean," Jello said.

"I'm afraid I do," I said.

"Are we going to do it now?" Sam asked.

"No time like the present," Jello said.

"There are worse ideas than handling a living, pissed-off python," I said. "I just can't think of them."

"We're not directly handling it. I have gloves," Jello pointed out. "Come on, R-Man."

It strangely felt like this was the third time he'd asked. "Well, I suppose," I said.

"I don't like it," Dad said.

I spun around to see Dad standing behind us on the porch. "What?" I asked, stunned.

"I don't like it," Dad said again, his eyes lingering on Jello's face.

Jello looked away.

"Since when do you come out of your room so much, O intrepid trekker?" I asked.

Dad ignored me. "Those animals are dangerous."

"So are guns, some would say," I said.

Dad's lips puckered. "Pythons too."

"Since when do you care so much?" I snapped at him. "You haven't cared so much in, oh, two years. My heart is beating wildly in my chest with all of this caring that you're doing."

Dad gripped the porch railing hard.

"Anyway, pythons don't really even bite. They kill by squeezing," I said, shooting a look at Jello, "and we'll just be holding it out. With leather gloves. At arm's length."

"You are planning on *holding a python*."

"Come on," I said to Jello and Sam. "Let's go."

Jello didn't move. He looked at Dad.

"Ronney. You will not go," Dad said.

"You're not going to stop me," I said. I met Dad's eyes and stared him down. "We've been doing without you just fine, animals or no animals. And anyway, if you're ignoring the doctor's orders and not doing your stupid arm exercises, how can you possibly tell me what to do?"

I could feel him shrinking in front of me. But now I was on a roll. "Do I tell you to change out of your pajamas every day? Does Mom tell you that you can't spend the entire day in your room? Do I tell you to get out of the house and do some actual grocery shopping? Or pick Mina up from school? Or, when she hugs you, to fucking hug her back?"

The determined look on Dad's face started to waver. He ran his hand through his hair, twice, and his shoulders slumped.

"No, we don't tell you any of this. We let you do your shit. So let me do mine. And let me remind you that two months ago when the car broke down with the four of us, you let Mom flag down a stranger to help us and do all the talking, all the while you sat in the passenger seat *with your eyes closed*. Did anyone tell you to help her? Did anyone tell you to deal with the auto mechanics instead of making her do everything? Does anyone tell you to take out the garbage when it's spilling onto the floor—"

At that point Dad's face twisted up, and before I could react, he snatched a potted plant from the railing of our front porch, raised the pot over his head, and smashed it on the sidewalk below. Then he went inside the house, letting the screen door slam behind him.

That terrifying feeling came again, and again I pushed it down.

A thick silence fell over Jello and Sam and me. Jello shifted from one foot to the other. Sam looked at the ground. "Let's go," I said to them, and my voice was thinner than I expected it to be.

"I don't think your dad is actually letting us do this," Jello said slowly.

"You saw him leave, didn't you?" I snapped. "I don't know about the two of you, but I'm leaving for Jello's. We've got work to do."

First, though, I stopped to pick up the broken pot shards and put them in the trash. I didn't realize how shaken I was until I felt pain on the palms of my hands, I was gripping the shards so tight.

Truth be told, I wanted Dad to put his foot down and end the stupidity, but he couldn't do it. I was pissed at him for backing off but then also pissed at myself for challenging him when I really wanted to shout *Fuck no, Jello, Dad says no!* and now here I was stuck in Python World.

I mean, why couldn't I just have listened to him? That's what I was wondering as we biked to Jello's house. And then I realized: I wasn't going to follow orders from a loser dad, someone who was just going to walk away. I couldn't follow orders from a dad like that. That's no way to live.

I found myself wishing for a full-time dad again, and I was stunned because I could have sworn that thoughts like that had died long ago. Just then I realized what that strange, terrifying feeling had been, twice now: hope. An awful pain crept into my chest. *I'm not going to let myself be hurt again,* I thought. *I can't.* I knew from personal experience that the pain would grow until it near consumed you, unless you had a way to go numb or shut it off somehow. Or bury it for good.

So I decided to shut it off by thinking about the python, which wasn't all that hard with Jello and Sam prattling along beside me.

Jello was keeping a python in his garage. I didn't know just how fast a python could move, but I did know that its entire body was freaking iron muscle. If we held it and it didn't want to be held, how would it wrap itself around us? And how could we get it off? A box cutter would be too small. Maybe a butcher knife?

I did a quick mental check: It wasn't Thursday. There, at least, was that. And I had to admit that even a really bad idea could be exciting once you put your mind to it. In a bad-idea kind of way.

"So," Jello was saying, "gloves. We need gloves."

"Smart," I said.

Jello went to his closet and pulled out a pair of leather gloves.

I looked at him. "You're giving the two of us one pair of thin leather gloves."

"We only need one pair," Jello said, "for the person holding the head, right?"

"Right," Sam said. "Can I hold the head?"

"No," I said, and I grabbed the gloves from Jello. My stomach knotted up. "Ski masks?" I asked.

"For what?" Jello said.

For if it lunges at our faces, I wanted to say, but then I realized how much of a loser I sounded, so I stopped. "What about a butcher knife?" I asked.

Jello looked at me blankly.

"If that thing is around one of us, we're going to need a way to get it off," I said.

Jello looked thoughtful. "Good idea." He grabbed at the pile of dirty dishes by his computer. "Here's a steak knife."

"A steak knife is not a butcher knife," I said.

"It'll be fine," Jello said.

"A steak knife is a toothpick to a python," I said. "Where's your butcher knife?"

"We can't use it. It's my mom's. She'd kill me if she found out. And anyway, we probably won't even need a knife."

"Probably," I said.

Jello checked his camera gear. "I think we have everything," he said. "Ready?"

"Ready," Sam said.

"I guess," I said.

"R-Man, you don't have to do this—" Jello said.

"Shut up," I said.

We climbed back out through the window, although that was pretty lame-ass, since we had to haul the gear through the window too, and we could have just used the door.

We trudged to the garage. Jello looked at us and smiled. He put his hand on the doorknob. His face was a billboard of excitement. "This is going to be so awesome," he said.

"Yeah," Sam said.

"Yeah," I said.

Jello rubbed his hands together. "So we're going to go in, and I'm going to open the garage door so we get more light," he explained. "Ronney'll tip the python box over, and the two of you will pick up the python, one at each end. While you're figuring that out, I'll adjust the side lighting and then be shooting the whole thing. I'll also be letting you know where to stand to get the best angle. You guys shouldn't be holding the python for more than a minute or two, tops."

"Easy," Sam said.

"Splendid," I said. Then I thought of something. "What are we going to do with the python when we're done?"

Jello adjusted his camera strap around his neck. "We could call it in, I guess. Or we could dump it in the woods."

"That would be cool," Sam said. "Maybe it'll kill a deer."

My stomach didn't feel too good. "Tell me again why you want these pictures so badly?" I said to Jello.

Jello sighed. "Because, my dear Ronney, I'll turn around and submit them to the *National Geographic*. How could they say no?"

Jello turned the doorknob and pushed the door open. The garage was pitch black. Jello went in, and Sam and I followed him. Jello hit the garage switch, and the garage was suddenly filled with a tinny, fluorescent light.

"It's probably sleeping," Jello said, and he sounded like a Discovery Channel commentator. "The python's been in the dark for almost twenty-four hours."

That was precisely when we noticed that the python box was tipped over on its side, lying on the ground, empty.

"Uh-oh," Jello said.

"Fuck," I said.

"Wow," Sam said.

We inched closer to each other in the middle of the garage, scanning the ground.

"You didn't put a lid on the box, did you?" I asked. It was more of an accusation.

"I did too," Jello said.

"Was it a locking lid?" I asked.

"No," Jello said. "It was a piece of cardboard."

"Did you put something heavy on top of the lid?" I asked.

"I didn't think of that," Jello said.

We looked in every corner of the garage. There was no python.

"It mysteriously disappeared," Jello said. He scratched his arm. "How could it do that?"

"Here," I said. I pointed to a space beneath the work bench: There was a mouse hole. I looked back at them. "Good-bye, python."

Jello swore.

"Darn," Sam said.

My stomach felt better. Kind of.

Jello was quiet for a moment. Then he stalked around the garage until he found a flashlight and peered into the mouse hole.

"It's dark," Jello said, on his hands and knees.

I couldn't think of anything a friend would say right then, so I shut up.

"I thought the garage was secure," Jello whined.

"That's a bummer," Sam said.

"Really too bad," I said.

Jello started pouting at that point—and watching Jello pout is as much fun as having my leg inserted into a wood chipper. So Sam and I left Jello to mope and stare at the mouse hole.

I was about to have Sam and me bike back to my house, but Sam had other ideas. "This way," he called over his shoulder, and took off. We biked across town until we came to this area that was starting to be developed, where new houses didn't dot the land and trees and stuff grew. We ditched our bikes by an old, fallen tree, partially covered in long grasses. Beyond that was a wooded area, the kind of place where a tiger would live, but I pushed that thought aside.

"What's this? You going back to nature or something?" I asked.

"Shh," Sam said, and it felt right: I was being too loud.

We hiked through the bramble. The woods kept going back for a ways, and the trees glowed like some cool-ass movie. It reminded me of a time when Dad and I were hiking in this forest, in a state park pretty far away, and we got our asses lost. The trails kept branching, and there were no signs or anything. I was starting to panic when Dad said, "Ronney, just look at these trees. They're *glowing*." And sure as shit, there it was, this whole crazy forest of glowing light in every direction I looked. Pure magic.

That's what these trees were like too, except we weren't lost, which was nice. Sam kept going deeper into the woods, and I followed him, shivering as the wind picked up. After a while a little creek stretched out in front of us, and some big stones sat in the middle of the stream. Sam plopped down on one stone, and I took another.

"Not bad," I said.

Sam smiled faintly; I could tell he was pleased.

We sat there for a while on those rocks, not saying much of anything. The sunlight was warm.

Suddenly Sam turned to me. "This is where we went."

Now *that* made sense. "How often?"

"Pretty often." Sam dipped his hand into the creek, grabbed a handful of stones, and began to throw them, one by one, into the water. I had the feeling that he did that a lot. "Nick would always sit on that rock too," Sam said, nodding to the rock I was sitting on. "He would teach me how to catch minnows, or we'd mess around with the mud, or sometimes we wouldn't do anything at all."

"Don't need to," I said.

Sam's face brightened: I got it. "And one time, Nick and I played hide-and-go-seek, and I hid in this pile of leaves and he couldn't find me," Sam said, leaning back to catch some sun. He smiled. "He was starting to get all worried, and he was standing right next to me! So I jumped up and the leaves went flying everywhere and Nick screamed like a girl—though he made me promise not to tell anyone about that, ever."

"Your secret's safe with me," I said, trying to imagine a deep-voiced Nick screaming like a girl. I smiled.

"One day I skipped school and came here," Sam said.

"Was that the day of the shooting?" I asked.

Sam startled. "Yeah, how'd you know?"

"Mina said you weren't in class that day."

Sam paused, then nodded. "Yeah, I was here. I . . . I just missed Nick." He stuck his feet in the water, shoes and all.

"You picked an awesome day not to go to school."

"My parents didn't even know, because with the shooting, the teachers were so panicked no one remembered to call." Sam smiled faintly.

"Nice work."

Sam's smile disappeared. "And this other time, Nick showed me his hiding place for—you know. When he drinks."

"Really."

Sam squirmed on his rock. "He'll never come home," he said, and he kicked at the water.

"You don't know that," I said.

"I just know," he said. He looked away.

"Hey," I said.

Sam looked at me.

"You gotta be ready for everything," I said, and I was surprised at how firm my voice was.

"I know," Sam said quietly.

"And *everything* means he might come back."

Sam's face brightened. "Yeah, right?"

"Right. You never know what'll happen," I said, but I felt kind of disgusting right then: I knew better than to get the kid's hopes up. God knows what happens when they fall for good.

18

IT WAS A THURSDAY WHEN GEORGE APPROACHED me in the school hallway. We were between classes; I was going to biology, and I knew she was heading to art class. She came up to me excitedly and said, "Hey, guess what?"

I looked away from her. "Hey," I mumbled, and tried to veer to the other side of the hallway.

She tagged behind me. "Ronney," she said.

I stopped and turned around, my heart thumping wildly in my chest. "What?" I said.

Her breath caught in her throat, and her face immediately flushed. "Um," she said. It was clear that she hadn't expected me to respond.

I peered at her. I'd never seen George taken off guard.

"Have you . . ." She fidgeted as she searched for things to say. "Um . . . heard that the tiger killed three cats last night?" she asked me. "Not big cats. Little cats. Pets."

"Really?" I asked, even though I had already heard this.

"They're saying that the tiger shouldn't be killing these cats with everything it's already killed and eaten. They're saying that the tiger isn't killing for food anymore—it's killing just to kill." She paused. "You better be careful."

"You too."

George watched the kids in the hallway for a while, and when she finally looked at me, her eyes were sparkling. "Ronney, I just got accepted into an elite architecture competition for high school students. We'll compete at Stanford University, on-site, and if we're in the top of our group, we're guaranteed massive scholarships, maybe even a full ride. Imagine that—guaranteed!"

"That's nice," I said flatly. I felt like an ass, but I just couldn't pull off trying to be happy for her. She was standing right in front of me, but I wasn't seeing her; I was seeing George's finger looped so casually around Jello's, and I wondered again how often she and Jello had been texting about the safari before she showed up at my door. Lying through her teeth.

George's excitement deflated at my response, but she kept going. "Dad and I will fly out there only for two days—there and back—because I don't want to miss school." She bit her bottom lip.

"Of course not. Good luck," I said, and I started walking toward class.

"Ronney," she said, and she reached out and touched my arm.

I stopped. "Yeah?" I tried to say it nicely, but it still had an edge.

"Ronney, I—" She looked up at the ceiling suddenly, then glanced back at me, her eyes all wet. "I . . . Ronney . . . I miss you." Her voice was thick.

I wouldn't have noticed if an ice cream truck bulldozed over me just then. "What?" I repeated, even though I'd heard her perfectly fine.

"I miss you," she said more strongly. "Jello's been talking about you helping him with these photos, and the more he talks about you, the more . . ." George looked away.

Students were passing us by, parting around us like water around rocks in a river. I stuck my hand in my Thursday-jeans pocket and jingled my coins, including my Thursday coin.

The stupid-ass thing was, I didn't know what to say. Doesn't that suck? When a really great, awesome, smart, *hot* girl comes up to you and says she misses you, and you lose all ability to spit out a couple of words in response—I repeat: Doesn't that suck? Because you can't say just any words when those amazing-girl-words have been spoken. No. You need *words*. You need words that will be as cool and awesome sounding as the words she just said, and the truth is, your ass can't think of *any*. Hell, I was so uncomfortable right then I would have even grunted if I could have gotten away with it, but I had to say something. Anything. Well, not anything, but something good. Something great. Something amazing. So, I said, "I know."

George frowned. "You know?"

At that point I should have turned to grunting and shut the

hell up, because the truth was that I didn't know what I had just told her I knew, that I was only saying something because something obviously needed to be said and I couldn't grunt like how I wanted, but maybe grunting really was the way out of this mess, because I continued opening my big-ass mouth and said, "Yeah. I know you've missed me."

The look of shock and disgust on her face was not a pretty one.

"You *what?*" George asked, though I'm sure she'd heard me perfectly fine.

I really wanted to teleport out of that place, right at that moment. And I suppose, if I were some sort of linguistic genius, I would have taken her question as a last-ditch escape hatch and said something like *But not anything like how I've missed you* or some shit that would have saved my ass. Unfortunately, I'd skipped too many English classes to learn how to smooth over fuckups like that, and so, in the vacuum that was my brain, the only answer that sprang to mind for her *What?* was to, quite literally, repeat what I'd just said.

"I know you've missed me," I said.

George turned her face away from me, her cheeks flushed and her mouth slightly open, and she exhaled for a good number of breaths. I could almost hear her counting in her head, trying to calm down. It was all that I could do to hope to God that she understood that I wasn't trying to be a dick; I was just being stupid and didn't know how to get myself out of the hole that I had just dug and fallen into.

"Ronney," she said slowly, "I don't think you're trying to be a dick, but you can be really stupid sometimes, you know?"

"You have no idea," I said, digging my hands into my pockets.

"Maybe I do," she said, crossing her arms over her chest.

I resorted to grunting at that point.

After a moment George shifted her weight from one foot to the other, and I could tell she was struggling to find words for whatever she was going to tell me next. My heart thumped wildly.

"Do you remember that day of the windstorm, when the animals got loose?" she asked me. Some of her honor-student friends passed us by in the hallway and called out to her, but she didn't notice, she was so focused on me.

"I was at your house. You were crying about that test. Pretty hard."

George bit her lip. "I wasn't crying about a test, Ronney," she said.

My eyebrows furrowed. "What?"

"I was crying about you." She paused. "About us. About . . . how trapped I felt."

I remembered what Jello had said: *George would start crying, kept saying that we had to tell you, and soon.* Maybe Jello wasn't a lying asshole, I thought.

George wrapped a tendril of hair around her finger, then unwrapped it. "I knew how devastated you would be if you ever found out. When you found out. I mean, I know . . ."

"You felt trapped?" I prompted, not wanting her to finish the sentence she had just been trying to finish: *I know how you feel about me.*

George met my gaze. "I felt like I was trapped between how much I care about you and how I feel about Jello," she said. "Either way, someone was going to lose—either you or him—and I was going to lose too, either way. Maybe we all were."

I had no idea what to say.

"So that day of the windstorm, I was so upset about all of this, and I didn't want to keep lying to you, but I didn't know what to do, and I felt like I was going to explode. Jello and I had talked a lot about what we should say to you, and when. But I just . . . I don't want to lose you. And I was afraid that once you found out . . ."

I remembered that day like it was yesterday. I could practically feel George in my arms again, the solidness of her back and her arms and her heart beating in her chest. She kept telling me about those four questions on her AP Chemistry test, kept moaning about how she was afraid to get that A-. I had held her for a long time that day, maybe twenty minutes, maybe thirty, until she calmed down, telling her over and over that it's okay not to be perfect, it's okay to make a mistake. *I'm here for you*, I kept saying. I could smell the shampoo on her hair, and her hair was so soft. . . .

"So there was no test?" I asked slowly.

The warning bell sounded for class. We had a couple minutes left.

George shook her head. "I had to give you a reason," she said. "At that point, I was losing sleep with keeping it a secret from you. So was Jello."

"So you lied to me," I said, my voice strengthening. "In many ways."

George bowed her head.

I swallowed hard. "But why Jello?"

The question hung there between us for what seemed like two weeks. Just when I thought she wasn't going to answer, she said, "At first, when we were lab partners in AP Chemistry, we worked so well together. Like we could read each other's minds. Then I found out he understood me in a lot of other ways."

"Why not me?" I had to ask, and my voice cracked.

The saddest expression fell across her face. "I can't help it. I just don't see you like that, Ronney."

"Not even once?" I asked, even though I knew I was begging.

George went quiet for a long time. "So it's not true anymore then, is it?" she asked.

"What do you mean?"

"You're not going to be here for me?" Her eyes grew watery.

It was my turn to look away. What could I say? How could I say that it was perfectly fine for my two best friends to deceive me? Of all the people in the world, they knew how thick my armor was, but the one chink it had, the one fucking chink, there they were, knifing me exactly in that tiny space, right where they could make a fatal blow.

When I looked back at George, she was still watching me, waiting for my answer. Her eyes pleaded with mine.

"I don't know," I said.

George winced, and she turned her head to look down the hall-way, where her next class was. We were nearly alone at that point, and the bell was going to ring. "Go to class—you're going to be late," I said.

"And you?" she asked.

"I don't know; I need to think about stuff," I said. My brain felt like scrambled eggs at that point, and I just needed to get outside, get some fresh air.

George swiped her cheeks, gave me a sad smile, and said, "I get it. Take your time, Ronney."

Then she walked away.

It was as if Dad had cameras around the house, because he knew exactly when I got home that day. "Ronney?" Dad called from his bedroom.

I sighed inside. After talking with George, Dad was the last person I wanted to talk to. Or semi-talk to. "Yeah?"

Silence.

I unclenched my teeth and went to the refrigerator. Astonish-ingly, Dad came out of his room in jeans and a T-shirt. I mean, he wasn't decked out for the Taj Mahal or anything, but he was wearing actual clothing. Like, *clothing*. And he had combed his hair. I stared at him.

"You want to go bowling?" Dad asked.

This was the first time he'd asked me to do something in a long-ass time, since way before his suicide attempt. He'd stopped things like bowling and fishing years ago. I didn't even know his mouth remembered how to say the word "bowling."

"Nice shirt," I said. "Good color."

"You want to go bowling?" Dad asked again.

Something inside me froze. Truly froze. I didn't know how to handle this; just like I didn't know how to handle George saying nice shit to me. I don't know, maybe I'm not wired for nice shit anymore; maybe I had gotten sick of having nice shit get my hopes up—whether it was building chocolate chip cookie houses or working on the car—and then something happens that brings it all down. Maybe that's what it was; I'm really not sure. All I know is that somewhere a numbness took over, like there was a rock in my gut. I said to Dad, "No. Bowling's lame."

Dad's face fell.

He retreated to the living room, didn't even turn on the TV, and I felt like a bucket of piss right then. I mean, listening to Dad was one thing, but hanging with him was another; Dad was asking me if I wanted to spend some quality time together, and I just shoved it in his face. But the worst thing, I know, would be to say yes. Because then you're taking those chains off the house you just locked up nice and tight, and hell, if you have a good time bowling, maybe that front door even opens a little. Before you know it, your dad comes into that house and starts sledge-hammering all your shit—your shit on the walls, your furniture shit, all the shit you know and love—and you'd be one sorry ass, because your dad is in your now-unlocked house, ripping everything to hell. Just like you knew he would.

The house was silent. It was the kind of silence where things were breaking, and it was because of you that it was so broken. Truth be told, I did want to hurt Dad—so he'd finally know how it feels to be me, to be trampled on so long and so hard that you think there's no rebounding, ever. But as soon as that thought crossed my mind, I knew that I was now part of the problem. I was turning into Dad. And I would rot in hell before I turned into him.

I paused in the kitchen as I was making my sandwich. "Dad?" I asked. I knew he could hear me in the living room.

Silence.

"Dad?" Pause. "Do you want a sandwich? I can make you one," I said, even though I didn't really want to. But I would.

From the kitchen, I heard him get up off the couch. When I peeked into the living room, I saw him in front of the window, looking out.

"Dad?"

Silence.

I went back into the kitchen, leaned on the edge of the kitchen counter with both palms, took a deep breath, and exhaled. When you're a dick, sometimes life lets you do things over again. But sometimes it doesn't.

19

WHILE DAD WAS STILL IN THE LIVING ROOM, Sam dropped by. Sam didn't need to say anything; he had a huge bruise on his face. I sighed inside: This was one long Thursday.

"So, what is it this time?" I asked, handing him my sandwich. I was hoping to God he wouldn't say it was his dad.

"Nothing," Sam said.

"Right," I said, tossing him a granola bar.

"Really," Sam said, catching the granola bar with his free hand.

Even with the windows closed, you could hear gunshots in the distance. These days you never knew if people were shooting at a wandering python, the air, or each other.

"So you punch yourself in the face often, then?" I asked. We went to the dining room.

Sam smiled faintly. "I got in a fight at school today."

I sighed a little in relief. "Nice," I said.

Sam was shaking his head. "With this kid named Caleb. He's an ass."

I snickered. Sam sounded like me just then.

Dad was seated on the living room couch and he turned his head toward us. He stared at Sam, then at me.

"What happened?" I asked, ignoring Dad's look.

"Caleb was making fun of Brian, and I didn't like that, so I told him to stop, and when he didn't, I hit him."

"Why didn't you let this Brian take care of himself?" I asked, rummaging in the pantry for something better. I found a bag of cookies, grabbed a handful, and passed it to Sam.

Sam didn't take any. "Brian can't take care of himself."

"I doubt that."

Sam gave me a look. "He's dead."

My thoughts had a total train wreck. "What?" I asked.

"Brian was the kid who died from the cheetah," Sam said. His eyes strayed to the window, and he watched a neighbor walking her dog. "He was my friend."

"Wow," I said.

"And Caleb was being an ass, making some joke that Brian couldn't handle a little cat—that pissed me off."

Again, Dad stared. A part of me was seriously annoyed that he was eavesdropping on our conversation, but hey, Sam was turning into a younger version of me. How cool is that?

"I told him to stop, and he kept laughing, so I hit him."

"Good," I said.

Sam nodded. "I got him hard on the third and fourth punch. Anyway, we started fighting on the playground and the teachers came over and Caleb was crying like a baby, said I started everything. I was going to get a suspension until I said that he had been making fun of Brian."

"Really," I said.

"Yeah. When I said that, the teachers made Caleb and me talk about it until we could both say 'I'm sorry.'"

"That's bullshit," I said.

"Yup. Bullshit." Sam paused, looked at the bag of cookies, and took a handful. "Then they called home, talked with Mom," he said.

I tensed up. "Oh?"

"She said she was going to talk with Dad about it."

My stomach lurched.

"He gets home around seven o'clock." Sam paused again. "I didn't want to stay home. So I told Mom I'm hanging out with you."

"I don't blame you," I said.

Sam grabbed some more cookies. "My dad's an asshole."

"Dads can be," I said loudly.

"Nick's an asshole too," Sam said.

I paused. "I don't know about that one," I said.

Sam stood up. "How can you say that?" he said, his voice rising. "He's an asshole, I swear to God." Sam's hands clenched into fists.

I raised my hand. "Hey, calm down. I mean, you two were

pretty close. He might not be a total asshole. Just a partway ass-hole."

"He's not coming home," Sam said. "It's been six months already. That's *total asshole* to me."

I winced and led Sam outside, away from Dad's prying ears. Sam was young to lose hope in his brother. He was what, ten years old going on eighty? I mean, it's not like Sam had a whole lot going for him in the first place. And that was *with* Nick. We threw around a football for a while as I wished beyond wishing that I could give him something to hope for. A small something.

"Hey," I said. "Want us to kick this football over the house?"

Sam's eyes lit up and he nodded. But dammit, the moment I launched that football over our roof, that heaviness settled back into his eyes. There wasn't another football, and I wasn't in the mood to go looking around in the grass. For the record, there was a python slinking around. And a tiger.

Then I got an idea. "Sam, we got a couple hours before your dad gets home, right?"

Sam nodded.

"You want to go bowling?"

Sam cocked his head and looked at me kind of funny. "Bowl-ing's lame," he said.

I grinned. "So you know how to bowl, then?"

"Not really . . ." Then he grinned back. "Let's go."

The guy behind the counter at the bowling alley was a douche-bag and made me prepay for our two games, probably because

I'm young and he was thinking we were going to bowl and ditch. Total jackwad. I do have to say I'm glad I didn't know anyone there, because I truly suck at bowling. Sam too; he slipped and fell on the bowling alley lane. We threw gutter after gutter and gave each other shit about who was worse. Every once in a while my thoughts would turn to Dad and how maybe this was how he wanted to spend an afternoon with me. But I didn't know what to do with that thought. What do you do when somebody is asking you to give them a second chance? And how much will you risk for your hope that maybe this time it'll be different? Honestly, there was such a huge chasm between Dad and me, I had no idea where to begin if I even did want to cross it.

Anyway, bowling with Sam was the most fun I'd had in a long, long time.

By the time we left the bowling alley, it was dark. I walked Sam home and made sure I saw him let himself in the house. It would be rough, him facing his dad, but sometimes hard things just need to be done. No way around it. Still, I hoped it wasn't too hard.

The moment I walked in from the garage, Mom and Mina were pulling up the driveway. The car stopped for a moment, and Mina got out and flung herself into my arms. "Ron-Ron!" she cried, and burst into tears.

"What is it?" I asked, alarmed.

She mumble-sobbed something into my T-shirt.

"I know. Flute lessons can suck," I said.

"It's not the flute lessons," Mina moaned. "Sam lost my bouncy ball."

I tried not to laugh. "It's just a bouncy ball," I said.

That made her cry harder. "No it's not," Mina said, wiping her snot on my shirt in the way she loves to do. "That was the bouncy ball you gave me."

"Oh," I said. "Don't worry; I'll get you another one."

She shook her head, and her spiral curls wobbled. "You can't get me another one, because it's gone. It's *gone*."

Mom parked the car and approached us. "She's been like this all the way home," Mom said. She looked weary as she adjusted the purse on her shoulder.

I rubbed Mina's back. "It's okay," I said again.

"And I don't like him anymore," Mina said, wiping her eyes with the palm of her hand.

"Because of the bouncy ball?" I was incredulous.

"Yes." She paused. "He lost it on purpose."

It was my turn to pause. "Really?"

Mina nodded dolefully. "He was bouncing it really hard, really really super high on the playground, and I told him that if he did that he'd lose it somewhere, and he said no he wouldn't, but then he bounced it and it went somewhere in the grass and then I spent the rest of recess looking for it, but the baseball field is huge," Mina said, her eyes growing big. "Huge."

"He was just having fun," I said. "He didn't mean to."

"With *my* bouncy ball." Mina broke away from me and started crying all over again. "I gave it to him as a gift and look what he did with it. He was reckless." She balled up her hands to her eyes. "Reckless."

"Nice use of a spelling word," I offered.

Mina cried harder.

"And then he couldn't even help me look for it because he was fighting with Caleb," Mina said between hiccups. "I was alone."

"I'm sure you looked really hard."

"I was alone."

"No you weren't, you . . ." The lie died on my tongue.

I didn't know what to do right then, and I hated seeing Mina cry. I really hate it—so I tickled her until she was half laughing through her tears, which was a whole lot better, at least for me. But she kept saying how reckless Sam was with her bouncy ball, and how alone she felt, and I could tell she was going to start crying again. I didn't know what else to do except to plop her ass on her bike and ride down to the 7-Eleven with their stupid vending machines, where I stuck quarters into their bouncy-ball machine trying to get an orange one for Mina. Of course, since it was a Thursday, a blue one rolled out, and I was about to try again, but Mina touched me on the shoulder and said, "It's okay, this one is fine."

"No it's not. It's not orange."

Mina stopped for a moment, looking down at the ground, and I thought she hadn't heard me and was going to repeat myself, when she said quietly, "It's not about the color."

I guess she really meant it too, that it wasn't about the color, because while I was taking my shower, Mina initiated phase two of Special Project De-Orange: She had put out into the hallway everything that was orange—which, believe me, was a lot. Her desk. Her comforter. Her beanbag chair. Her desk chair. Her shoes. Her *shoes*, for chrissake. When Mom went to ask her what was wrong, Mina shrugged and said to her, "I don't want orange anymore." Which was true, even for a bouncy ball. At first Mom was mad that Mina was throwing away half of her belongings and bitched about how much it'd cost to replace them, but then I heard her sigh and say, "My little girl's growing up." Which goes to show how lame Mom is.

So there was a mountain of orange Mina stuff in our hallway, and when that mountain got too big, Mom had Mina put it out in the garage for Goodwill. Which was a great idea unless Sam went to the store and bought it all back, I thought with a quiet chuckle. But Goodwill or no Goodwill, it sucked seeing all that orange shit go, like it was a tumbled mess of sunshine about to leave our house. I can't explain it; it just sucked.

And who knows, maybe even Mina thought that it sucked too, because she woke me up later in the middle of the night, screaming. When I heard the first scream, I jolted out of bed. The darkness in her room was thick, and with all her shit gone it was like I was on the shadowy surface of a barren, frigid moon.

"Shhh. It's okay, Mina," I said. I rocked her softly.

I could feel Mina slowly wake up in my arms.

"He was reckless," Mina said finally. I couldn't see her face, but her voice trembled.

"You had a nightmare about Sam?" I asked, slightly confused.

"No. Dad." She paused. "I was so alone."

My brain was still groggy. "Looking for the bouncy ball?"

"I was in the living room again." Mina tilted her head up to mine. She swallowed. "Ron-Ron, why did he do it? Why did he leave us?"

I was about to say *He didn't leave us*. But then I had to admit that he had. "What else was your nightmare about, Mina?" I asked.

"Then the color in the world drained away," she said softly, "and when the last of the color left, we died."

"Who's 'we'?"

"You, me, and Mom. Everyone else in the world. Only Dad was left alive, alone."

I exhaled. What the hell could I say to that?

"Then I had another nightmare," Mina continued, and for some reason she sounded guilty.

"About what?" I asked.

"I found the key," she whispered.

"The key?"

"Yeah."

"The key to what?" By now I was really confused.

"Never mind," Mina said. "It was just a bad dream, right?"

I rocked her for a long-ass time that night. She didn't fall back asleep; her muscles were too tense—I could tell. I wished I could say something that would make her happy, or at least happier, but sometimes life just isn't happy, not even a little, and trying to make something out of nothing would be fake-ass and lame. So I held her in the suckiness, and she let herself be held in that same suckiness, until I got tired of rocking her and kind of sleepy myself.

"Mina?" I asked.

"Yes, Ron-Ron."

"Are you going to be okay here by yourself? I'll be right next door, in my room."

"Is it okay that I threw out all my orange stuff?" Mina asked.

I paused, a little surprised by the question. "Well, you liked orange because you didn't want it to be lonely, right?"

"Yeah. And unloved."

"Well, is it lonely now?"

Mina was quiet.

I rubbed her arm. "Yeah, it's okay you threw out your orange things. You're still you. Although I have to admit, I'll miss seeing orange around the house."

Mina still didn't say anything.

The next day after school Sam was seated on the bench by my school's parking lot, waiting for me. He looked glum.

"What's up?" I asked.

"Nothing," he said.

"Liar," I said. "Let's try that again. What's up?"

A police car sped down the road, lights flashing.

"Well," Sam said, sighing, "my teacher is really mad I stopped doing my homework."

I sat down, propped my ankle up on my other knee, and let the sunshine soak in. "Math again?"

"All of it."

"All of math?" I asked, uncomprehending.

"No. All homework. All of it," he repeated.

My eyes grew big. "Are you serious? You stopped everything, cold?"

Sam stood up, uncomfortably, and started scuffing the sidewalk with the bottom of his shoes. "I'm done with school," he said.

I snorted. "You forgot to count the next seven years, kiddo."

Sam shook his head. "What does it matter?" he said. "Nick's not coming home. My dad blows. So does my mom."

"So not doing your homework will help things?" I asked.

"So doing my homework will help things?" Sam said.

"Well, at least you won't be having trouble with school," I said.

"I'm done with school," he said, fiercely this time.

I paused. Could I blame him? I mean, how many times have I skipped school to work on the house? "Okay," I said slowly. "So what else are you going to do?"

Sam looked at me. "What do you mean?"

"Well, if you're not going to do your homework, what *are* you going to do?"

Sam thought about that for a while. "I don't know," he said. "Maybe I should run away."

I looked at him sharply. "I must say, that was not funny."

"That wasn't supposed to be funny," Sam said.

"You are the fount of non-funniness," I said.

"Stop it, Ronney," Sam said. He sat back down on the bench so his legs dangled, and he swung them lightly. "I'm serious," he said, his voice quiet.

"So where would you go?" I asked, trying to keep my voice level.

Sam shook his head. "I don't know," he said, "but it would be better than here. Than this." He looked up at the glowing clouds overhead. "If Nick could do it, why can't I?"

"Nick's like, eight years older than you."

"Seven," Sam said.

"That's still more than half your life," I said.

Sam was quiet. I wanted to stop talking about this, so I told Sam he could meet me at my house and I'd take him out for ice cream later that evening if he wanted. Sam shrugged.

I guess that shrug meant a no, because Sam never showed up. In fact, he never showed up at home, either.

He was gone.

20

I DON'T KNOW WHY KIDS LIKE TO RUN AWAY from home. Actually, scratch that. I *do* know why kids like to run away from home: They have no more options left. At least, none that they can see. On the night that Dad shot himself, Mina could have come and hung out with me, or she could have started screaming at the top of her lungs, or she could have climbed that tree in our backyard and fallen from it and been driven to the hospital herself and been nice and taken care of. But she ran away because she didn't see any options, just like Sam didn't see any options, just like Dad hadn't seen any options. So then it's not about kids running away—I guess adults run away too. Except they don't run away from homes, they run away from people, just like how Dad was trying to get away from us.

I asked Dad once why he did it. It was right after he was released from the psych ward; he'd undergone a couple weeks of solid therapy at the hospital. In the very beginning, when he was in the ICU, I was kind of scared for him, but once I knew that he'd live, the reality of what he'd done hit me. That evening the psych ward released him, I was waiting for him to get home and feeling angrier and angrier with each passing moment. I mean, what right did he have to fuck with our lives like that? Who did he think he was, making everything we cared about come to a careening stop?

Mom drove him home, and after she turned off the car, she went around and opened his door for him, even though it was his left arm that had gotten hit and he could have opened the door himself. Anyway, I went outside and met them on the driveway. It was hard to see his face because the sun had mostly set and his skin blended in with the darkness. Also, the automatic lights on our garage decided to break then too, and with everything breaking and in the darkness, I walked up to Dad and put my face maybe an inch from his. I was his height, which was awesome, and I looked at him for the longest-ass time, but I couldn't see his eyes, only the shadows of where his eyes should have been. My chest suddenly felt ripped up.

"You're a jerk," I said.

"Ronney, be nice to your father," the silhouette of Mom said. "He's just gotten home from the hospital."

I ignored her. "So, why'd you do it?" I asked, my voice hard. "Why'd you try to leave us?"

Dad's shoulder was bandaged up pretty bad. Even in the shadows, I could see him look away. "I didn't try to leave you."

I waited.

"My life . . . had . . . gotten too heavy."

"What the hell is that supposed to mean?" I asked.

"Ronney," Mom said. She came and put a hand on Dad's good arm, leading him into the house.

"Don't let him run away," I said to her. I turned to him. "What does that mean, 'life had gotten too heavy'?"

"I just . . . didn't know how to get out of it," Dad said.

"Out of what? Your life?"

Dad was silent.

"You're pathetic," I said.

In the shadows, Dad hid his face in his good hand.

"What about us?" I asked him, and my voice broke on those words. "You were thinking of yourself. Trying to escape your life," I said, and I tried like hell to make my voice solid, but I couldn't and my voice broke again. "Well, what about that whole 'appreciate life' bit you talked about when we went fishing, huh?"

Dad shook his head.

"You're a hypocrite," I said, and I swallowed back the thickness in my throat. "Fuck you."

"Ronney!" Mom said, and pulled Dad inside the house.

"You'll like the new carpet I just installed," I called after them. "Don't mess it up again."

I watched them flick on the lights.

I had thought a lot about what Dad had said: *Life had gotten too heavy. I just didn't know how to get out of it.* Those two phrases ran themselves over and over in my mind, whirring endlessly through the nights, itching under my skin in the day. I lost sleep thinking about it all: What could possibly make someone up and shoot himself? Mom tried to talk with me about it, but someone had to make money for the family, and so she was working long-ass hours to make up for him.

But still: How could life get too heavy? He's got a family that's pretty good—okay, we have our moments, but we're not crap—he had a job, and we went on vacations every summer. What's so bad about that?

What's so bad about *us*?

These questions kept at me, gnawing at the edges of my brain, and I guess they did for Mom, too, because a couple nights after Dad came home I was roaming the house because I couldn't sleep, and I almost bumped into Mom, who was roaming the house because *she* couldn't sleep.

"Ronney," she said, startled.

"Sorry, Mom," I said. "Didn't mean to scare you."

"That's okay," she said, and her voice sounded full and sad. "How long have you been up?"

"Up as in awake, or up as in walking around the house?" I yawned as I said that, and I made her yawn too.

"Oh, Ronney," Mom said, and her voice sounded old and weary. "I'm so sorry you have to witness all of this."

I didn't know what to say to that.

"You want me to make you some tea?" Mom asked.

"Tea sucks."

"Okay, then maybe—"

"No, that's okay," I said.

"I just wish I could make things better for you."

I thought about that for a while.

"You know what would be nice?" I asked.

"What?" Mom said, suddenly eager.

"It'd be nice to walk around the house together."

For a moment she just stood there, in silence, in the dark, and I wasn't sure how she was taking that. But then I started walking to the living room and she was with me, by my side, and though it was awkward in some spaces, we walked around the house together for hours that night. After a long time I started to hear sniffling behind me. I tried to ignore it at first, but the sniffling continued, and as we rounded the corner to go into the living room, I caught Mom's hand brushing her cheek. Before I knew it, I turned around, and I was holding her as she sobbed in the night, and I was tall enough that she was sobbing into my shoulder. That was the only sound in the house, besides Dad's snoring coming from down the hallway.

Finally, we both went back to bed, and in the morning, for the first time in years, I didn't put my shoes in the middle of the kitchen floor. Though she was out the door early for work, as usual, she left me a note on my pillow that night: *Thanks for walking with me.*

You bet I still have that note.

Sam left two words for us: *Good by.* And because he didn't do his homework, he didn't know that he had misspelled the goddamn word. But that was the only way that we knew that he hadn't turned into tiger food, at least not yet. Beyond that, there was no explanation, no hint. As soon as Sam's mom called me, I raced over to his house, and there were flashing police cars there, his parents talking to the cops. When his dad saw me, he said, "There he is," and pointed.

I grimaced. Coming over was a bad idea.

There were three police officers there, and two of them were talking to Sam's parents one-on-one. Out of the corner of my eye, I spied one officer with a buzz cut and his chest thrust out: He was looking at me, his face lingering on my skin in the way that I hate. A moment later he was in my face with a pen and pad of paper in his hand. The badge on his uniform said LIEUTENANT KOWALSKI.

"So, how do you know Sam?" he asked me.

"We were friends. Are friends," I corrected myself. "He would hang out at my house a lot."

"Really?" He gave me a little smirk, as if I was such a loser that the only friend that I could have was a ten-year-old kid.

"I have a sister his age," I said coldly.

"I see," he said in the way that made it quite obvious that he did not believe me. He jotted something down on his pad of paper. Probably noting that I was some sort of pedophile.

"Did Sam say anything about where he would go?" Lieutenant Kowalski asked me.

"No," I said.

"Are you sure?"

"Really, I'm sure."

"Mmmm," he said, disbelievingly.

He peered at me then, and his eyes lingered on the shape of my nose, the shape of my eyes, my dark, straight hair. I knew what he wanted to ask me next so I beat him to the punch. "I was born here," I explained, meeting his gaze. I knew I was edging toward the line of being an asshole, but I couldn't help it.

Lieutenant Kowalski jotted more notes. "How often do you two hang out, and where do you go?"

"Every couple of days or so. He usually comes over to my house."

"What was his mental state?"

For that last question the only thing I could say was, "He lost hope."

Lieutenant Kowalski raised an eyebrow. "Lost hope?"

"Yeah," I said. "He's been waiting for his brother to come back."

The officer flipped through his papers. "He ran away too, huh?"

"Yeah."

He whistled softly. "No clue where this brother Nick is?"

"No," I said. "But I did talk with him."

"With Nick?" He raised an eyebrow.

"Yeah. He found my number and called me."

"What did you talk about?"

"We told each other to go fuck ourselves."

Lieutenant Kowalski stared at me.

I shrugged.

The cops took down whatever helpful information they could,

and I was at Sam's place until late into the evening. After they had left, Sam's mother looked at me, a little awkwardly, and invited me to stay for a soda.

His dad frowned. "I'm tired," he said loudly, and yawned the fakest yawn I'd ever seen.

His mom stiffened. "Oh." She didn't meet my eyes. "We're pretty tired. Maybe next time."

I wanted to tell her to grow some balls and get a new husband, but I held my tongue. I didn't want to stay there, anyway. It was too stifling.

On that Thursday when Mina ran away from home and Dad was in the hospital getting his bullet removed, there was a moment when I entertained the same notion of running away myself. I'm not sure exactly why I wanted to run away, but I had this fear for him and then a larger, clawing fear for us all. I mean, if Dad could do this to himself, what else could happen? It's like if your town is getting bombshelled, you do not just stand around with your finger up your ass. No, you get the fuck out of there. You go somewhere. Anywhere.

When I realized that Mina had beaten me to it, I still went through the house, calling her name, even though I knew she wouldn't answer because she was gone. Regardless, I went to the bloody living room, the kitchen, her room, my room, and then to the bloody living room all over again, letting the reality of it all sink in. My empty house.

So I left the house and started looking for Mina, my younger sister who had done precisely what I wanted to do and who was hiding somewhere. At first I was afraid that she was on her own, but when I realized she was creamed shit if she truly had tried to set out by herself, I also realized that she was smart enough to know that too. That's when I calmed down and started looking under bushes in the neighborhood, behind people's porches, that kind of thing.

I have to say, it was cool when Mr. Smith, my neighbor, came out to help me look. Then Mr. Gomez and Mr. Jaffe joined us, until it was the group of us looking, and that's when I really calmed down. There's no way that any kid could get past a fanned-out brigade of dads and me. It felt great; before, it was just me looking for Mina in the whole entire world, and now somehow that world grew smaller by the moment, or maybe the dads and me grew bigger by the moment, until we were one motherfucker battleship scanning the ocean depths.

Or something like that.

We finally found her crouched in someone's big old bush, bawling. When she saw me, she cowered even deeper into the bush, crying, "I'm bad, Ronney, bad. If I hadn't gone to the movies and left Dad alone, this wouldn't have happened," like it was all her fault or something, and I had to crawl in there because she didn't want to come out. We sat in that bush, and I held her for a long time. The neighbors were relieved, of course. They were also concerned and asked where Dad and Mom were, and I said the hospital. Maybe one of them eventually told my parents about Mina running away, but

I doubt it, because once word got out about why they were in the hospital in the first place, well, it's kind of an embarrassing thing to chitchat about, and I could see no one wanting to add more shit to what was already there.

For the record, Mina has not been back to the movie theater since.

The first two nights after Sam left I didn't sleep. I mean, maybe fifteen minutes here and there, out of sheer exhaustion, but nothing really close to resembling sleep. That third night the tiger made another appearance; it was found slinking around the edge of a parking lot at the high school football game and tried to attack two kids who were making out, but the good thing was that the kids were in a car and had locked the doors. Still, the tiger had gashed up the car and even hopped on top of the roof and tried to dig through it. Normally, I would have watched the online videos of this one, but not anymore.

On the fourth day I put my phone in my pocket and hopped on my bike.

It was a nice day, which sucked, because I felt crappy inside. I tooled around town hoping I wouldn't run into anyone who would report my ass to the principal, and luckily the streets were quiet. I didn't know where I was going, and I didn't realize I was headed back to that forested place until I got there.

I lay my bike in the ditch, shoved my hand into my pocket and took out my phone, waiting for him to text, to call, to pop out from behind a bush.

"I'm here, Sam," I said to no one.

The sunlight filtered through the trees.

I gripped my phone.

When my hand started to cramp, I shoved my phone back into my pocket, wandered on the forest paths, and sat down on that rock in the stream that I'd sat on before. I sighed. Sam, for as much as I liked the kid, didn't have that same sense about him as Mina did: He would actually run away. I talked to Sam's mom every day to check and see if they'd heard anything. They hadn't. The police hadn't either.

That's when the realization crushed me: I should have taken better care of him. I should have talked with his dad or done something to convince Nick to come back, or maybe talked with Sam more about how running away is stupid-ass shit. Something to prove that I'd done everything I could do to help Sam, because the truth is, I wasn't sure I had really done my best.

Okay: I knew I hadn't gone all the way. I had failed him.

I put my head in my hands.

After a while I biked home, but the ride didn't take the weight off my chest like I thought it would, so I got Dad to buy a garbage disposal from the hardware store and went to work replacing ours with the new one. The old one made a hell of a lot of noise—the kind of noise you'd expect it would take to purée a small cat—and it was slow and didn't even do the job very well: The best it could do would be chunks of cat. I had to do the installation twice because the first time I didn't put waterproof putty around the underside of the drain flange like I was supposed to, so the water started spraying out like a liquid firecracker. I was installing it for the second time when Dad came out of his room, into the kitchen.

"Any word yet?" Dad asked. He jingled the coins in his jeans.

"No," I said. I stood up and wiped my hands on my pants.

Dad watched me, then looked at the sink. "Does it work?" he asked.

I ran the water and flipped on the switch, and the disposal ran like a charm. "Looks like it does," I said.

Dad looked at my pants. "You're wet."

I shrugged. "I forgot the putty," I said.

Dad nodded. "What do his parents say?"

"The police are over every day, giving updates, but there's not much to say," I said. I looked away, and my throat tightened. "You ready for me to tear down that moldy wall in the living room? The paint job is only a temporary solution. We really gotta rip it out."

Dad shook his head. "Not yet."

I made a face. "What does that mean?"

Dad looked away.

"Whatever," I said. "We gotta do it sometime. It's going to suck now just like it's going to suck later."

"His parents really don't know where Nick is either, huh?"

"This is what you call evading a question."

Silence. Dad grimaced, which is exactly how I felt.

"No, his parents don't know either," I said. I shifted uncomfortably. I didn't want to be talking about Sam or Nick with Dad. "The driveway is starting to crack. It needs to be sealed over."

"Two sons gone."

"Yup," I said.

"His parents must be worried," Dad said.

"Duh," I said.

"You too," Dad said.

I started. "A little."

Dad nodded. "I understand."

"You don't even know him," I snapped.

"You've been taking care of him."

"Trying to," I said. My neck muscle twitched.

"I understand," Dad said again.

He might as well have shot me himself.

"What, exactly, do you understand?" I stood up and stared at him incredulously. "Taking care of people? You had a great fishing trip, as far as I can remember."

"When you were four years old with bronchitis, I stayed with you in the hospital for nights on end—"

I sneered. "When I was four years old—what about last year? Or the year before that? Where the hell have you been?" I slammed my hand on the kitchen counter.

"You can't put all that on me," Dad said, running his hand through his hair.

"You know nothing about taking care of people," I continued, grabbing the plastic from the garbage disposal package and ramming it into the garbage. "I just fixed this disposal because you wouldn't. I care about the living room walls because you don't. I'm going to reseal the driveway because you're going to be in your bedroom, online, doing God knows what, drooling your life away."

"Ronney," he said. He ran his hand through his hair again.

"You can't tell me you 'understand' about taking care of people." My hands clenched into fists. "You're taking care of absolutely no one now. Face it: You crapped all over your responsibility, and here's fifteen-year-old me, staying at home fixing shit when I should be going after girls"—just thinking about George made my throat clench up—"or hanging out with my friends instead of playing parent to Mina." I paused. "I know you wake up when Mina screams in the middle of the night. But who goes to her? Me. It's sure as fuck not you."

Dad crossed his arms over his chest, but he wasn't angry.

"So I don't want you to be my pal," I continued, "or my guru, or telling me you understand, because if you really understood what you did to us, you wouldn't be showing your ugly face around here."

Silence.

"How long are you going to crucify me, Ronney?" Dad said quietly.

My stampede of anger suddenly slammed to a halt, leaving me feeling more exposed than I ever wanted to be in front of Dad. "It's not my fault," I said, walking to my room. My voice was barely a whisper. "Just leave me alone."

Then I closed my bedroom door.

21

THE NEXT MORNING I WOKE WITH A HEADACHE
and felt like crap. Why did Dad have to come into the kitchen
and talk with me? Doesn't he know that it's just easier for us not
to talk? Why is he trying to care? It was so much easier when he
didn't—then things could proceed in their typical crappy way.
I mean, yeah, it's a crappy life, but at least it's *my* crappy life.
Not that I really wanted that, mind you, but at least it's stable.
Predictable.

I had to admit, though, there was a tiny part of me that wanted
Dad to put his arm around my shoulder and take me fishing again.
I'd even offer to watch him eat a worm. Isn't that weird? That you
can be so angry at someone you want to be with so much?

However, I couldn't stop the annoying question: If you
want to be with him so much, why are you acting like a dick?
The truth was, Dad didn't deserve me being nice to him. For
everything he did to us, he deserves everything he gets, and it's

not my fault: He's the one who caused all this suffering. If I'm pissed, that's his problem. That's what I was thinking as I put on my non-Thursday clothes. We floundered for two years, and I finally found my footing—without him—and I'm not going to throw that away. There were a lot of nights that I cried myself to sleep, and I'll be damned if I'll go back to whimpering under my sheets like a kid.

Anyway, even if it was possible for Dad and me to hang like we used to, I have no idea how that would happen, what that would feel like, what I would need to do to get there.

However, there was no guarantee he was going to continue to care about us. He already tried to leave us once. There was no guarantee he wouldn't try to pull that trigger again, and I was not going to be the sucker that would let him kill me twice. In a bizarre but very real way he was like a stranger to me. And you don't just go around trusting people you don't know.

Damn, I had a fuckload of a headache as I thought about all of it. And though that headache was probably because of Dad, it could have also been because of Sam. Doesn't everyone know that the longer a kid is gone, the smaller the chances get that he's okay? It was now the fifth day, and there were no calls or texts or messages falling from the sky. At first I was like, *Okay, the kid's hanging out somewhere and will come back when his underwear gets crusty.* But it was five days now and nothing. The police were over at his house all the time, updating his parents, but there was nothing to update except that the police had been looking and asking. The newspaper even ran an article on Sam, but that didn't turn up anything new like the police had hoped.

Sam's dad was pissed. He didn't like me, which was fine because I thought he was the biggest jackwad I'd ever met. In fact, he defined the word "jackwad."

"So, Ronald, with all the times Sam's been with you, you don't have any idea where that idiot has gone?"

"No, Mr. Smaldwell—"

"It's Caldwell."

"—I don't know where he is and haven't heard anything from him. Trust me, I would tell you, first thing."

Sam's dad frowned. "I don't trust you," he said. "That's the thing." The thin wisps of his hair fell over his eyes, which somehow made him look like a balding, overweight goat.

"Jack," Sam's mom said. "Ronney here is just trying his best."

"Shut up," his dad said. "I wasn't talking to you."

I stiffened. Then I smiled. Then I left.

The longer that Sam was missing, the more I was pissed with myself. Why didn't I see that he needed help? Did I not care enough? What was wrong with me?

I was so preoccupied with Sam it barely fazed me when George came up to me in the hallway a day or so later.

"I haven't seen you around much," she said. She was wearing this glittery barrette or whatever in her hair that looked really nice. And her lips were shiny too.

"I haven't been here much," I said.

She nodded. Everyone knew that Sam had run away. The two brothers. There were rumors that Nick and Sam were starting up some sort of underground colony for other runaways. I wanted to find those people who were talking and punch them.

"I'm sorry about Sam," she said, and fidgeted, twirling a strap on her backpack around her finger.

I shrugged. "Nothing to do."

Her eyebrows furrowed. "You look tired," she said.

"Yup," I said.

George ran her fingers through her long hair. At that point I realized she was wearing her tight jeans. Before, both of these things would have driven me crazy. Now, my eyes wandered the hallway, watching the kids. Of course, this was a high school and none of them would be Sam, but by this point it was automatic. I wondered if he had eaten anything so far that day.

"Well . . . ," George said, "let me know if I can help."

I gave a small smile. "Sure."

"No, I mean it," she said.

"So do I," I said.

George's eyes flicked down the hallway, and she waved to some of her other valedictorian-track friends. Then she turned back to me. "Ronney."

"What?" I said, slightly agitated. I wanted to skip my next class and walk around the block. Get out of here.

"I'm leaving for that competition tonight, on the late flight."

She smoothed her hair again with her hand. "I've been prepping for it nonstop."

"That's great, hope it goes well," I said noncommittally. But I wasn't really excited. Maybe if there wasn't this missing kid or this huge hole in my chest, fine, but under the circumstances, a scholarship competition just wasn't cutting it on the Interest-O'-Meter. Not even with George.

"I have something for you," she said tentatively.

I looked at her. I didn't want pity. "I'm fine, thanks," I said, shaking my head.

"No, really," she replied, and looked through her backpack, took out a photo, and pressed it into my hand. She held her hand over mine so I couldn't look at it.

"I've thought a lot about that day we made a cookie house," she said. The barrette sparkled again in her hair.

I looked down at my shoes for a second, then back up at her. "Did you ever eat it?" I asked.

"No," she said. "It's still on my desk. It's like a rock by now, you know?" She threw me a small smile and drew her arm back. When I opened my hand, I saw a picture of our cookie house with a newly vaulted ceiling. And she had made the sunroom bigger with a bay window.

At that moment Jello came up to us, his backpack casually slung over his shoulder. He looked at me warily for a second, and then his face took on his normal chill expression.

Jello glanced at the photo in my hand. "Hey, the cookie

house," he said. "George worked on that for a long time."

George, standing between the two of us, suddenly looked as awkward as I felt.

"How are the bruises?" I asked, simply because I didn't know what else to say.

"You mean this one?" he said, pointing to his right cheek side to side. "Or maybe this one?" he asked, lifting up the side of his shirt.

I whistled. "Dang. They're faded."

"Yeah. About that. To answer your question, they all sucked, thanks to you," he said, grinning in a typical Jello fashion. Even though his grin was not as wide due to the bruise that remained on his cheek, it was the same grin that I had known all my life. And sure as shit, I felt myself relax. Maybe it was going to be okay.

"Does this mean I can't punch you in the arm anymore?" I asked. "Like this?" I mock punched him in the arm.

"Hey, hey!" he said, dodging my blow and throwing his arms up. "We'll see about any future punching. My people will talk to your people."

George looked back and forth like a spectator at a tennis match. Someone in the hallway called out to Jello and George in the same breath, and they both turned their heads and greeted one of George's friends. The whole school knew that they were together. This was not news. I felt stupid and foolish and blind, and my chest tightened, even though I wished to God that it could have just turned to stone and saved me the humiliation.

Instead, I felt a little wobbly inside as I started to walk away.

"Wait, Ronney!" George said, waving at me.

I turned to look at her, even though I wanted to keep walking, even though I was bleeding all over since my heart had not, in fact, turned to stone. "We'll talk later, right?" George called out to me.

"Sure," I said numbly.

"My dad wants to bake again," she said with a hesitant smile. "Think about it?"

My face softened. Then I left and took that walk around the block.

The tiger was getting worse. Even a kid could tell you that.

"The tiger is getting worse," Mina announced at dinner that night.

"What do you mean, Mina?" Mom said.

"It's stopped going after cows," Mina said.

"Well, that's nice," Mom said.

"Now it's going after humans," Mina finished.

Dad's eyebrows lifted.

"The tiger attacked Mr. Marren when he came home from work," she said, stuffing her mouth full of food.

"From Marren's Corner Store?" I asked.

"Oh my gosh," Mom said. Mina had her undivided attention.

Mina swallowed. "The tiger was sitting by the front door, hiding in a bush. It leaped on him and bit him in the thigh, and as he was screaming, a neighbor came and started hitting it with flowerpots and everything, and it ran away."

I swallowed hard. I kind of felt bad right then for stealing shit from his store and freaking out his wife.

"I'm scared, Mommy," Mina said, and Mom opened her arms and took Mina into them. After a while Mina looked at Dad. "Daddy?" she asked him. He hesitated, then gingerly reached out and patted her on the shoulder.

"How did you hear of this?" Mom asked as she stood up to switch on the TV, which I had plugged back in after Mina's reluctant approval.

"Mr. Marren is Sarah's uncle, who's in my class," Mina said.

Mom flipped the TV to the news, which was always a risk since Mina had freaked out with the lion shooting. A reporter was interviewing some county official. Guys were putting up yellow police tape in the background.

"... and why is it that you haven't been able to kill this tiger?" the reporter prompted.

The official puffed out his chest. "Everything about this creature is designed for stealth. Its paws are deadly silent. It has laser vision. Let's face the hard fact: A tiger is a killing machine."

The reporter took back the mic. "But this is the twenty-first century. I don't understand how it hasn't been found yet."

"Look, we've found almost all of these fifty-four animals. We've—"

"But not the python," the reporter interrupted.

"No, not the—"

"Or the camel."

"Right. No, not the camel. Not yet." The official cleared his throat. "But let me tell you, we're tracking them. There's dogs and helicopters and boots on the ground. We're doing everything we can to round up the last ones. It's like Darwin's . . . um. Darwin," the official said, fading off. "The survival of the fittest. And these last ones are the fittest. We need everyone's cooperation." He looked into the camera, and his nose shone red like a lobster claw. "Please, people: Call in anything you see or hear. Getting these animals is not just our job—it's everyone's job."

Later that evening another incident of the tiger stalking a human was reported.

The next day I sealed the driveway. Sealing a driveway isn't hard; it just takes time. You need a nice, sunny day, a thick brush, and tons of sealant, and you paint the sealant on like you would on a huge canvas. My back hurt from being bent over all morning, but I was in a pretty good mood from talking with George yesterday: Her cookie-house picture was in my back pocket.

I was about halfway done when Dad came out. "You're not at school?" he asked, looking at my work. "I didn't call in for you."

"It's Saturday."

"Oh." He cleared his throat. "So, did you hear the update about Mr. Marren?" Dad asked.

I continued brushing on the sealant. "Not yet."

"They say he's going to make it," Dad said. He stood there awkwardly. "I'm glad he's going to survive."

"Me too," I said, and I meant it. I took a deep breath, cleared my mind, and dipped my brush back into the sealant, continuing my long, slow way down the driveway. You need solid strokes when you do this work, and I knew my shoulder was going to be sore tomorrow, as well as my knees, with how they were grinding into the cement. Frankly, though, it all felt great.

Except that Dad was still standing there, watching me.

I looked up. "What?"

He shifted. "I'm feeling better."

He paused as I squinted up at him.

"I'm feeling better," he repeated. "Not terrific, but better."

"Shall I write a thank-you note to your shrink?" I asked.

Dad shoved his hands into his pockets. What did he want me to say? Did he expect me to give him some sappy hug?

"Well, congratulations," I said. I wanted to ask him if this meant he wasn't going to try to blow his brains out again, but I held my tongue. I was proud of that, mind you.

"Have you heard anything about Sam?" Dad asked.

"Have you thought about getting a job?" I asked.

"Have you thought about being a decent human being?" Dad asked. "Or is this the best you got?"

I stared at him, mouth gaping. I had no idea what I was going to say, but as I opened my mouth to reply, the phone rang.

Dad hasn't answered the phone in years. It's one of the many things you can't count on him for. So I stood up, and he watched me wipe my hands on my jeans and run into the house.

I got it on the fourth ring, just before it went to voice mail. "Hello?" I said.

"Hey," the voice said.

I'd know Nick's voice anywhere. Somehow, hearing from Nick proved, again, that Sam was gone. Really the fuck gone.

"So, Nick, how have you been holding up?" I said, not trying to hide the edge in my voice, and I didn't know if it was because of him or Dad or both.

"Where's my brother?" Nick said.

"Oh, you've finally heard about Sam?" I said. "It's been seven days. You're slower than I thought."

"Where is he?"

"Why, he's with you forming a colony for runaway kids."

A pause. "A what?" Nick said, disbelievingly.

"That's what they're saying, at least."

"Sam's not with me," Nick retorted.

"I assumed as much when I heard your lovely voice. I figured you wouldn't call just to say hello." I paused. "Though that would have been endearing."

"Knock it off. Where is my little brother?" Nick said again.

"I don't know if anyone's told you, but the definition of 'missing' is that no one knows where he is." That last part was surprisingly difficult to say. I swallowed back the lump. "I know you get along splendidly with your dad. What did he say?"

"I haven't talked with my parents," Nick admitted.

"Oh, I'm the first? What an honor."

"I figured you would have heard . . . something."

"The last thing Sam said was that he wanted to be like you and run away."

"He didn't say that," Nick said, surprised. "Did he?"

"Something like that," I said evenly.

"He didn't."

"He did."

"He didn't."

"He did."

A long pause this time.

"Hello?" I said.

"I didn't mean for this to happen," Nick said, and his voice wobbled.

"Well, surprise. Life happens how it happens," I said. "Sam wanted to be like you, and now he's disappeared. He's well on his way, don't you think?"

Then the most unexpected thing happened: Nick began to cry.

I shit you not, I lost all words at that point. I truly didn't know what to say. So I said, "I'm going to go."

"Okay," he said. I guess he was too uncomfortable for it all too.

I hung up and let him cry.

Later, Mina came home from a trip to the library, and she walked on the grass so she wouldn't mess up my sealant job. It was drying really well, and the sun was out and warm, which helped. I was raking up the leaves, which was a good thing, since I needed to think, and raking always helps me think. I couldn't get over the fact that Dad had said that I wasn't a decent human being. That I wasn't doing my best. I dug the rake into the earth as I thought about that. I take care of Mina. Now I'm taking care of Sam. I mean, I'm not perfect, but at least I show up. What about him? It's not like he's some sort of superhero himself. How could he accuse me of shit when he doesn't even take out the garbage? If I weren't doing my best, I wouldn't be raking the fucking lawn, especially without anyone having to ask me. Right?

Mina joined me in the yard. I noticed that she was walking differently: She used to look like that orange bouncy ball the way she would enter places—sometimes she would actually hop on one leg, just because—but now she walked. She just walked. Nothing more, nothing less. And a non-orange Mina, walking—I didn't know what to make of it. I had this random urge to hit something when I saw her walk like that.

"How's it going?" I asked her, stopping to wipe the sweat off my forehead.

"Pretty good, Ron-Ron," Mina said. "Have they found Sam yet?"

"Not yet."

Mina looked at my raking job. "Can I help?"

"No, I got it," I said, and propped my rake on the ground.

"Where's Dad?"

I snorted. "Where do you think?"

"He met me at the bus stop yesterday after school."

"Really?"

Mina nodded. "I couldn't get a ride home yesterday, so I had to take the bus. Maybe Dad will meet me on Monday," she said hopefully.

"Don't count on it," I said, and I started raking again. I paused. "Maybe," I corrected myself, although it felt weird to say that.

Mina watched me rake for a while. "Ronney?"

"Yes?"

"Have they caught the tiger yet?"

"No, Min-o," I said. I stopped raking. "There are no updates today."

"What if I'm walking home and the tiger comes out?"

"You get a ride home from school. That won't happen."

"So what if I'm on my bike and the tiger comes out?"

"Hope it isn't hungry," I offered.

Mina was silent.

"That was a joke," I said, giving her a light jab on the arm.

"That wasn't funny," Mina said.

"I don't know what you should do. You can't run away. The tiger's too fast."

"Climb a tree?" Mina suggested.

"Tigers can climb."

"Oh." She looked at the ground and picked up a leaf. "So I'm not safe, then?" she said, turning the leaf over in her hand.

"That's not true," I said. "I'm here to protect you."

"Like at school with the shooting," Mina said, lost in her thoughts. "There's danger everywhere."

"Hey," I said, putting my hand on her shoulder. She looked up at me, and the way her eyes were so open and trusting, my chest suddenly ached. "Remember, there's protection everywhere too."

"And the tiger?"

"Don't worry about the tiger," I said. "It's been eating cows, anyway." I paused. "Well, a couple humans, but it's a smart tiger. It'll realize that cows are much better."

Mina looked at me skeptically.

"Why would it continue going after tiny humans when it could go after big cows?"

She thought about that for a long while. "That makes sense."

"It does, doesn't it?"

"So I shouldn't be afraid of the tiger."

"I don't see what that would do for you."

"The tiger doesn't care about me, anyway."

"Probably not."

"Fuck the tiger," Mina announced, nodding her head.

"What?" I asked, incredulous.

"Fuck the tiger," Mina said again. Then she looked at me and smiled.

My jaw dropped.

Mina laughed.

22

UNSURPRISINGLY, I WAS LOOKING FOR SAM. Well, okay, I wasn't actively *looking* for him at this point, with it being a week out already, but my eyes kept going over people in a crowd—even when I knew everyone there—and my ears were always straining to hear his voice.

I wasn't sleeping well, and neither was Mina. They had gotten some counselors in to talk with the kids from Sam's class, in case the kids needed to talk about his running away. Mina talked with a shrink, but I don't think it helped very much, because she was still sleeping in my bed every night, and I could hear her cry, even though she tried to be quiet. That's when I would rub her back and we would both lie there in the night, waiting for a phone call that never came.

At least, not from Sam.

On the eighth morning after Sam disappeared, the phone rang. I jumped for it.

"Hello?" I said.

"Hey," Nick said.

I swallowed back my disappointment and paused for a moment to collect myself. When I did, I said, "What's up, O missing brother of the missing Sam?"

"Meet me tomorrow," Nick said. "I can't stand this."

"What, so you can cry on my shoulder?" I said.

"I want to talk about him. I want to make a plan."

"You going to be drunk? Drunk people do not plan very well," I pointed out.

"Shut up."

"Well? Will you be?"

"No," Nick said through clenched teeth.

"Good. I hate liars, by the way," I said. "If you come drunk, I'll fucking hit you for wasting my time."

"Tomorrow at Rogers Park, three o'clock, by the statue."

"Fine."

I put down the phone and smiled for the first time in days.

Mina could tell I was feeling better. Later that evening, when the four of us were eating dinner, she looked at me. "What happened, Ron-Ron?" she asked.

"About what?"

"I don't know. You're happy."

"No I'm not."

"Yes you are."

"No I'm not."

Mom sighed and continued eating her goat stew.

Mina ignored her. "Yes you are. I can tell. What happened? Did they find Sam?"

"No, they didn't."

Mina's face fell. "The counselor at school said that this is an extreme time of unknown circumstances, and that it's typical for us to be really stressed out." She put down her fork.

"You know what?" I said. "I don't give a f—"

Mina was looking at me.

I looked at her.

"A fart," I said slowly. "I don't give a fart what that counselor said."

Mina giggled.

Dad stared. Then a slow half smile grew on his face.

"Did you hear about the tiger?" Mina said.

"What now?" I said.

"It got into someone's house."

"And?" I asked.

"They were able to scare it away."

"Well," I said, shoveling more food into my mouth, "they were butt wipes for letting the tiger come in in the first place."

Mina giggled. "Butt wipes."

"How do you let a tiger into your house, anyway?" I continued. "Do you open the front door for it? Does it ring the doorbell?"

"Yeah, right?" Mina said. She sounded like me.

Dad watched us. That half smile lingered for a long time.

The next day—the day I was supposed to meet up with Nick—I went to school. It always amazes me how many kids are there. I mean, I look at all the students milling about, and I'm kind of shocked that they choose to go to school every goddamn day. I was standing in the hallway between classes, looking at all of them, when I spotted George in a sparkly T-shirt, her hair tied back. When she saw me, she dashed over and threw herself on me.

I was shocked. Especially since "throwing herself on me" does not mean an attack.

She was *hugging* me.

"Oh, Ronney," she said, crying into my shoulder.

My hands went around her. I couldn't help it.

"What is it?" I asked, alarmed. Then I remembered. "Was it the competition? You didn't win?" I asked.

She shook her head. "I finished in the tenth percentile," she moaned.

"That's not that bad," I said, trying as hard as I could not to rub her back.

George tilted her head up at me, and I leaned my head down. "I was in the tenth percentile *from the bottom*," she whispered.

"Oh."

Tears streaked her face. "Don't tell anyone, Ronney, You can't let anyone know."

"I won't, trust me."

"My life is over," she said, pulling away slightly.

"Not really, George," I said, looking into her eyes. "You'll be fine."

"But what am I going to do now?"

"Maybe not be an architect?"

That's when she slapped me. Kids stopped and hooted.

Her hand went to her mouth. "Ronney, I'm so sorry," she said, her voice watery.

"Yeah, me too," I said.

"No, I'm really, really sorry," she said, and I had the feeling she wasn't talking about just having slapped me.

"I know. And it's okay to feel shitty." I paused, took a deep breath. "I'm here for you, George."

I put my arms back around her, and we stayed like that until well after the bell rang.

After school that day I went to the park and sat right at the base of a statue of some guy on a horse. Just as I was supposed to.

I knew it was Nick from a mile away. For the first thing, there was no one, absolutely no one, else in the park. For the second thing, he walked like someone who was guilty as hell. As he got closer, I could see his firm jaw and his sandy hair combed to the side. I was surprised he actually combed his hair.

"You're uglier than I thought," I greeted him as he approached. He was wearing a T-shirt and flannel that seemed too thin for late fall.

"You're not too beautiful yourself," Nick said. He eyed me a little longer than necessary.

"What?" I asked.

"No, I—" Nick looked away. "Um." He blushed. Then he cleared his throat. A foghorn went off in the distance, and then another one, and then another one. But it seemed like Nick didn't even notice; his eyes kept darting around the park.

"Chill out, commando," I said. "It's not like there's a squadron of police here or anything. I didn't tell anyone."

Nick didn't reply, but he seemed to relax a little. "What's with the animals?" he asked. That was, after all, Makersville's official new greeting.

"What's with you?" I asked back. "Are you drunk?"

"If you have to ask, then I'm not," Nick said.

"Just wanted to see if you were a liar on top of it all," I said.

Nick scratched the back of his neck. "What do you have against me?" he asked.

"Where do I start? You ran away like a loser when your parents tried to help you."

"They didn't try to help me."

"I'm talking. You left your brother with your dick father. You refused to come home and protect him."

"I had my own stuff to take care of," Nick muttered.

"I said, I'm *talking*. Then when I let you know that your little bro is waiting for you to come home, like fucking *pining*, you really couldn't give a shit."

"That's not true."

"It's not?" I gave a little smirk. "Then you pulled a good one, because that's exactly what it seems. Or did you run away because you cared about Sam so very much?"

"You have no idea what my life is like," Nick said.

I snorted. "You want mine?"

"I don't have to defend my choices to you," Nick said.

"No one said this had to be a love fest," I said.

"Hey, hey," Nick said, putting up his hands. "Sam."

"Ah, yes. Sam."

"You gotta find him," Nick said.

I snorted. "Why? So you can hide away in peace?" I crossed my arms over my chest. "Look. You know what that kid wants."

Nick sighed and massaged his neck. "I can't go back."

"This," I said, "is why you're a dick."

"You don't get it! You're not listening to me!" Nick shouted suddenly. His face was red.

I stiffened.

"It's a problem, okay?" He walked away from me. Then he came back. "There. I said it," he said, waving his arm in the air. "It's a problem. I didn't think it was a problem. I thought I had it under control." Nick took a deep, shaky breath.

I didn't say anything. *Oh please*, I thought, *for the love of God, don't cry.*

He didn't. He started pacing. "I know how stubborn Sam is."

I nodded.

"He's not coming back," Nick said. "Unless something makes him."

"Like a stalker-killer who chops up little kids and hides them in his freezer?" I suggested.

"Shut up!" Nick made as if to lunge at me, then caught himself. He backed away a couple steps, as if the space between us would keep him sane. Gunshots went off. I thought just then of a hungry tiger, but instead of mentioning that, I asked, "You said you had a plan?"

"I said I wanted to *make* a plan."

"So make it," I said. I wasn't feeling all that generous.

"Fine," Nick said. "How about you go to those places you and Sam went to before, talk to people with big mouths."

"Yeah? And?"

"You leave them a message that would hopefully get back to him."

That's when it hit me. "Wait. 'You'? What's this 'you'? What about 'we'?"

Nick smiled. "I don't see any other volunteers, do you?"

"Yes, I do," I retorted.

"I don't. You told me to make a plan, and I'm making a plan. You going to do it or not?"

I stared at him. "You're a fucker."

Nick grinned wider. "Well?"

I grimaced. "Fine," I said sharply. "I'll do it. What's the message?"

Nick looked away for a long time.

"Hello, princess?" I said. "I'm waiting."

Nick kept staring into the distance. Finally he turned to me with a strange expression on his face. "The message is: Nick's coming home."

23

MINA WAS WATCHING HER FAVORITE TV SHOW
that afternoon when another gunshot went off. It came from
down the street, and Mina jumped, just slightly. Then an empty
look settled over her. It was creepy: The look on her face changed,
and even though she was still staring at the TV, I could swear she
wasn't seeing it.

"Maybe they got the tiger. Or the python," I said. Like I had
to remind her.

"I know," she said, still with that distant look in her eye.

Then another gunshot, and another. Mina looked away from
the TV, wrapped her arms around her legs, and started rocking
gently. "Make it stop, Ronney," she said quietly.

"I can't," I said as I stood there, and my heart broke.

Three gunshots went off in quick succession.

Mina continued rocking, almost doubled over. "I hate this.
Please, Ronney," she said a little louder.

Another gunshot. Mina's body jerked.

"Daddy's dead," she said.

"No he's not," I said, and I sat down next to her on the couch, but when I touched her, she jumped again, and I drew my hand away.

Another gunshot. Mina shook her head. "He kills himself again and again and again and again and again and—"

I would've done anything to stop those guns for her, and right then I felt like an absolute, helpless ball of shit. That was when Dad came into the living room. He actually noticed that Mina was all weird.

"Mina, are you okay?" Dad asked, and his voice sounded funny, with a mixture of concern and shame.

"Does she look okay to you?" I snapped. "After two years, you're finally figuring out that Mina is in fact not okay?"

"Does she need a doctor?" Dad asked as he watched her rocking. He didn't make any move to approach her.

"Give me a break," I said, standing up and facing him squarely. "I can't believe that you're even saying this. You know what she needs."

Mina wrapped her arms around her knees so she was an even smaller Mina ball.

Another gunshot went off.

Mina tightened the grip on her arms and tucked her head into them.

Dad looked at Mina. "Honey, I think they're trying to get the tiger," he said to her. He looked at her for the longest time, then ran his hand through his hair and started to walk back to his room.

I snorted. "Is this the best you've got?" I called out after him.

Dad stopped. Then he turned around sharply, his face red. "You have no right to say that to me," he said.

I gave a little laugh. "Oh, you can't take your own medicine? Well, do you have any idea how to deal with this?" I asked as I waved my hand toward Mina. "What we've been through? No, Dad, you have no idea, and you never will."

"Maybe we should have her—"

"Shut up, Dad. Let me tell you something: The little things fucking matter. For instance, you could sit down next to her and try to give her a hug. But you don't. It's little, but it matters."

"—see a therapist or something."

"The problem isn't her, it's you."

Mina lifted her head. "Daddy, I want to sit on your lap." But it was more of a question. Mina hadn't said this in over a year.

Dad rubbed his chin with his hand and looked at her for a long time. "Maybe later. Are you okay?" he asked again.

"I'm fine, Daddy," Mina said blankly.

I scowled. "Bullfrogs," I said.

She giggled. In that moment Mina came back. She tilted her head up and smiled at me. "You're funny, Ron-Ron."

I threw Dad a look. "It's all the little things."

Dad walked back down the hallway to his bedroom.

"You're such a fucker," I muttered.

The smile disappeared from Mina's face, and she looked down at the ground: At that moment I realized that what I had just said was a little thing too.

I winced and wished I could take those words back, but of course I couldn't.

"Sorry," I said quietly to her. She looked up at me, startled, and that was when I opened my arms to her. Mina crawled off the couch and gripped me tight around the waist. I rubbed her back in the way that calms her down.

"Ron-Ron, you're the best," she said into my left rib.

"Not really," I said.

"Well, maybe I could sit down for a couple of minutes," a voice came from around the corner. We both looked over to see Dad walking back into the living room. He hesitated when he saw the two of us hugging. "I mean, Mina, if you want to," he said, gesturing to the couch with his chin.

Mina gave a *squeeee* of excitement and launched herself onto Dad, who was still standing up, and the two of them lumbered their way over to the sofa. He sat down, and she climbed all over him like he was a tree and she was a squirrel. After her explosion of excitement, she settled down into the crook of his side, and he draped his arm over her. He didn't say anything at all, he just held her, and Mina started to wordlessly sing to herself. She was about to climb all over him again, when he slowly stood up. "Okay, honey," he said. "That's enough."

"But, Daddy," she said pleadingly. Her voice grew thick with tears.

"Next time," he said, and he held her chin in a tender way that made my stomach flip.

"Please don't go, Daddy." The tears started to fall down her cheeks.

"It's okay," he said. "Next time, I promise."

At that her face brightened. "Next time? Promise?"

"Yes," he said.

I had to leave so that I could go around town delivering Nick's message. It was a good thing, too, because I was so jumbled up at that point I couldn't stand being there one moment longer.

I seriously wished that I had those question-mark jeans, because I would've been wearing them as I delivered Nick's message. I mean, what the hell was that? I had witnessed Dad do something . . . *fatherly*. He actually made Mina happy, which is something I couldn't remember him doing for years, for her or any of us.

My crappy, stable world had just experienced an earthquake. I couldn't argue with the fact that Dad had actually acted like a dad with Mina. *What do I do now? Do I give him a second chance?* But even as I thought that, my stomach tightened: *Just because he did something great once doesn't mean that he's going to do it again. Don't trust this. And yet, if I don't trust him and he is proving himself, does that mean that I'm wrong?*

It was a good thing that I was biking around town from store to store, because there were a number of times when I biked as hard as I fucking could, trying to get some of these thoughts out of my head. After I hit the third store, Jello texted.

How's the animals?

Not bad, what about for you?

I got a mangled-up raccoon in my garage, been feeding it.

A raccoon is not a safari.

I know, but I found it, the tiger probably attacked it, and I want you to help me with another photo shoot.

No go, I'm getting out a message for Sam, you want to help me?

I already did help.

One more time?

A long pause. In the time he was deciding, I hit another place.

I'm waiting.

Fine, I'll help you, but then you'll help me with my raccoon.

No, I won't.

Come on, R-man, help me.

No.

There was another long pause. Then my cell phone rang.

"What do you mean, no?" Jello said, and I could hear the tightness in his voice. "This is the third time I asked."

"And this is the fourth time I'm saying it. No." The words felt strange in my mouth.

"Come on."

"No. Fifth time."

He gave a weird yelp. "Jesus, Ronney. Do it."

"No. Sixth time."

Jello tapped his phone's microphone a couple times. "I don't know, is this thing working? I keep hearing this strange word, and it keeps sounding like *no*."

"I think your phone *started* working, nice and clear," I said, feeling like the king of the world.

A long silence.

"Wow, R-Man, you got balls," Jello said. "What the hell happened?"

"So you can help me with Sam if you want, but I'm done with safaris." My voice was strong, firm.

I could hear Jello's TV in the background.

"Hello?" I said.

"I'll be there. Give me ten minutes," he said.

I don't know who was more surprised, Jello or me.

It was a lot faster with Jello helping out, to say the least. We got to the same businesses Sam and I had gone to before, making doubly sure to hit the corner stores and other places where a ten-year-old might buy shit. Which was actually pretty depressing. I mean, if Sam was going into a corner store, what would he buy? Beef jerky? Toilet paper? Or would he be stupid and buy a car air freshener, just because he could?

Jello was a sport and stuck with me until the whole town knew that Nick was coming home. The most surprising thing was, a lot of people already knew Nick—not just about him, but actually knew him—and were genuinely happy to hear the news. Like he was some decent guy or something.

Take, for example, when we were talking to Mrs. Marksteiner, who manages the local burger joint in town, Happy Dog. They don't sell hot dogs, by the way; Mrs. M really loves her dog, who—you guessed it—is named Happy Dog, after the seemingly endless smile he has on his face.

Or may I say, had.

Mrs. M let Happy Dog out to go roam the neighborhood sometimes—she says that everything likes its freedom—and for the whole day Happy Dog would paw at people's front doors and wait for them to throw him food. Mrs. M. demonstrated her keen sense of judgment when she continued to let her dog out with the tiger on the loose: One day Happy Dog had gotten close to the tiger and got hit with a stray bullet. He probably still had that smile while he was bleeding to death, which is pretty fucked up, if you ask me.

"He was such a great dog," Mrs. M said. This was her answer to "How are you?"

"I'm sure he was," I said.

"He had looked at me confused, like he had done something wrong," she said, and her voice got watery.

"I'm sure he had."

"He didn't."

"You're right, he didn't." I paused. "It was one bullet?" I asked, despite my urge to run from Happy Dog.

"Two, if you count the one we used to . . ."

"Oh, yeah. Right." I fidgeted. I couldn't stand this conversation. "And Sam—"

"Ah, yes, I know him."

"You do?"

"Well, I knew his older brother. Nick. Such a sweetie," she said, smoothing her Happy Dog shirt.

"He was?"

"Yes. Just like my Happy Dog."

I refrained from snorting.

"Well, Nick is coming home," I said.

Mrs. M's face brightened. "He is?"

I nodded.

"That's wonderful," she said happily. "He would always order my Happy Dog double burger with everything on it, and he would tell me stories about school and his baseball and whatnot." She shook her head, remembering. "There was that great story, the one about the ice cream. You ask him about the ice cream. Then you tell him to come in here, and I'll give him a free Happy Dog Meal. On the house."

I promised her exactly that.

On the way home I stopped by Sam's favorite place in the woods and tied a message to a tree:

Nick's coming home. Miss you, bud.

I choked up as I was putting up that note. It was harder to write that I missed him than I thought. I was almost not going to write that part, thinking that I might sound like a wimp, but before I could stop myself, I was writing those last three words and getting all choked up about it.

As I turned to leave, I heard something: shouting. In the distance. I cocked my head; was I going crazy? Was I hearing shit because I wanted to? I'd already checked the woods. Sam wasn't here.

Then I heard it again. Shouting. Actually, screaming.

I turned and sprinted toward the voice across the clearing and veered around a fallen tree that I hadn't seen before. I kept running, pumping my arms, well off of any path. "Sam?" I shouted, my voice loud and raw and catching. "Sam?" Twigs snapped beneath my feet.

The screaming grew louder.

I ran harder, stumbling on some underbrush. I looked around wildly, my ears straining. I had no idea the forest was this big.

There the shouting was again. I raced toward it, deeper into the forest, stopping when I had to catch my breath, hands on my knees. When I finally stood up, I shouted, "Sam?"

Off a ways, there was a tent. In the middle of the woods.

Then I saw him.

He was on the ground with a fifteen-foot python coiled around his thigh.

"Get away!" Sam was screaming, trying to pull his leg from the python, and his screaming dissolved into hysterical sobs.

The python's body shuddered, and it curled around one of Sam's hips.

I ran through the forest and launched myself at them, trying to pry the python off with my hands. Its body was solid iron. I stood up and looked around wildly, grabbed the biggest rock I could find, one that was at least twenty pounds, and slammed it down on the part of the python that wasn't yet curled around Sam.

The python yanked its head backward, its mouth open, small fangs exposed.

Then, before I could do anything, it bit Sam's stomach.

Sam screamed, and I slammed that rock onto the lower half of the snake's body over and over again. That didn't stop it: The python slithered upward, toward Sam's other hip. If it crawled a couple more inches to Sam's stomach, he was as good as dead.

Out of desperation, I spied a good-size branch on the ground; the part where it had broken from the tree was heavily splintered. I ran and got it, then grabbed the python close to the head with one hand and started jamming the splintered branch into its eyes with the other.

Sam yelped as the python's body seized tighter. Then it slacked slightly. I kept beating the snake with the splintered branch. "Get out, Sam!" I shouted, and Sam, who had been in a daze watching me, started struggling against the python's body. I kept hitting the python's head and Sam kept struggling until he was able to wriggle free—up to the knee, then the ankle, then the foot, and Sam leaped to his feet, out of breath. That was when I threw the stick away, grabbed the large stone, and smashed that python until snake blood oozed on the ground and its body went limp.

Sam vomited.

When he turned back around, I said, "Let me see the bite." His skin was puffy and red. "Can you walk?" I asked.

Sam nodded.

"Come on, let's get out of here," I said.

Sam kicked the python's body as we left.

I kicked it too, for good measure.

"Wait," Sam said. He went back inside his tent, and when he came out, what he had in his arms made me stop short.

The question-mark jeans.

"Sam, you still have your brother's jeans?" I asked. I couldn't believe it, not after all that Nick had done to Sam, all the ways that Nick had failed Sam, all the ways that Nick had abandoned him.

"He's my brother," Sam said fiercely.

I didn't know what to say. I mean, sure, Nick is Sam's brother, but he was also a dick. And yet that didn't make much of a difference to Sam, even to the point where Sam was carrying his brother's jeans as he ran away. If I were Sam, I would've cut Nick off a long time ago, walked away, and never looked back. Yet Sam was carrying them in his freaking arms, wadded up in a question-mark ball. It didn't matter that Sam couldn't answer any of the questions that Nick had left him with. The questions didn't matter as much as the fact that Sam was holding those questions carefully, almost reverently. Somehow, through it all, Nick was still Sam's hero. A fallen hero, but a hero nonetheless.

I swallowed back a lump in my throat.

• • •

It was a long way out of the forest, and Sam's leg was wobbly. We walked slowly, even though I wanted to run out of there. But I kept my pace slow for the kid.

"That was crazy," Sam whispered.

"One more inch and—"

"I know."

"You're a little fucker for running away," I said.

Sam nodded. "I didn't know what else to do."

"So you've been staying out here?"

"Yeah," Sam said. He sighed. "I brought a sleeping bag and everything. I just didn't think the python would be out here with me."

"How did it get you?" I asked.

"I was taking a nap. That's when it started curling around my leg." He paused. "I didn't know pythons could travel that far. I mean, Jello's house is a ways away."

I shook my head. "Maybe someone found it and didn't want to call it in, threw it in the woods."

"That would be dumb," Sam said fiercely.

"That's what Jello was going to do."

Sam was silent. We kept walking. Sam walked with a heavy limp.

"I looked by the place where we hung out before," I said.

"I knew you would," Sam said.

"Food?" I prompted. The ground was soft beneath my feet.

"That's been running out," he said guiltily.

I nodded, a bit worried. He did look thinner.

"I've been stealing stuff from Marren's Corner Store," Sam continued, running his hand over the top of a bush as we passed by.

I snorted. "Who doesn't?"

Sam looked at me, surprised. I'd never told him I stole from Marren's.

He paused. "Thank you, Ronney."

I shook my head. "You're a crazy fuckwad idiot," I said, but I smiled with my eyes.

Sam smiled back. "You say crazy a lot, you know that?"

At the question, an image of Dad popped into my head: Dad aiming a gun at himself. Suddenly my chest felt like it was caving in on me, and I didn't know what to do, had no idea how to respond to that, and so to avoid Sam seeing my face, that's when I gave Sam the hug I had wanted to give since I saw him. That kid buried his head in my chest as if he were in the middle of a great storm and was afraid of getting ripped out of my arms. I didn't say anything and neither did he, but I could feel his heart beating wildly in his chest, and after a while the word "crazy" started to fade away and I could hear other sounds, like the wind rustling the leaves of the trees and a shotgun going off in the distance. And since Sam probably hadn't seen any of our signs yet, that was when I told him about Nick.

While we were headed back from the woods, I texted George.

I FOUND SAM! ☺ AND I NEVER USE SMILEY FACES! ☺☺☺☺☺

THAT'S GREAT, RONNEY!!! ☺ Is he okay?

Yes, mostly. He got bit by the python, but he should be fine.

By the WHAT??? Well, that's fantastic he's okay!...I'd invite you over for a hug but my eyes are almost swollen shut. I look awful.

From crying?

Yeah. My world is falling apart, Ronney. What am I going to do about my Twenty Steps to Be an Architect? I was on step fourteen!!!

Where are you?

At home.

Where's Jello?

At his home. He doesn't want to talk to me.

What?!!!

Don't ask.

I dropped Sam off at his house because he didn't want me to go inside. He said he wanted time with his parents, which made sense. But I made sure he went in. Both of his parents' cars were in the driveway, and I made Sam promise me that he'd get his snakebite treated, pronto. Then I biked my ass to Jello's, dropped into his room, and found him dicking around with photos on his computer.

"Why aren't you with George?" I asked. I stared at him. "She's freaking out."

Jello looked miserable. "Yeah, I was texting her for a little while but had to do something else."

"Like what? Play with photos?"

"I just . . . what am I supposed to do? George is hysterical, crying all the time." Jello rubbed the back of his neck. "I can't help her."

"You can be there for her."

"But how?"

"How?" I asked. I wanted to say, *You caress her gorgeous hair and sit with the crap, with the questions, with the awful moments as they pass by.* But then I realized that he'd never had to sit with the crap, or the questions, or the awful moments, because, for Jello, they had never passed by.

He just didn't have it in him.

"You . . . ," I said, pacing, "sit next to her. Tell her you're there for her. Hold her, goddammit."

Jello looked uncertain. "But my photos—"

"Fuck the photos!" I shouted, and grabbed his shirt. Jello cowered like I was going to hit him again for real.

I released his shirt and watched him adjust it back into place. "George is more important than your photos, Jello."

"I know that, but . . ."

"I know it all sucks, but just because it sucks doesn't mean you turn into a loser and hide in the basement. Now get out of here and go to her house, or I swear I'll hit you for real. Be the boyfriend, dammit," I said, and I stumbled over the last words.

He mumbled some semblance of thanks as he wheeled over to her house.

I turned around and texted George.

Jello's on his way.

I can't believe he just left me.

He's coming.

He said he needed to work on his photos. ☹

He can be a jackwad, but he's coming.

Are you going to come too?

If he can't make it for whatever reason—

Mom arrived home from work. I'd slipped my shoes off in the middle of the kitchen floor and turned on the TV while I was texting George. Mom looked down, saw my shoes, and walked by. Then she backtracked, walked right up to me, and looked me in the eye.

I started first. "Mom, I found—"

"I'm worried about Mina," she said.

"Duh," I said. "But—"

"What do you mean, 'duh'? I'm really worried about her."

"But Mom, I found—"

"Will you stop thinking about yourself for once?" Mom exploded. Her black hair quivered, she was so upset. "When will you actually listen to me? I'm telling you, I'm worried about Mina."

I paused. This exploding Mom was rare. Very rare. As in, it-never-happens rare. I gave up. "What did Mina do?" I asked.

"I got a call from her teacher. She hit one of her classmates."

My eyebrows popped up. "For real?" I asked. I wanted to say,

Atta-girl, but I had the feeling it wasn't the best time to cheer her on. "Mina's in her room if you want to talk to her."

"Not yet. After dinner," she said.

"Was it bad?" I asked.

"She gave him a black eye."

My eyebrows lifted. "Niiiice." I couldn't help it.

That was when Mom started crying.

"This is so hard," she sobbed. "This is just so, so hard."

I didn't know if she was talking about Mina or Dad or life in general. A part of me wanted to give Mom a hug, tell her it's going to be okay, and that I'll help her. But I just couldn't. Instead, I stood there awkwardly, not knowing what to do with my hands.

"Gee," I said. That was the best I could muster.

She wiped her nose. "I'm sorry, Ronney," she said. "I guess I need some time to cool down, get my thoughts together."

"Sounds good," I said.

"Maybe I'll go for a drive," she said distractedly.

"Be careful," I said, and pulled up a chair at the kitchen table.

Mom left through the back way, by the patio door.

George texted me.

What, you left me too?

No, no, I just got sidetracked.

What do I do if there's no plan? If there's no Twenty Steps?

I was in the middle of responding when Dan the News Man

came on the TV screen in the kitchen, jabbering about a tiger sighting in town maybe a half hour ago.

I wanted to say, *Another day in Makersville.*

"Ronney?" Dad called.

I ignored him. I went back to my phone and to George.

It'll be okay. Not sure how, but it'll be okay.

I'm a failure, Ronney. I failed so bad. I failed. Oh God.

I'm still here for you. You don't have to be perfect. It's okay to fail. Life goes on.

I have boogers on my hands.

"Ronney?" Dad said. He was coming down the hallway.

That's nasty, but funny, too bad you can't wash the phone.

Haha.

"Ronney." Dad was looking at me now from the entryway to the kitchen. He ran his hand through his hair. "Why didn't you answer me?"

"Because," I said, still looking down at my phone, "you would only ask if I'm here, which you can certainly see that I am. What's the point of responding?"

Dad ran his hand through his hair again. "That's not why I was calling you," he said.

I looked up. "Fat chance of that. Anyway, you were in your bedroom while Mom was out here crying just a couple minutes ago."

"She was?"

"You expect us to respond to you, but then you turn a mysteriously thick, deaf ear to everyone in this house." I was getting heated up, despite myself.

"That's not true," Dad said.

"Like when Mom was crying," I said. "Why the hell didn't you hear her? Why didn't you call for her when she was crying?"

Dad's face twisted up. I couldn't tell if it was embarrassment or guilt or anger, but it was still a big score for the R-Man.

My phone buzzed. George just texted me. I wanted to see what she said, but I had Dad in front of me, which annoyed me further.

"I couldn't hear Mom crying," Dad said, his voice tense.

"Well, I couldn't hear you, either," I said.

"I don't like your attitude," Dad said.

I feigned shock as I glanced from my phone and stood up. "Why, look at that. That's something a father would say. I'm sorry, I don't know what that's like, to be the son of a real father; it'll take me a moment to adjust."

"So adjust," Dad said flatly.

I addressed an imaginary audience. "All right, folks, suddenly having a father is harder to adjust to than one thinks. This might take a little more than a moment," I announced. I turned back to him. "I must say, I don't know that being a father suits you." I gave him a look. "Maybe you've outgrown it, *Dad*."

Dad ran his hand through his hair for a third time.

Touchdown. I tried to hide a smile. Then I glanced back down at my phone to see what George had said.

That's when Dad came over and snatched my cell phone from my hands.

I stared at him. "Give it back," I said, in shock.

He held on to it. "Pick up your shoes from the kitchen floor."

I kept staring at him. "What?" I said, though I'd heard perfectly well what he said.

"You heard me. Pick up your shoes from the kitchen floor," he repeated, slowly, like I was stupid. He pointed to my shoes. "Be like any normal human being and put them where they belong."

I looked at him. "Are you serious?"

Dad gave a little laugh. "Do I look serious?"

That pissed me off. "So you think you can drop in on my life whenever you want and tell me what to do? What about all those times we needed you and you had checked out? Huh?"

Dad was grim. "Those times are over."

I stood up from my chair. "Well, isn't that marvelous that you changed from Clark Kent to Superman. I'm thrilled."

"Pick up your shoes," Dad said.

"Too bad no one needs saving," I said.

"Really." Dad laughed again. "I don't care what your opinion is. Pick them up."

Fuck, I was hot. The temperature in that kitchen must have exploded or something. I stomped over to my shoes, picked them up, and threw them onto the shoe pile with a flourish.

"Content, Superman?" I said.

Dad walked back to his bedroom.

I followed him down the corridor. "You think you can do that, huh? Show up, be all tough, and then retreat back to your safe little cave whenever you want to? Well, let me tell you the truth, Dad Who Makes Son Put Away Shoes: We fucking floundered because you left us, and I needed to do the shit that you wouldn't. So go ahead, be all proud that you—"

"It doesn't matter," Dad said. "I'm still the father of this household."

"Could have fooled me," I said.

Dad spun around and grabbed my arm surprisingly hard. "You will not talk to me like that," he said.

I tried to yank my arm away but couldn't. "Let me go," I said, and my voice cracked.

Dad did, but I suddenly felt all claustrophobic in the hallway, my back almost against the wall. Still, my mouth kept going. "What were we supposed to do? Huh? Twiddle our thumbs for two years while you got your shit together?" I waved my arm in the air. "Sorry. I got news for you: Life goes on."

Dad looked at me incredulously. "You see what a hypocrite you are? You berate me for leaving you, but listen to yourself. You've left *us*."

There was suddenly a strange smell in the house, but I couldn't pin it down. I shook my head at Dad. "If I'm a hypocrite, then you're a pathetic mess. You're powerless. You fucking failed us," I said, but at that moment, something inside started to stutter, to break down. Because with those very words I remembered just how powerless I had been with Sam. How deeply I had failed him.

Just like Dad.

I had to get out of there. I stomped down the hallway and into the living room, and when I got there, I stopped cold.

There was a tiger looking at me.

A live tiger. In the living room.

It growled.

Mom must have left the door ajar.

I froze. The sharp, thick smell of musk saturated the house. My nostrils flared. Every single goddamn hair on my body stood on end.

Dad was on my heels. When he got into the living room, he stopped too.

"Um . . . ," I said.

"Ronney, get out of here," Dad said. His voice quivered.

"Right," I said, my eyes still locked on the tiger. "Trying."

I inched toward the kitchen door, and the tiger approached me. One step. Two.

I stopped and put up my hands as if it were a holdup.

"Ronney," Dad said.

The smell of musk was everywhere. Fucking dripping. I could barely breathe.

"Dad," I said. My voice was high and whispery.

Dad made another step toward me.

The tiger swished its tail and growled again. Its eyes locked on Dad. Dad stopped.

"What if we run for it?" I said.

"Once we turn our backs, it'll jump," Dad said.

"So then what?"

"Go slow."

The kitchen door was a million fucking miles away. I swear to God. I swallowed thickly and inched again toward the kitchen.

The tiger crouched low and made a couple steps after me. Stalking me.

I stopped. "I don't want to die, Dad," I whispered. My entire body trembled and dripped in sweat.

"You won't, son," Dad whispered back. "Just go slow and steady."

I kept walking to the kitchen door, step by agonizing step, and the tiger kept countering each step of mine with a step of its own. Each paw was the size of my face.

"It's going to jump—I know it," I whispered. "Look, Dad, I'm sorry for—"

"Ronney, stay focused," Dad said.

It took everything that I had not to turn and run for that door. But I knew Dad was right: If I lost my focus, it was over.

It was as if that tiger knew the plan, knew what doors were, and knew what I was heading for. The growl came thick from its throat, and its eyes narrowed into slits. It crouched even deeper.

"Dad?" I squeaked.

"I'm here," he said.

"What do I do?" I asked.

"Keep going," Dad said. "You're getting there."

"I won't make it."

"Ron-Ron?" a voice said. I wrenched my eyes from the tiger and saw Mina maybe twenty feet away.

Holding the gun.

The tiger leaped.

Dad threw himself between the tiger and me, his arms outstretched and wide, trying to make himself into a living wall.

"Nooo!" Mina howled. She squeezed her eyes shut and fired once, twice, three times, four times.

Dad screamed and went down.

"Dad!" I shouted, and fell onto him. Dad didn't move. I didn't know where the blood was coming from, just that it was awful and thick and dripping down my hands.

That smell of blood. I would recognize that sickeningly sweet smell anywhere. And it was everywhere. Dark and thick. On the carpet. On my hands. I saw myself running to get the phone. Slapping Mina.

I blinked.

Then I remembered the tiger.

The huge body of the tiger was lying in the middle of the living room floor, blood gushing out of multiple places on its body. The very tip of its tail curled, then uncurled, curled, then uncurled, then finally lay still on the carpet.

Dad groaned and shifted beneath me. His shirt was a deep red, and the red was spreading quickly. I could hear Mina dashing for the phone. "Dad, I'm sorry, okay? I'm really, really sorry. I'm sorry for everything," I whispered to him. "Hang in there. Dad. Don't die. Oh God. Please." Then I started to cry, and before I could stop myself, my crying turned into sobbing, and I was shaking as I held him, I was sobbing so hard.

I don't know how he did it, but Dad slowly raised one heavy arm, draped it over my back, and held me like that while I cried. He was still holding me when the paramedics came in to take him away.

24

IT TURNED OUT THAT MINA HAD SHOT DAD IN the shoulder—the same shoulder, of course. He was out of the hospital quickly this time, released the same day he went in, though he had to start all over with his physical therapy, which must have sucked. I had the feeling that he'd do his exercises better than he did before, if only because getting a gunshot wound while saving your son's life was a hell of a lot better reason than trying to blow off your head.

I had to admit, I didn't quite know what to do with Dad. I had really just been kidding about that superhero bit, but now it held true: I had a Superman dad who saved my ass from a tiger. Well, ultimately Mina saved my ass—she saved both of our asses—but I'll get to her later. The upshot about Dad was that he was walking around the house all confident and shit, doing his new physical therapy exercises with gusto.

Gusto, goddammit.

What do you do when someone saves your life? How do you thank him in a way that isn't lame? I mean, if it had been some cop instead of my dad, that'd be cool, because I'd bring him a steak or whatever, and then I'd be done with it. But when it's your dad, well, you live with the guy, right? You can't bring him a steak every time you see him, because that'd get expensive and annoying. A part of me was also floundering inside because I couldn't make my usual Dad comments—it just didn't seem right anymore. A part of me was really tempted to make the same Dad insults that I always had, just because it was familiar. But I shut that voice up because that was something a dickwad would do, and truth be told, I really didn't mind having some awesome dad who had saved my life walking around the house. So I was mostly quiet around him and made sure to put my shoes nice and neat in the shoe pile, which I think he appreciated.

However, I did seek out Jello soon after the whole tiger bit. He was on his computer when I dropped into his room.

"Hey," I said, and I went up to him and fake punched him in the arm.

Jello fake fell over. "Hey," he said.

I helped him up. "Thanks for saving my life," I said, and my throat felt tight.

Jello sat his ass back on his chair. "But I didn't. Your dad did." His brow furrowed in confusion. Then he grinned. "Your kid sister did."

"No, not that. I meant that one day. On the lake."

"Oh, that," Jello said, waving his hand. "That's nothing."

I shook my head. "You saved my life. I owe you," I said, and at that moment no words existed to express how indebted I felt toward him.

Jello looked at me oddly. "That was years ago, R-Man. It's fine."

"Yeah, well, I'd still be dead without you, years later."

"What's this about?" he asked, as he grabbed the camera next to him and started cleaning the lens.

I winced. How could I tell him how much it meant that he had come through for me, that something he did actually *was* my business, that I had needed him, that it was okay to need someone?

I shrugged.

Jello squirmed in his chair and fiddled somewhere with his camera. "It's cool. You're welcome." Then he gave a little laugh. "It's too bad you didn't go all sappy on me last week, because you know I'd have found something for you to do."

His mangled-up raccoon had died, a prisoner in captivity, a couple days ago. On its back, its legs stuck in the air.

I nodded, feeling damn lucky indeed. "So that's the end of the safari," I said.

Jello gave a sly smile. "Not really."

"Jello, they're all dead. Except for the camel. Game over."

"Not really," he said again.

I gave him a look. "What do you mean?"

"Promise not to tell?" Jello said.

My stomach twisted. "I promise."

Jello's eyes shone. "Well, with all these animals around, the newspaper has been covering different angles on them, right?"

"Go on."

"They covered this story about a lady who had purchased a baby lion cub a couple years ago and is raising it in her house."

I stared at him. "Are you for real?"

"All of it. And I called her up."

"Wait. Where is she? In Makersville?"

Jello's eyes sparkled. "I'm not going to tell you. But it's safe, you know? This is a domestic lion cub."

I snorted. "A domestic lion. God, are you naive sometimes."

"But determined," Jello added, and grinned. "And I'm going to get my driver's license in two months. So I can drive out there."

"Shit," I said, almost admiringly. Leave it to Jello to get his way.

"And, R-Man, you have to admit: Playing with a lion cub in some woman's house is a whole lot better than going on a safari."

I fake punched Jello in the arm again. He fake fell off his computer chair again, then climbed back onto it. "It's a whole lot better," I said. "You're brilliant."

Jello's eyebrows lifted. "Are you being sarcastic?"

I smiled. "Maybe. Maybe not."

Jello's eyes latched onto his computer screen, and he shifted uncomfortably. "And hey, thanks for kicking my ass with George."

I suddenly felt awkward.

"I needed some major ass-kicking," he said.

"I know. You were pathetic."

Jello nodded, then turned to grab a bag of chips that was sitting on his bookshelf. "You were right. She needed me."

I felt even more awkward. "Well, I should get going," I said.

"But somehow," Jello continued, "she knew that you and I had talked. She kept saying, 'Ronney told you to come back here, didn't he?' And when I asked her how she knew, she just rolled her eyes and said, 'Please. Put Ronney in any situation, and he'll know what to do.'"

My eyes bugged out. "She said that?"

Jello shrugged. "Yeah. Although I thought that was a little generous. *Any* situation? Come on, man. I've seen you really mess up situations."

So had I, but that still didn't stop the grin on my face all the way home.

The day after I'd talked with Jello, Sam and I were hanging at my house when the doorbell rang.

I told Sam to stay in my room and went to the front door. It was Nick, who came just as he said he would. Right on time. My insides bounced around.

"Hey," Nick said. I could see his car in our driveway, loaded down with his shit.

"So you're really doing it," I said.

"That's what I said I'd do," he said, and the stubborn glint in his eye was exactly the look that had so often come from Sam. He paused. "No news about Sam?"

I shrugged.

"I can't believe that nobody's heard anything," he said.

I shook my head.

"Who is it?" Sam asked as he entered the foyer. Nick and Sam both did double takes, then triple takes, and then Nick's face broke open. Sam gave a whoop and ran into his arms, and Nick picked that kid up like a bag of leaves, then fell to his knees and pressed his face into Sam's tiny shoulder. Sam's arms wrapped around Nick's neck like a vine, like nothing in the world could wrench them apart.

After what seemed like the longest time, Nick drew Sam away, looked him in the eye, and said, "You're so stupid."

Sam fidgeted. "So are you," he said.

Nick winced, then pressed his lips tightly together. "Sam, I'm sorry. But I'm back now, okay?"

Sam nodded. The thing that almost got me, Sam's face softened until he looked like a ten-year-old kid again. I'd only seen that look on his face once, with me.

I swallowed thickly.

Mina, of course, was a hero. No one else but a ten-year-old girl could shoot that tiger, the mayor proclaimed, and she made the front-page story in the paper for four days straight.

She was famous.

All the kids at school wanted her photograph, and a lot of the kids were upset that she didn't get a picture with the bloody, dead

tiger. After school she was followed home by journalists and reju-
venated gun rights fanatics and gun control fanatics all asking
her the same things: How could you shoot an animal like that?
What were you feeling? And then when they heard about Dad,
they pounced on her like a freaking beast, asking her questions
until she burst into tears. That was when Dad stormed out into the
front yard, looked at Mom, who was with her, and ranted at them
all, flailed his arms, and told them to leave a crying child alone, or
he would call the police. That was the only thing that made them
go away.

After Dad did that, Mina was happier than I'd ever seen her,
and she bounced her non-orange bouncy ball just as if it were the
orange one. Dad let her crawl onto his lap any moment she saw
him sitting down—on the couch, at the kitchen table—though
he drew the line when he was driving the car. Dad seemed to like
all the fussing too; they even had a special handshake they did
before he left for his therapy sessions. Mina never really went
back to the color orange like I was hoping she would, but when I
asked her about it, she whispered in my ear that her heart was the
color orange, and that that was a secret between her and me: Even
though it totally wasn't true, in a way, it was.

She still had nightmares, though; now she had nightmares that
she was shooting Dad. One night I heard her yelling in her sleep,
and I stumbled out of bed, when who did I bump into but Dad,
who was also making his way into her room.

"After you," I said.

"No, after you," he said.

So we went into her room together.

"Hey, Min-o," I said softly, turning on her bedside lamp.

She murmured.

"Honey," Dad said, and touched her arm.

"Ron-Ron?" Mina said. "*And* Daddy?"

"What was your dream about this time?" I said, crouching at her bed, down by her feet.

"I was . . ." She swallowed. "The gun . . ."

"It's okay," Dad said, smoothing her hair.

"I closed my eyes again," she said.

"What?" I asked.

"It's not okay," Mina said, her voice wobbling. "I never should have closed my eyes. And I keep doing it. I keep closing my eyes."

"What are you talking about, honey?" Dad asked.

"I closed my eyes when I shot it. It's all my fault. If I hadn't closed my eyes, I wouldn't have hit you, Daddy." She burst out crying.

Dad slid himself onto Mina's bed and held her, supporting her with his good arm. "You did your best," Dad said.

"And you died. In my dream, you died." Her body started to shake.

"Hey, hey," Dad said. He started to rock her.

Mina whimpered loudly.

"And, Mina, my little girl," Dad said, still rocking her, "I'm here for you."

I gave a start and stared at him in the darkness. I was glad he couldn't see the absolute shock that must have been on my face when he said that: *I'm here for you.* Is that not exactly what I've been telling George? Is that not exactly what we needed to hear from Dad all this time?

Meanwhile, in that same darkness, Mina sucked in a breath. "Really, Daddy?" she asked.

I don't think he meant for me to hear, but I could hear Dad swallow hard. "Yes. I'm here for you," Dad repeated. "I'm not going to leave you."

"Same here, Min-o," I said. "So you go right on back to sleep, because we're watching out for you."

She didn't have nightmares as much after that.

Dad still regularly went to his shrink sessions, and he had let it slip that he had found some good medication, but I didn't give him shit about it anymore. I mean, if you need it, you need it. I guess it was working pretty well, because after I replaced the carpet a second time, he came up to me one weekend morning as I was eating my cereal.

"Ronney," he said. He took a swig of his coffee. "That living room wall is really bad, isn't it?"

"Yeah," I said.

"It looks pretty good on the outside."

"But it's all rotten on the inside."

"It'll take a lot of money to fix it."

"It'll be worth it."

Dad paused. "So we gotta rip it all out, huh?"

I looked up from my bowl. "'We'?"

Dad shuffled his feet. "Well, if you want some help, that is. It's a big project."

I looked at him, dumbfounded. "Yeah, it is," I said. I scratched my arm, like I didn't know what to do with myself. "Thanks, Dad."

Dad didn't say anything to that, but while he was taking another swig of coffee his eyebrows lifted slightly, like he was smiling into his cup.

After looking long and hard, the authorities finally found the camel: It was in the backyard of Mr. Lulloff's house, because Mr. Lulloff had decided he didn't want the camel shot, like all the other animals had been, so he hid the camel in his basement. Only when he finally let the camel out to get some fresh air did some nosy neighbor report his ass. Mr. Lulloff brought out his gun when the authorities came by, telling them that there was no way they were going to shoot that camel, and only when the authorities convinced him that a camel is a camel and is in no danger of being shot did Mr. Lulloff finally agree to let the authorities into his house and take the confused but grateful camel. I say "grateful" because instead of the pizza that Mr. Lulloff had been feeding it, the authorities had brought with them camel food, like hay, which was a good thing for everybody.

And speaking of good things for everybody, that was the last of the animals—except for the monkey, which was just seen once and then never again—and the feds and the state warden and the media and all their pals finally packed up and left Makersville. Just for old time's sake, and maybe to still feel special, people in town continued to greet each other with "What's up with the animals?" even though no one ever had a good response.

It took a few days for Dad and me to rip out that wall and get the new wall installed. We had to get advice from the guys at the hardware store a couple times, but hell, it sure felt great to get it done. On the second day of wall installation, Dad was out on a quick supply run when the doorbell rang. I went to the door and peeked through the side window.

It was Sam. He was looking down at the ground.

"Hey, kiddo," I said, opening the door to a gust of cold air. "What's—"

"We're moving." He glanced up at me, and his gaze wavered.

"Huh?" My heart flipped.

"Nick convinced Mom that we needed to leave. So we are."

I swallowed back the lump in my throat. "When?"

"I don't know. But he told me it was going to happen soon. A different town. I don't know where."

Silence.

"Sam, this is great news," I said quietly.

Sam's bottom lip trembled. He nodded and looked at me again.

"This is what you've needed for a long time." My voice was thick.

Sam looked down at the ground again and whispered something.

"What?" I asked.

"I don't want to go."

"Don't be dumb. Of course you want to go."

His eyes flicked up to mine. "You can come with us?"

I looked at him, and my heart crumbled. "No, Sam," I whispered. "I stay here."

He turned away. And in that silence I could hear the years of shouting and screaming and hitting and hiding and smallness, and then also, like a balm, the times of Sam and me and potato chips and football and wall repairs and question marks and dinners and wooded areas and rescues and hope.

"Hang on a sec," I said to Sam. "I have a poster I want to give you. Signed."

"Soon" turned out to be sooner than soon: The very next day, Sam, Nick, and their mom were gone. Earlier, Nick had texted me while my hands were all mucked up with wall dust:

Dad just left the house. Now's the time. We're leaving. Come outside, quick.

Now?

Now.

I almost didn't catch them at all, because I was an idiot and didn't believe Nick's "now" meant *now* and stopped to wash my hands. When I got outside, Sam's mom was driving slowly past our house—inching, really—and I ran to the car. Sam was in the back seat and rolled the window down, and I walked beside the car and extended my hand out to him, into the car, and he took it, his tiny hand in mine. Tears streamed down his face.

Sam's mom rolled down her window. "I'm sorry, Ronney, we'd stop if we could but—"

"No, that's okay," I said. I was still walking beside the car. "You gotta go. I get it." Nick nodded to me, gave me a thin-lipped smile.

That was when I saw the John Lennon poster in the back seat right next to Sam. My eyebrows lifted.

Sam saw me looking at the poster, then at him, and his face crumpled up again.

"Hey," I said, and I stopped walking. Sam's mom stopped the car. Sam threw the door open and bear-hugged me.

"You'll be okay," I said to him.

"No I won't."

"You shut that up," I said. I looked at his teary face. "You're a fighter. You'll be okay. And do your homework."

Sam nodded.

"Now go," I said, my voice wobbling.

Sam got back into the car and kept his hand extended out the window, as if to eternally take mine in his.

Then they drove away.

The next day I was taking out the rest of the drywall that Dad and I had torn down, cleaning up, still thinking about how Nick and Sam and their mom were finally on their own. They'd be fine, I knew: They were all survivors. But I felt exhausted inside.

The air was crisp, like snow was going to come soon, and my mind slowly drifted to the things that the house needed for winter. I was wheeling the garbage out to the curb, because it was a Thursday, a garbage day, and the wind had picked up again; if it got any stronger, stuff would start blowing around. I shivered because I was only in my flannel shirt, and I heard a voice behind me.

"Ronney?"

I turned. "Yeah, Dad?"

"Need some help?" he asked.

"Sure," I said, and we loaded the drywall into the trash cans.

"You want to go ice fishing this winter?" Dad asked.

"Fuck no, it's cold," I said.

Dad laughed. "We'll have heaters in the shelter, Ronney."

I thought about that. "We won't fall through?"

Dad grinned. "Not because of the heaters. The ice is too thick. Now, if you decide to walk into the fishing hole, all bets are off."

I thought about the two of us drinking hot chocolate and huddling around the heaters, with our fishing poles dangling over a patch of dark, inky water.

"What would we do?" I asked, despite myself.

"It's a lot like regular fishing," Dad said.

"You mean you'll eat a worm?" I asked.

Dad laughed again, and his laugh was loud and free. "Maybe."

"In that case, why not?" I asked.

Dad put his arm around my shoulder as we headed back to the house, and our feet matched each other's in unison.

The next day I went to visit George. Her father opened the door, and I even smiled nicely, asked if George was home. He grinned at me like I was some awesome superstar kid, now that my family was in the papers, and went to get George. We sat in the sunroom, which was warm and appropriately sunny. She looked tired, but there was a light in her eyes that I hadn't seen before.

"How've you been sleeping?" I asked.

George made a face. "Getting better. I've been doing a lot of thinking."

I waited.

She leaned over and plucked a white flower off of a nearby houseplant, then rolled the stem between her fingers. "My classmates—you know, the valedictorian-track ones—wanted to know what happened at the competition." She gave a little snort. "When I wouldn't tell them, they thought that I must have gotten the full-ride scholarship and didn't want to say anything, like, rub it in their faces. Some kids thought that by *not* saying anything I was still rubbing it in their faces, and they started talking about me."

"Kids can be fuckers."

George looked down at the flower that she was rolling between her fingers. "People can be superficial, you know? I mean, it's just grades."

I stared at her. "Whoa. Wait. This is coming from George?"

"There's always going to be someone better than you. Sometimes a lot of someones," George said, looking up. "But I'm not going to let a lost scholarship ruin me."

My face must have gone slack, because when she looked at me, she started laughing. "Here, let me show you something." George stood up and took me by the hand to her bedroom. Over her bed, where her Twenty Steps to Be an Architect sign had been, was a new sign:

TWENTY-ONE WAYS TO KICK ASS AT LIFE, NO MATTER WHAT

The moment I saw that new sign, I hooted and gave her a huge high five. Then I froze. "Wait. So this means you're not going to be an architect?"

"The tenth percentile means the tenth percentile," George said, looking away. "Maybe I'll be something else."

"Maybe you were with inhuman brainiacs and you shouldn't judge yourself against them."

"Maybe I'll keep an open mind about things," George said. "Lots of twists and turns to life—you gotta keep going, right?" George said, blushing a little.

I shook my head with admiration. "Balls of steel, woman."

George gave me a pointed look and a devilish grin. "I think you mean 'ovaries.'"

"What?" I asked. Heat instantly inflamed my face.

"Ovaries of steel," she said, nice and slowly, lingering on each syllable. "Ovaries, Ronney. You know." George pointed to her abdomen.

"Um . . . yeah . . ." I fidgeted and scratched the back of my neck. I had no idea what to say, and I sure as hell couldn't look at her.

George laughed, a laugh loud and strong.

When my face no longer felt like a furnace and George's laughing died down, she hugged her arms across her chest. "I just . . . wish I hadn't lost friends over this stupid scholarship."

"They weren't friends."

She sighed. I knew that sigh. It was an *I wish this had never happened, but I'm not running away* sigh. And there was that look again, one I never thought I'd see in George's eyes: the look of a fighter.

"Sometimes you just have to go through the shit," I said. "No other way around." I paused. "So you and Jello are doing better?"

George nodded. "Yeah," she said quietly. "We're better."

I looked into her eyes. God, she was beautiful. "You're happy?"

She nodded again and tucked a strand of hair behind her ear.

I took a long, slow breath. "Good," I said, and dammit, I meant it. Then I remembered something. "Thanks so much for that photo of the cookie house," I said. I hesitated. "I have something to give you, too." I dug around in my pocket and brought out my lucky Thursday medallion. "Here," I said, handing it out to her. "This is for you."

She cocked her head. "What is it?"

"I've carried this around for a while," I said. "You never know when you're going to need a little bit of luck."

Her fingers closed around it.

She shook her head and gave me an unguarded smile. "You're so strong, Ronney, dealing with all kinds of things. I always wondered how you did it. Now I guess I know, at least a little—you've got a whole lot of strength, resilience, and a lucky coin. You're really incredible."

I took her hand. She gave me a surprised look.

"You're really incredible too," I said. My heart started to pound. Her hand was so soft.

"Ronney—I'm seeing Jello," she faltered, but she didn't pull her hand back.

I will never be able to hold her hand like this, I thought as I held her hand. *This may be exactly how Jello holds her hand all the time and doesn't even think about it. And it's true: I'll be there for her; it's certainly not how I want it to be, but it doesn't have to be perfect in order for it to be good. Maybe even very good.*

That's what I was thinking as George stood there and looked at me hesitantly. A couple moments later her look deepened.

Then, before I could stop myself, I leaned in and kissed her.

Her lips were soft, warm.

It was heaven on my lips when she kissed me back.

Let me repeat that: George was freaking kissing me.

I can't tell you how badly I wanted that kiss to go on forever, but at some point I pulled away and said thickly, "So go ahead and see Jello."

"Okay, I will," she whispered, biting the lip I had just kissed. Her eyes were sparkling.

I gave a small smile. "Put Ronney in any situation, and he'll know what to do, eh?" I asked.

"Yeah," George said softly. "I stand by that."

And it was a Thursday.

ACKNOWLEDGMENTS

This was a story six years in the making. I could not have pulled it off without the following support: Jennifer Ung, my editor, who is heroic in so many ways; Tina Wexler, the best agent and ally I could ask for; Silvia Gomez, who saw a squirrel falling from a tree in a windstorm; Stacy Jaffe, who lovingly encourages me onward; Timothy Smith, who will always have my heart; Zachary Lulloff and Karen Brailsford, my dear spirit friends; Regina Rodríguez-Martin, who strengthens; J. Michael Sparough, S. J., my (sneaky) mentor and guide; Allen Ellis DeWitt and Max Kowalski, who gave just the right critiques at just the right time; Miriam Busch, whose fire, brilliance, and generosity propelled me on; Kathi Appelt, my deep friend; Mike Pelko, who inspired Ronney's voice; the Cenacle Sisters and Bob Raccuglia, who help make this all possible; Ephathatha, who will always be with me; the YMCA treadmill, on which I imagined a small boy keeping pace with me; Ben Jaffe, Esther Hershenhorn, Deborah Doering,

Susanne Fairfax, Erica Hornthal, Emily Kokie, Tom and Kristin Clowes, Colleen Berry, Joe Metz, Amber Evey, Beth Miller, Tim Schmidt, Monica Martinez, Emanuele Solomon, Juan Carlos Linares, Susann Revelorio, Mara Anastas, Liesa Abrams, Chriscynethia Floyd, Sarah Creech, Jodie Hockensmith Nicole Russo, Catherine Hayden, Lauren Hoffman, Amy Hendricks, Chelsea Morgan, Christina Pecorale, Emily Hutton, Michelle Leo, Anthony Parisi, Janine Perez, Anna Jarzab, Kristin Reynolds, Brian Luster, and finally, my mom, stepdad, brother, and dad; and finally-finally, a thanks to the squirrels, who needed to step out of the spotlight (although you know I will always love you).

ABOUT THE AUTHOR

Crystal Chan watched with amazement at the exotic zoo outbreak in Zanesville, Ohio, in 2011, where scores of animals—including hungry lions, panthers, and tigers—ran loose around the county. That incident helped inspire this story. When Crystal isn't writing, her passions are giving diversity talks to adults and kids alike, telling stories on Wisconsin Public Radio, and hosting conversations on social media. Her debut novel, *Bird*, was published in nine countries and is available on audiobook in the United States. She is also the parent of a teenage turtle (not a ninja).